ALSO BY HANIF KUREISHI

SCREENPLAYS AND PLAYS

My Beautiful Laundrette

Sammy and Rosie Get Laid

London Kills Me

Outskirts and Other Plays

My Son the Fanatic

Sleep with Me

FICTION

The Buddha of Suburbia

The Black Album

Love in a Blue Time

Intimacy

Midnight All Day

Gabriel's Gift

NONFICTION

The Faber Book of Pop
(edited with Jon Savage)

INTIMACY
a novel

——————— AND ———————

MIDNIGHT ALL DAY
stories

Hanif Kureishi

SCRIBNER PAPERBACK FICTION
Published by Simon & Schuster
NEW YORK LONDON TORONTO SYDNEY SINGAPORE

SCRIBNER PAPERBACK FICTION
Simon & Schuster, Inc.
Rockefeller Center
1230 Avenue of the Americas
New York, NY 10020

First Scribner Paperback Fiction edition 2001
Intimacy and *Midnight All Day* were first published individually in Great Britain in 1998 and 1999 respectively by Faber and Faber Limited.

SCRIBNER PAPERBACK FICTION and design are trademarks of Macmillan Library Reference USA, Inc., used under license by Simon & Schuster, the publisher of this work.

For information regarding special discounts for bulk purchases, please contact Simon & Schuster Special Sales at 1-800-456-6798 or *business@simonandschuster.com*

Designed by Kyoko Watanabe

Manufactured in the United States of America

1 3 5 7 9 10 8 6 4 2

Library of Congress Cataloging-in-Publication Data
Kureishi, Hanif.
[Intimacy]
Intimacy : a novel ; and, Midnight all day : stories / Hanif Kureishi.
1st Scribner Paperback Fiction ed.
p. cm.
1. Great Britain—Social life and customs—20th century—Fiction.
2. Man-woman relationships—Fiction. 3. Separation (Psychology)—Fiction. 4. Midlife crisis—Fiction. 5. Men—Fiction. I. Title: Intimacy ; and, Midnight all day. II. Kureishi, Hanif. Midnight all day. III. Title: Midnight all day. IV. Title.

PR6061.U68 I58 2001
823'.914—dc21   2001041168

ISBN 0-7432-1714-4

CONTENTS

INTIMACY

7

MIDNIGHT ALL DAY

125

Strangers When We Meet   *127*

Four Blue Chairs   *176*

That Was Then   *186*

Girl   *212*

Sucking Stones   *229*

A Meeting, at Last   *261*

Midnight All Day   *274*

The Umbrella   *296*

Morning in the Bowl of Night   *309*

The Penis   *322*

INTIMACY

IT IS THE SADDEST NIGHT, for I am leaving and not coming back. Tomorrow morning, when the woman I have lived with for six years has gone to work on her bicycle, and our children have been taken to the park with their ball, I will pack some things into a suitcase, slip out of my house hoping that no one will see me, and take the tube to Victor's place. There, for an unspecified period, I will sleep on the floor in the tiny room he has kindly offered me, next to the kitchen. Each morning I will heave the thin single mattress back to the airing cupboard. I will stuff the musty duvet into a box. I will replace the cushions on the sofa.

I will not be returning to this life. I cannot. Perhaps I should leave a note to convey this information. "Dear Susan, I am not coming back . . ." Perhaps it would be better to ring tomorrow afternoon. Or I could visit at the weekend. The details I haven't decided. Almost certainly I will not tell her my intentions this evening or tonight. I will put if off. Why? Because words are actions and they make things happen. Once they are out you cannot put them back. Something irrevocable will have been done, and I am fearful and uncertain. As a matter of fact, I am trembling, and have been all afternoon, all day.

This, then, could be our last evening as an innocent, complete, ideal family; my last night with a woman I have known for ten years, a woman I know almost everything about, and want no more of. Soon we will be like strangers. No, we can never be that. Hurting someone is an act of reluctant intimacy. We will be dangerous acquaintances with a history. That first time she put her hand on my arm—I wish I had turned away. Why didn't I? The waste; the waste of time and feeling. She has said something similar about me. But do we mean it? I am in at least three minds about all questions.

I perch on the edge of the bath and watch my sons, aged five and three, one at each end. Their toys, plastic animals and bottles float on the surface, and they chatter to themselves and one another, neither fighting nor whingeing, for a change. They are ebullient and fierce, and people say what happy and affectionate children they are. This morning, before I set out for the day, knowing I had to settle a few things in my mind, the elder boy, insisting on another kiss before I closed the door, said, "Daddy, I love everyone."

Tomorrow I will do something that will damage and scar them.

The younger boy has been wearing chinos, a grey shirt, blue braces and a policeman's helmet. As I toss the clothes in the washing basket, I am disturbed by a sound outside. I hold my breath.

Already!

She is pushing her bicycle into the hall. She is removing the shopping bags from the basket.

Over the months, and particularly the last few days, wherever I am—working, talking, waiting for the bus—I have contemplated this rupture from all angles. Several times I have missed my tube stop, or have found myself in a familiar place that I haven't recognized. I don't always know where I am, which can be a pleasurably demanding experience. But these days I tend to feel I am squinting at things upside down.

I have been trying to convince myself that leaving someone isn't the worst thing you can do to them. Sombre it may be, but it doesn't have to be a tragedy. If you never left anything or anyone there would be no room for the new. Naturally, to move on is an infidelity—to others, to the past, to old notions of oneself. Perhaps every day should contain at least one essential infidelity or necessary betrayal. It would be an optimistic, hopeful act, guaranteeing belief in the future—a declaration that things can be not only different but better.

Therefore I am exchanging Susan, my children, my house, and the garden full of dope plants and cherry blossom I can see through the bathroom window, for a spot at Victor's where there will be draughts and dust on the floor.

Eight years ago Victor left his wife. Since then—even excepting the Chinese prostitute who played the piano naked and brought all her belongings to their assignations—he has had only unsatisfactory loves. If the phone rings he does a kind of panicky dance, wondering what opprobrium may be on the way, and from which direction. Victor, you see, can give women hope, if not satisfaction.

We find pubs and restaurants more congenial. I must say that when Victor isn't sitting in the dark, his eyes sunken and pupils dilated with incomprehension and anger, he can be easy-going, even amusing. He doesn't mind whether I am silent or voluble. He is used to the way I dash from subject to subject, following the natural momentum of my mind. If I ask him why his wife still hates him, he will tell me. Like my children I appreciate a good story, particularly if I've heard it before. I want all the details and atmosphere. But he speaks slowly, as some Englishmen do. Often I have no idea whether he is merely waiting for another word to occur or will, perhaps, never speak again. I can only welcome such intervals as the opportunity for reverie. But will I want monologues and pauses, draughts and pubs, every day?

Susan is in the room now.

She says, "Why don't you ever shut the bathroom door?"

"What?"

"Why don't you?"

I can't think of a reason.

She is busily kissing the children. I love her enthusiasm for them. When we really talk, it is about them, something they have said or done, as if they are a passion no one else can share or understand.

Susan doesn't touch me but presents her cheek a few inches from my lips, so that to kiss her I must lean forward, thus humiliating both of us. She smells of perfume and the street.

She goes to change and returns in jeans and sweatshirt, with a glass of wine for each of us.

"Hallo. How are you?"

She looks at me hard, in order to have me notice her. I feel my body contract and shrink.

"Okay," I reply.

I nod and smile. Does she see anything different in my face today? Have I given myself away yet? I must look beaten. Usually, before seeing her I prepare two or three likely subjects, as if our conversations are examinations. You see, she accuses me of being silent with her. If only she knew how I stammer within. Today, I have been too feverish to rehearse. This afternoon was particularly difficult. And silence, like darkness, can be kind; it, too, is a language. Couples have good reason for not speaking.

She talks of how her work colleagues have let her down.

"They are not good enough," she says.

"Is that right?"

It has been difficult for her since the publishing house was taken over. But she is a woman of strong feelings anyway, of either dislike or enthusiasm. Generally they are of dislike. Others, including me, infuriate and frustrate her. It is disturbing, the way I am compelled to share her feelings, though I don't know the people. As she talks I see why I leave the bathroom door open. I can't be in a room with her for too long without feeling that there is something I must do to stop her being so angry. But I never know what I should do, and soon I feel as if she is shoving me against the wall and battering me.

The boys' bath water drains away slowly, as their toys impede the plughole. They won't move until the water is gone, and then they sit there making moustaches and hats with the remaining bubbles. Eventually I lift the younger one out. Susan takes the other.

We wrap them in thick hooded towels. With damp hair and beads of water on their necks, and being so tired and all, the boys look like diminutive boxers after a match. They argue about what pyjamas they want to wear. The younger one will only wear a Batman T-shirt. They seem to have become self-conscious at an early age. They must have got it from us.

Susan gives the younger boy a bottle, which he holds up to his mouth two-handedly, like a trumpeter. I watch her caressing his hair, kissing his dimpled fingers and rubbing his stomach. He giggles and squirms. What a quality of innocence people have when they don't expect to be harmed. Who could violate it without damaging himself? At school—I must have been eight or nine—there sat next to me a smelly boy from a poor family. One day, when we all stood, his leg slipped down behind the bench. Deliberately I jerked it up, trapping his leg. The look on his face of inexplicable and unexpected pain has stayed with me. You can choose whether to do others good or harm.

We take the children downstairs, where they lie on cushions, nonchalantly sucking their dummies, watching *The Wizard of Oz* with their eyes half open. They look like a couple of swells smoking cigars in a field on a hot day. They demand ginger biscuits, as if I am a butler. I fetch them from the kitchen without Susan noticing me. The boys extend their greedy fingers but don't look away from the TV. As the film runs they not only murmur the dialogue but echo the sound effects too. After a while, I pick up the crumbs and, having considered what to do with them, fling them in a corner.

Susan works in the kitchen, listening to the radio and looking out at the garden. She enjoys that. Her own family life, like mine, has mostly been unpleasant. Now she goes to a lot of trouble to shop well and make good meals. Even if we're having a takeaway, she won't let us eat in a slew of newspapers, children's books and correspondence. She puts out napkins, lights candles and opens the wine, insisting we have a proper family meal, including nervy silences and severe arguments.

She likes auctions, where she buys unusual pictures, prints and furniture, often with worn velvet attached to some part of them. We have a lot of lamps, cushions and curtains, some of which hang across the middle of the room, as if a play is about to start, and from which I try to stop the boys swinging. There are deep armchairs, televisions, telephones, pianos, music systems and the latest magazines and newest books in every room. Most people don't have comfort, plenty and ease like this.

At home I don't feel at home. In the morning I will let go of it. Definitely. Bye-bye.

I sit on the floor near the boys, releasing the buckle of my belt when I locate it finally in the loose folds of my belly. For a change I neither pick up the newspaper nor follow the film, but examine my sons, their feet, ears, eyes. This evening, when I am both here and not here—almost a ghost, already—I will not drink, get stoned, or argue. I have to be aware of everything. I want to develop a mental picture I can carry around and refer to when I am at Victor's place. It will be the first of the few things I must, tonight, choose to take with me.

Suddenly I feel as if I might vomit, and I slap my hand over my mouth. The feeling passes. But now I could howl! I feel as if I am in a plunging aeroplane. I will see the children as often as I can, but I will miss things here. The disorder of family life: the children's voices as they sing their scatological version of "The Teddy Bears' Picnic"; watching them watch television through their new binoculars; the three of us dancing to the Rolling Stones, the older one balanced perilously on the coffee table, the other plunging through the sofa; seeing them on their bikes, as they speed away from me, yelling; them walking down the street in the sunshine, umbrellas up, crooning "Singin' in the Rain." Once, when the older boy was a baby, he threw up in one of my shoes, and I didn't notice until I was in the taxi on my way to the airport.

If I come home and the children aren't here, even if there's plenty to do, I can wander from room to room waiting for their faces to come through the door, and for the world to be re-animated by their chaotic energy.

What could be more important? Lost in the middle of my life and no way home, what kind of experience do I imagine I am forfeiting this for? I have had a surplus of emotional experience with men, women, colleagues, parents, acquaintances.

I have read, thought and talked for years. Tonight, how will any of it guide me? Perhaps I should be impressed by the fact that I haven't attached myself to things, that I am loose and free enough to walk away in the morning. But what am I free for? Surely the ultimate freedom is to choose, to dispense with freedom for the obligations that tie one to life—to get involved.

This confusion isn't going to leave me alone. But by the morning my mind had better be made up about certain things. I must not descend into self-pity, at least not for longer than necessary. I have found that it is not my moods that frustrate me but the depth and indeterminacy of their duration. If I feel a bit low, I fear a year-long depression. If my once-girlfriend Nina became distant or sharp, I was convinced she was permanently detaching herself from me.

Tonight my predominant emotion is fear of the future. At least, one might say, it is better to fear things than be bored by them, and life without love is a long boredom. I may be afraid but I am not cynical. I am trying to be resolute. Tonight, don't worry, I will set the record crooked.

I should, too, consider what it is I love about life and other people. Otherwise I will turn the future into a wasteland, eliminating possibility before anything can develop. It is easy to kill oneself off without dying. Unfortunately, to get to the future one has to live through the present.

While considering these things, I have thought of several people who seem to have been depressed for most of their lives, and have accepted a condition of relative unhappiness as if it is their due. How much time have my numerous depressions wasted over all? Three years, at least. Longer than all my sexual pleasure put together, I should imagine.

I encourage myself to think of the pleasures of being a single man in London, of what there might be to look forward to. My sons look up as I giggle to myself. The other night Victor goes to a bar, meets a woman with a stud through her tongue and is invited to her loft in the East End. She likes to be tied up; she has the equipment. The stud roams his scrotum, like, as he says, a slug with a ball bearing in its head. They joke about misplacing the keys. His bottom smarts.

He calls at an unrespectable hour the next day and insists we meet for breakfast so I can hear about it. I inform him that the nanny, as nannies do, has lost the will to live and that it is difficult to get a baby-sitter first thing in the morning. But at last I arrive at the café, happy to be out and to have someone bring me breakfast, rather than running about, as I normally do, with slices of toast with jam which inevitably end up face-down on the floor.

Victor doesn't omit a moment.

"And what were you doing?" he enquires politely, at last.

I sigh. Wearing an old tracksuit and drinking beer in bed, coughing, smoking and listening to a late Beethoven quartet on my headphones.

He and the woman never meet again. Most nights Victor watches TV alone, a plate of saveloy and chips on his lap, a pickled onion or two on the side.

Another friend: a plump, middle-aged alcoholic who is an accountant. I envied his enthusiasm as he talked of the life that marriage, for the moment, was keeping him from. He had worked too hard to enjoy sufficiently his teenage freedom the first time. He leaves his wife, buys underwear, aftershave, cufflinks, a bracelet and hair-dye. He presents himself to me.

My eyes and mouth widen.

At last I say, "You've never looked better."

"As always, you're very encouraging," he says. "Thank you, thank you."

We shake hands and off he sets for singles clubs and bars for divorcees. He meets a woman, but she will only have him in her marital bed, to provoke her husband. He meets another. You remind me of someone, she says; an undertaker, as it turns out. My furious friend replies that it isn't *her* body he has come for. He soon learns that at his age he cares far more than formerly whom he spends his time with. What he wanted then he doesn't want now. He notices also that people become eccentric as they get older, and that there is a lot of them to take in.

"Shall I go back to my wife?" he asks.

"Try it," I say, the expert speaking.

But she regards him suspiciously, wondering why his hair has turned aubergine and whether he has had his name engraved on a bracelet to make him identifiable after an accident. She has realized that life is possible without him.

The boys have fallen asleep. I carry them upstairs, one by one. They lie side by side under vivid duvets. I am about to kiss them when I notice their eyes are open. I dread a second wind. I am a liberal parent, afraid of my occasional rages. I always regret any superfluous restraint. I wouldn't want them to fear me; I wouldn't want them to fear anyone. I don't want to break or discourage anything in them. Occasionally, though, I do want them to believe I am in charge. Soon they are leaping from bed to bed. When they make for the door, since I am too tired to grab them, I am forced to put on my "cross" voice. Their reluctance to go to sleep I don't understand. For months the highlight of my day has been the anticipation of unconsciousness. At least they regret the passing of each day, as do I, in a different way. Tonight we want the same thing, my boys and I: more life.

"If you lie still I will read to you," I say.

They regard me suspiciously, but I find a book, and make a place between them. They stretch out across me, occasionally kicking one another.

It is a cruel story, as most children's stories are, and it involves a woodcutter, as most children's stories do. But inevitably it concerns a conventional family from which the father has not fled. The boys know the story so well they can tell when I skip a bit or attempt to make something up. When they stop asking questions I put the book down, creep out of the room and switch off the light. Then I return to find their faces in the covers, and kiss them. Outside I listen for their breathing. If only I could stand here all night. Then I hear them whispering to one another and giggling.

Old wives; old story.

$$\star \quad \star \quad \star$$

From the beginning, starting with the girls at school, and the teachers in particular, I have looked at women in shops, on the street, in the bus, at parties, and wondered what it would be like to be with them, and what pleasures we might kindle. At school I would toss my pencil under the teacher's desk in order to crawl underneath and examine her legs. The desultory nature of the education system enabled me to develop an enthusiastic interest in girls' skirts—in the material and texture, and in whether they were billowy, loose or tight, and in which places. Skirts, like theatre curtains later, quickened my curiosity. I wanted to know what was under them. There was waiting, but there was possibility. The skirt was a transitional object; both a thing in itself and a means of getting somewhere else. This became my paradigm of important knowledge. The world is a skirt I want to lift up.

Later, I imagined that with each woman I could start afresh. There was no past. I could be a different person, if not a new one, for a time. Also I used women to protect me from other people. Wherever I might be, if I were huddled up with a whispering woman who wanted me, I could keep the world outside my skin. I could stop wanting other women. At the same time I liked to keep my options open; desiring other women kept me from the exposure and susceptibility of loving just the one. There are perils in deep knowledge.

Unsurprisingly, Susan is the one woman, apart from Mother, with whom I can do practically nothing. But now, when I am certain that I am able to speak to women without being afraid of wanting them, I am not sure that I can touch someone as I used to—frivolously. After a certain age sex can never be casual. I couldn't ask for so little. To lay your hand on another's body, or to put your mouth against another's—what a commitment that is! To choose someone is to uncover a whole life. And it is to invite them to uncover you!

Maybe that is what happened with Nina. One day a girl walks past and you want her. I've examined the moment a score of times. She and I would go over it repeatedly, in joy and in puzzlement. I can remember how tall and slim she was; and then there was the jolt, the violent jolt, when we met, and met. Something about her changed everything. But I had wanted people before, and I knew nothing about her. She was from another world. After a certain age you don't want things to be so haphazard. You want to believe that you know what it is you are doing. Perhaps that explains what I did.

My young gay friend Ian liked to stand with me outside tube stations where I would watch the flocks of girls in the summer, after I had finished work for the day, around lunch time. There were certain locations that guaranteed more interest than others. "A picture of impotence," he called it. With him, looks would be exchanged and off he would go, while I waited, having coffee somewhere. Sometimes he fucked five people in a day, shoving his arm up to the elbow into men whose faces he never saw. Every night of the week there were orgies he might attend.

"I've never understood all the fuss you straights make about infidelity," he'd say. "It's only fucking."

"Fucking means something," I'd reply. But what? I'd add, "Surely, for there to be beauty there must be mystery too."

"When there are other people there is always mystery," was his answer.

Susan has already laid the table. I open the wine and pour it. The man in the off-licence said it is an easy wine to drink. These days I find anything easy to drink.

Susan brings the food in and sets it down. I glance over the newspaper. As she eats, she turns on the TV, puts on her glasses and leans forward to watch a soap opera.

"Oh my God," she says, as something happens.

The noise presses into my head. You'd think, if she wanted domestic drama, she could look across the table.

But I am looking away, at a tree in the garden, at a print on the wall, longing for something beautiful or made with care. I have begun to hate television as well as the other media. I was young when the rock-'n'-roll world—the apotheosis of the defiantly shallow—represented the new. It was rebellious and stood against the conventional and dead. Television, too, remained a novelty throughout my youth—all those flickering worlds admitted to one room, Father making me hold the aerial up at the window on tiptoe. Every few months something new and shiny arrived: a car, a fridge, a washing machine, a telephone. And for a time each new thing amazed us. We touched and stared at it for at least a fortnight. We were like everybody else, and ahead of some people. We thought—I don't know why—that things would be enough.

Now I resent being bombarded by vulgarity, emptiness and repetition. I have friends in television. They talk constantly of their jobs and salaries, of the politics in which they're enmeshed, and of the public, whom they never meet. But if you turn on the TV and sit down hoping to see something sustaining, you're going to be disappointed—outraged, in fact, by bullying, aggression and the forcible democratization of the intellect. I am turning off; rebelling against rebellion.

A nerve in my eye is throbbing. My hands seem to be shaking. I feel hollow and my nerves raw, as if I have been pierced by something fatal. My body knows what is going on. If I am frightened now I will feel worse tomorrow, and the day after, and the day after that. All this, in the name of some kind of liberation. But terrible feelings go away after a time—that is one of the terrible things about them.

At university I met a woman as sad as me, if not sadder. For six years, before I met Susan, we lived together. To me now, that seems a long time. But then I imagined there would be time for everything. We slept in the same bed every night, and cooked and ate together. Our friends took it for granted that we were one, though at times we had other lovers. About once a month we would have sex. It was the late seventies, and relationships were nonchalant and easy, as if it had been agreed that the confinement of regularity made people mentally sick. I think I believed that if you didn't have children monogamy was unnecessary.

I want to say the smell of mimosa reminds me of her. I want to say she will always be with me in some way. But it has gone, and she is an unmourned true love.

But Nina has not gone from my mind. I am unable to let her go, yet.

I force myself to eat. I will need strength in the next few days. But no tomato has ever tasted so intransigent. Suddenly Susan touches my face with her fingertips.

"You," she says.

"Yes?"

Maybe she can sense the velocity and turmoil of my thoughts.

"Just you, Jay. It's all right. Only that."

I stare at her. The kindness of the gesture shocks me. I wonder if she does somehow, somewhere, love me. And if one is fortunate enough to be loved one should, surely, appreciate it. I have been anticipating an argument. That would certainly get me out of the house tonight. But I know I must do this sane and sober, and not run out of the door with my hair on fire, or while hallucinating, or while wanting to murder someone.

Tonight I want to be only as mad as I choose; not more mad than that, please.

This is not my first flight. You see, I have run away before. As a boy I would sit in my bedroom with my hands over my ears while my parents raged at one another downstairs, convinced that one would kill the other and then commit suicide. I imagined myself walking away like Dick Whittington, with a spotted handkerchief tied to a stick over my shoulder. But I could never decide on a destination. I did consider going up north, but *Billy Liar* was one of my favourite films and I knew that northern malcontents, when they could, were fleeing down south.

A few years later, one dreary afternoon, a friend and I walked out of the house and took the train from Waterloo to the coast, and then a ferry to the Isle of Wight, where we expected to catch Bob Dylan performing "Subterranean Homesick Blues." All night we lay out in the drizzle in our tie-dyed T-shirts and frayed jeans, returning home the next day, disappointed and afraid. My mother was crying "What have you done?" as I stepped back into the house. I was muttering, "Never the same again, never the same again."

I was right. My excursion was all round the school. It increased my standing with the hippies who had previously scorned me. They invited me to a party where I met their group—girls and boys from the local area, aged from thirteen to seventeen, who spent most evenings and all weekends together. They smoked pot, or "shit" as it was called, and took LSD, even during classes. In the houses of absent parents, the parties were orgies, with girls and boys openly copulating and exchanging partners. Most of the children were, like me, fleeing something: their homes. I learned it wasn't necessary to keep one's parents company. You could get out. A decent teacher had shown me a Thom Gunn poem, "On the Move", which I tore from the book and carried in the back pocket of my Levis. At parties I would lie on the floor and declaim it. "One is always nearer by not keeping still."

You gotta go.
Again.

After we have cleared up, Susan sits at the table writing invitations for the boys' party. Then, making a shopping list for next week, she says, "What meals do you fancy?"

"I don't want to think about it now."

"What's your favourite ice-cream flavour at the moment? Is it the nut crunch or the vanilla?"

"I don't know."

She says, "It's not like you to be unable to think of food."

"No."

I am considering how well I know her. The way she puts her head to one side, and the grimace she makes when concentrating. She looks as she must have as an eleven-year-old taking an exam. No doubt she will have a similar look at seventy, her gestures and movements unchanged, writing a letter to one of our sons.

How would I describe her? A characteristic image would be of her as a young teenager, getting up early to study in her bedroom, bent over a table as she is now. She would prepare for school, make her sandwiches, and leave the house, while her parents slept. She got herself into Cambridge, where she ensured she knew the most luminous people. She is as deliberate in her friendships as she is in everything else.

Though we exist at all ages at once, I can't say that I have ever seen her girlish. She is an effective, organized woman. Our fridges and freezers are full of soup, vegetables, wine, cheese and ice-cream; the flowers and bushes in the garden are labelled; the children's clothes are washed, ironed and folded. Every day there are deliveries of newspapers, books, alcohol, food and, often, of furniture. Our front path is a kind of thoroughfare for the service industries.

There are also people who come to clean the house, iron our shirts, tend the garden and cut the trees, as well as nannies, baby-sitters, child-minders and au pairs, not to mention masseurs, decorators, acupuncturists, financial advisers, piano teachers, accountants, the occasional drug dealer and people to organize all of the above and some of the below. When the numerous gadgets stop working, men come to mend them, one for each. Chalked on a board are instructions for the week, with several underlinings. Susan is always thinking of how to improve things here. She will, too, have strong, considered opinions on the latest films and music. In bed she reads cookbooks.

Being lower-middle class and from the suburbs, where poverty and pretension go together, I can see how good the middle class have it, and what a separate, sealed world they inhabit. They keep quiet about it, with reason; they feel guilty, too, but they ensure they have the best of everything, oh yes.

As with any other business, in marriage there soon develops an accepted division of labour, and a code of rules. But couples are never quite sure if they are both playing by the same ones, or whether they might have changed overnight, without the other having been informed.

It wasn't her wit or beauty that fascinated me. There was

never great passion—perhaps that was the point. But there was enjoyment. Mostly I liked her humdrum dexterity and ability to cope. She wasn't helpless before the world, as I felt myself to be. She was straightforward and firm; she knew how to get things done. I envy her capability, and wish I had half of it. At the expense of feeling weak, I enable her to feel strong. If I were too strong and capable, I wouldn't need her, and we would have to part.

Susan is too prudent to want much power, but at the office she is clear and articulate. It is not difficult for her to make less confident people feel ineffectual. She doesn't know how to protect them from her stretch and vigour, and can't understand how I might see the other side. After all, she is cleverer than her colleagues, and has worked harder. Like many girls brought up to be good and well-behaved, she likes to please. Perhaps that is why young women are so suitable for the contemporary working world. They are welcome to it. Not that Susan cannot be ruthless, intent, as she has to be, on concealing her more sympathetic aspect. However, ambition without imagination is always clumsy.

Unlike me she doesn't constantly lucubrate on the splendours and depths of her mind. She finds even interesting self-awareness self-indulgent. The range of her feeling is narrow; she would consider it shameful to give way to her moods. Therefore she keeps most of herself out of view, for fear of what others, and she herself in particular, would think. I would say this odd thing. Because she has never been disillusioned or disappointed—her life has never appalled her, and she would never lapse into inner chaos—she hasn't changed.

But to keep everything going she can be bullying and strict, with a hard, charmless carapace. You have to take care with her: she will rarely cry, but she could burst into flames.

She does, too, have a curious attachment to the minor and, when permitted, major aristocracy. I don't mind a little snobbery, just as one cannot object to the more poignant vanities; they are amusing. But she does have a penchant for anyone titled, as some girls will only go out with drummers, rather than, say, bass players. I find it a puzzling attachment to a class that is not even rotting, but which is completely uninteresting. Clearly one must tolerate all kinds of irritating tendencies in others, but what of the occasions when one cannot grasp the other person at all?

I can, when I am in the mood, make her laugh, particularly at herself, which is a kind of love, because something in her has been recognized. She envies my insouciance, I think. What other function I serve I am not sure, though I have always been urgently required by her. Having had a mother who had little use for me, a woman I could neither cure nor distract, I have liked being a necessity.

But I have been pushed and shoved because I haven't known my own mind, because I have become accustomed to going along with things, and tomorrow morning we will kiss and part.

Actually, forget the kiss.

I fear loneliness, and I fear other people, I fear—

"Sorry?" I say.

Susan is speaking—asking me to get my diary.

"Why?" I say.

"Why? Just do it, if you don't mind. Just do it!"

"Don't speak to me like that. You are so harsh."

"I'm too tired for a negotiation about diaries. The children wake at six. I have to spend the day at work. What do you do in the afternoons? I expect you sleep then!"

I say, "You're not too tired to raise your voice."

"It's the only way I can get you to do anything."

"No, it's not."

"You exhaust me."

"And you me."

I could strike her. She would know then. But at home we are necessarily politicians. Yet I am about to say, "Susan, don't you understand, can't you see, that of all the nights we have spent together, this is the last one—the last one of all?"

My anger, usually contained, can be cruel and vengeful. I would willingly spill my intentions at a time like this, to achieve an easy satisfaction.

However, I should be satisfied. It is not as if I want to discover tonight that Susan and I really are suited.

I murmur, "All right, all right, I'll do it."

"At last."

I shake my head at her.

Sometimes I go along with what Susan wants, but in an absurd parodic way, hoping she will see how foolish I find her. But she doesn't see it and, much to my annoyance, my co-operation pleases her.

I sit in front of her with my diary, flipping through the

pages. After today the pages are blank. I have left space for the rest of my life.

"The children look beautiful at the moment, don't they?" she says.

"They are healthy and happy."

"You love them, don't you?"

"Passionately."

She snorts. "I can't imagine you being passionate about anything."

She says how much she is looking forward to the weekend away that we have planned. We will stay at the country hotel we visited several years ago, when she was first pregnant. The weather was warm. I rowed her on a lake. We ate mussels and read the papers on the beach. It will be just us, without the children, and the opportunity to talk.

"What books should we read?" she asks.

"I'll find something in my study later," I say.

"The rest will do us good. I know things have been getting fraught here."

"Do you think so?"

"You are gloomy and don't try. But . . . we can discuss things."

"What things?"

She says, "All this." Her hands flail. "I think we need to."

She controls herself. "You used to be such an affectionate man. You still are, with the children." She reminds me that there are historic walks and castles in the vicinity of the country hotel. "And please," she says, "will you remember to take your camera this time?"

"I'll try to."

"It's not only that you're completely useless, but that you don't want any photographs of me, do you?"

"Sometimes I do."

She says, "No you don't. You never offer."

"No, I don't offer."

"That's horrible. You should have one on your desk, as I do, of you."

I say, "I'm not interested in photography. And you're not as vain as I am."

"That's true."

I pace up and down with my drink, in an agitated state. She takes no notice. For her it is just another evening.

Fear is something I recognize. My childhood still tastes of fear; of hours, days and months of fear. Fear of parents, aunts and uncles, of vicars, police and teachers, and of being kicked, abused and insulted by other children. The fear of getting into trouble, of being discovered, and the fear of being castigated, smacked, ignored, locked in, locked out, as well as the numerous other punishments that surrounded everything you attempted. There is, too, the fear of what you wanted, hated and desired; the fear of your own anger, the fear of retaliation and of annihilation. There is habit, convention and morality, as well as the fear of who you might become. It isn't surprising that you become accustomed to doing what you are told while making a safe place inside yourself, and living a secret life. Perhaps that is why stories of spies and double lives are so compelling. It is, surely, a miracle that anyone ever does anything original.

I notice that she is speaking to me again.

"By the way, Victor rang."

"Oh yes? Any message?"

"He wanted to know when you are coming."

She looks at me.

"Okay," I say. "Thank you."

After a bit she says, "Why don't you see more people? I mean proper people, not just Victor."

"I can't bear the distraction," I say. "My internal life is too busy."

I should add: I have enough voices to attend to, within.

"I can't imagine what you have to think about," she says. Then she laughs. "You didn't eat much. Your trousers are baggy. They're always falling down. You look like a builder."

"Sorry."

"Sorry? Don't say sorry. You sound pathetic."

"Sometimes I am."

She grunts. After a few moments she gets up.

"Put the dishes in the machine," she says. "Don't just leave them on the side for me to clear up."

"I'll put them in the machine when I'm ready."

"That means never." Then she says, "Are you coming upstairs?"

I look at her searchingly and with interest, wondering if she means sex—it must be more than a month since we've fucked—or whether she intends us to read. I like books but I don't want to get undressed for one.

"In a while," I say.

"You are so restless."

"Am I?"

"It is your age."

"It must be that."

Adults used to say that to me as a child. "It's only a phase."

For some people—Buddhists, I believe—life is only a phase.

Asif relishes the weekends. Occasionally I see the family on the towpath on Sunday mornings, the kids in yellow helmets on the back of the adults' bikes, on their way to a picnic. At university he was the brightest of our year, and was considered something of a martyr for becoming a teacher.

But he never wanted anything else. Soon after finals he and Najma married. One of his children has spent months in hospital and was lucky to survive. Asif nearly lost his mind over it. The child seems to have recovered, but Asif never forgets what he almost lost.

He doesn't often come into the city; the rush and uproar make his head whirl. But when he and I have an "old-friends" lunch I insist he meets me in the centre of town. From the station I take him to clamorous places where there will be fashionable young women in close-fitting items.

"What a picture gallery you have brought me to!" he says, rubbing his hands. "Is this how you spend your life?"

"Oh yes."

I indicate their attributes and inform him that they prefer mature men.

"Does such a thing exist?" he says. "And are you sure? Have you tried them all?"

"I'm going to. Champagne?"

"Just the one."

"I'll have to order a bottle."

Our talk is of books and politics, and of mutual university friends. I have had him confess that he wonders what another body might feel like. But then he imagines his wife putting out flowers as she waits for him. He says he sees her across the bed in her negligée, three children sleeping between them.

I recall him describing how much he enjoys sucking her cunt. Apparently he's grunting and slurping down there for hours, after all this time, and wonders whether his soul will only emerge through her ears. They massage one another's feet with coconut oil. In the conservatory their chairs face one another. When they are not discussing their children or important questions of the day, they read Christina Rossetti aloud.

"In five years," he says, "we will move house!"

When he yearns—he is not a fool—he yearns for what he has already, to play in the same cricket team as his son, for a garden pond with frogs, and a trip to the Grand Canyon. It is easy to laugh at bourgeois happiness. What other kinds are there? Asif is a rare man, unafraid of admitting his joy.

One afternoon I went to his house to pick up my children. While they played in the garden, Najma was drawing with crayons at the kitchen table. I love looking at crayons, and scrawling with them on big sheets of coloured paper. But the serenity made me uncomfortable, I don't know why. I couldn't sit still because I wanted to kiss her and push her into the bedroom, thereby, it seemed to me, smashing everything up, or testing it, or trying to see what was there, what the secret was.

Asif's happiness excludes me. After a time he and I can only smile at one another. I can't get a grip on him, as I can with Victor. It is unhappiness and the wound that compels me. Then I can understand and be of use. An atmosphere of generalized depression and mid-temperature gloom makes me feel at home. If you are drawn to unhappiness you'll never lack a friend.

If only I could see her face again. But I don't even have a photograph.

For Aristotle the aim of life is "successful activity" or happiness, which for him is inseparable from, though not the same as, pleasure. My unhappiness benefits no one; not Susan, not the children, not myself. But perhaps happiness—that condition in which there is completion, where one has everything, and music too—is an acquired taste. Certainly I haven't acquired it in this house. Perhaps I haven't sought it or let myself feel it. Doubtless there have been opportunities. That afternoon when . . . Their smiling faces. Her hand as it . . .

Yet velvet curtains, soft cheese, compelling work and boys who can run full-tilt—it isn't enough. And if it isn't, it isn't. There's no living with that. The world is made from our imagination; our eyes enliven it, as our hands give it shape. Wanting makes it thrive; meaning is what you put in, not what you extract. You can only see what you are inclined to see, and no more. We have to make the new.

Asif has integrity and principle. Without being especially pompous, he is not ashamed to say what he believes in. He refused all that eighties cynicism. His beliefs give him stability, meaning, and a centre. He knows where he is; the world is always recognizable to him. But why do people who are good at families have to be smug and assume it is the only way to live, as if everybody else is inadequate? Why can't they be blamed for being bad at promiscuity?

I have integrity too, I am sure of it. It is difficult to explain. I expect him to know my particular probity without having to go into it. I suppose I want to be loyal to something else now. Or someone else. Yes; myself. When did it start going wrong with Susan? When I opened my eyes; when I decided I wanted to see.

A few months ago we went into his study and I requested him to inform Susan that I had been with him when I had been with Nina.

He was dismayed.

"But don't ask me to do that."

"What?"

"Lie for you," he said.

"Aren't we friends?" I said. "It's a sensible lie. Susan doubts me. It is making her unhappy."

He shook his head. "You are too used to having your own way. You are making her unhappy."

"I am interested in someone else," I said.

"Who is she?"

I told him little of my relationships with women; he imagined such fabulous liaisons that I didn't want to disillusion him. He said to me once, "You remind me of someone who only ever reads the first chapter of a book. You never discover what happens next."

He asked questions, the first of which was, "How old is she?"

There was a discernible look of repulsion on his face, as if he were trying to swallow sour milk.

"It's only sex then."

"There is that," I said.

"But marriage is a battle, a terrible journey, a season in hell and a reason for living. You need to be equipped in all areas, not just the sexual."

"Yes," I said, dully. "I know."

Oh to be equipped in all areas.

After a certain age there are only certain people, in certain circumstances, whom we allow to love one another. Lately, Mother has been joking about wanting a younger man, and even looks at boys on the street and says, "He's pretty." It makes me shudder. Grandmother, at eighty, found a paramour with whom she held hands. She started to wear perfume and earrings. She imagined we would be pleased that she was no longer alone. How eagerly even the most seditious of us require strict convention! But Asif's favourite opera is *Don Giovanni,* and *Anna Karenina* and *Madame Bovary* his favourite novels. Testaments of fire and betrayal, all!

People don't want you to have too much pleasure; they think it's bad for you. You might start wanting it all the time. How unsettling is desire! That devil never sleeps or keeps still. Desire is naughty and doesn't conform to our ideals, which is why we have such a need of them. Desire mocks all human endeavour and makes it worthwhile. Desire is the original anarchist and undercover agent—no wonder people want it arrested and kept in a safe place. And just when we think we've got desire under control it lets us down or fills us with hope. Desire makes me laugh because it makes fools of us all. Still, rather a fool than a fascist.

When, in abstraction, I tried out the subject of separation, Asif said: "I can just about see why someone would leave their spouse, but I can't understand how someone could leave their children. To me just going to work feels like *Sophie's Choice.*"

It is the men who must go. They are blamed for it, as I will be. I understand the necessity of blame—the idea that someone could, had they the will, courage or sense of duty, have behaved otherwise. There must, somewhere, be deliberate moral infringement rather than anarchy, to preserve the idea of justice and of meaning in the world.

Perhaps Asif will consider it all as one would the death of an acquaintance—how foolish it was of them to die. Surely it is not a mistake one would make oneself! He will shiver and feel glad it hasn't happened to him. Then he will contemplate frogs.

*　　*　　*

You sat back in your chair. It was that place we went to, chosen at random in Soho. I was looking for it this morning, to remember. Somehow I hoped you would be sitting there, waiting for me.

That day, both lost in our own perplexity, we had hardly spoken. Then you tucked your hair behind your ears so I could see your face.

You said, "If you want me, here I am. You can have me."

You can have me, you can.

But that was before.

The comfortable chairs, old carpets, yards of books, many pictures, and piles of CDs, create a calming silence. I've always had a room or study like this.

I read and make notes here, but I don't work at home. For the last ten years I've rented an office a bus ride away, a place as bare and minimal as they get, with, if possible, a view of a dripping stairwell. I work in short bursts, without interruption, on adaptations and original scripts for television and the cinema. I pace up and down a lot, if I'm not walking about the streets.

I am more of an engineer than an artist, although as I become more accomplished I find myself putting more of myself into the stories than formerly. I like my work to be more difficult these days. But by the time I get to a piece most of the art has already been done. It does take some talent to put the right scenes in the right order. Organization in a work is more important than people realize. If only writers in the past had seen that in the future all written stories would be translated to the screen, it would have saved a lot of time for people like me. "Turning gold into dross," Asif calls it.

I extract my weekend bag from the cupboard and open it. I stare into the bottom and then put it on my head. What do you take when you're never coming back? I throw a book into the bag—something by Strindberg I've been studying—and then replace the book on the shelf.

I stand here for ages looking around. I am afraid of getting too comfortable in my own house, as if, once I sit down, I will lose the desire for alteration. Above my desk is the shelf on which I keep my prizes and awards. Susan says it makes the place look like a dentist's waiting room.

An inventory, perhaps.

The desk—which my parents bought me when I was taking my A-levels—I have lugged around from squat to squat, via shared houses and council flats, until it ended up here, the first property I have owned. A significant decision, getting a mortgage. It was as if you would never be able to "move" again.

I'll leave the desk for the boys. And the books? I can neither reread them nor throw them out. I have spent sufficient time with my face lost in a page, some of it dutiful, some of it pleasurable, some of it looking for sustenance only a living person could provide. Often I made the mistake, when young, of starting a book at the beginning and reading through to the end.

For a while I was some sort of Marxist, though I cannot any more recall the differences between all the varieties—

Gramsci-ists, Leninists, Hegelians, Maoists, Althusseurians. At the time the fine distinctions were as momentous, say, as the difference between hanging someone or shooting them.

I was keen on history too: E. P. Thompson, Hobsbawm, Hill. I had an uncle who, when middle-aged, made himself "master" Roman history, and spent years memorizing "the classics." Yet, at the end of his life, as well as being unable to remember a tenth of it, he couldn't even recall why he'd sought such learning or who it was for.

You might say that without a general culture nothing can be understood. But the general culture isn't getting me any-where tonight. I can't keep my loneliness and longing away.

I must do something. But what?

And, more importantly, why?

At university I shared a flat with a friend, a handsome, intelligent man, who would sit at a table for days with only a pack of cigarettes as distraction. People might come in and out of the flat; they might be troubled or unhappy, or might want excitement, sex. Yet still he would sit there. I don't know if he was depressed, indifferent or stoical. But I envied him. Pursuing nothing, he waited. He and I discussed the possibil-ity of living on cereal, eating it twice a day, with an orange for lunch. We discovered that one could survive on this regime for weeks without injury to one's health, if not to one's out-look. I expect to hear one day that he has killed himself.

But to be able to bear one's own mind, to wait while the inner storm of intolerable thoughts blows itself out, leaving one to contemplate the debris with some understanding—that is an enviable state of mind.

*   *   *

What puzzles me more than anything? The fact that I have struggled with the same questions and obsessions, and with the same dull and useless responses, for so long, for the past ten years, without experiencing any increase in knowledge, or any release from the need to know, like a rat on a wheel. How can I move beyond this? I am moving out. A breakdown is a breakthrough is a breakout. That is something.

One makes mistakes, gets led astray, digresses. If one could see one's crooked progress as a kind of experiment, without wishing for an impossible security—nothing interesting happens without daring—some kind of stillness might be attained.

You can, of course, experiment with your own life. Maybe you shouldn't do it with other people's.

I like walking to school at lunch time with my long-haired sons, pulling them along and joking with them. But as soon as we enter the Victorian playground, the smell and the teacher's dogged look—her voice carries to the street— remind me of futility. If the teacher spoke to me as she does to my elder boy, I would smack her face. A braver man would take the boys home. But I drop them off and slip round to a quiet pub for a pint of Guinness, a read of the paper and a cigarette, glad it's them and not me.

I paid no attention to my schoolteachers. They had bored and scared me, unless their legs provided some compensation. But my first weeks at university shocked me into attention. I had to get home to read *Teach Yourself* books, and *The Children's Guide to* . . . When there was no compulsion and my mind began to run, I got through Plato, Descartes, Hume, Kant, Marx, Freud, Sartre.

Philosophy was formal, abstract, cool. I chose it because I loved literature, and didn't want stories that had been poisoned by theorizing. For me that was like food that had been chewed by other people. I am ready to study seriously again—music, poetry, history. At this age, coming to my senses as a human being at last, I am not done with learning. I know I am no longer ashamed of my ignorance, nor afraid of liking things.

At university we went to the theatre several times a week, since my group of friends worked as dressers and ushers at the Royal Court, at the newly opened National, and at the RSC in the Aldwych. At the interval I would pick up girls in the audience. During the more boring plays they would slip out and talk to me. I have never found that the man being in a subordinate position has put women off. In fact, for some people, the more subordinate you are, the more "genuine" they imagine you to be. People are afraid of too much power in others. But when I had these women I never quite knew what to do with them.

I am still standing upright, but something is moving and I would rather it didn't. Yes, it is me. I seem to be swaying.

I sit still a few minutes, head in hands, taking deep breaths, hoping for some deep calm. During one of our turbulent periods, Susan and I attended yoga classes in a hall at the end of the street. There were, in this class, many attractive women, most in bright leotards and all taking up adventurous positions reflected in the polished mirrors. In such circumstances I found infinite desirelessness a strain to bring on. As our souls lifted into nirvana on a collective "oommm" my penis would press against my shorts as if to say, "Don't forget that always I am here too!" Sexual release is the most mysticism most people can manage.

Fuck it, I will leave everything here. My sons, wandering in this forsaken room, will discover, perhaps by mistake, the treasures they need.

After school or college, in my bedroom, I would pile up Father's classical records on the spindle of my record player, and the symphonies would clatter down, one by one, until supper. It was rebellious in those days to like music that didn't sound better the louder it was played.

Then, restless at my desk, with my father's bookshelves around me, I would reach up and pull down a few volumes. Father, like the other neighbourhood men, spent most of his days' energy in unsatisfying work. Time was precious and he had me fear its waste. But browsing and ruminating at my desk, I figured that doing nothing was often the best way of doing something.

I will regret forfeiting this room. For though I have never been taught the art of solitude, but had to learn it, it has become as necessary to me as the Beatles, kisses on the back of my neck and kindness. Here I can follow the momentum of my thoughts as I read, write, sing, dance, think of the past and waste time. Here I have examined dimly felt intuitions, and captured unclear but pressing ideas. I am speaking of the pleasures of not speaking, doing or wanting, but of losing oneself.

But it was in this room, late at night, when she and the children were asleep and I sat here listening to the street, that I saw how I yearned for contact and nourishment. I never found a way to be pleasurably idle with Susan. She has a busy mind. One might want to admire anyone who lives with vigour and spirit. But there is desperation in her activity, as if her work is holding her together. In some ways, it is less of everything that I want.

I know how necessary fathers are for boys. I would hang on to Dad's hand as he toured the bookshops, climbing ladders and standing on steps to pull down rotting tomes. "Let's go, let's go . . ." I'd say.

How utterly the past suffuses us. We live in all our days at once. The writers Dad preferred are still my favourites, mostly nineteenth-century Europeans, the Russians in particular. The characters, Goriot, Vronsky, Madame Ranevskaya, Nana, Julien Sorel, feel part of me. It is Father's copies I will give to the boys. Father took me to see war films and cricket. Whenever I appeared in his room his face would brighten. He loved kissing me. We kept one another company for years. He, more than anyone, was the person I wanted to marry. I wanted to walk, talk, laugh and dress like him. My sons are the same with me, repeating my phrases in their tiny voices, staring admiringly at me and fighting to sit beside me. But I am leaving them. What would Father think of that?

What embarrassed Nina about me embarrassed me about him. I don't yet read the newspapers wearing gloves, as Father did to prevent his fingers getting soiled. But I know many local shopkeepers, and I do bang on their windows as I pass, and will stop and ask them personal questions about the minutiae of their lives. Father would invite in any passing religious freak with a shopping bag full of pamphlets and engage in a ferocious debate.

But I lack his kindness. Of all the virtues it is the sweetest, particularly since it isn't considered a moral attribute, but as a gift. Nina always said that I am kind; she said I was the perfect man for her, and that I had everything she could want. Would she still say that?

My younger son, his nose in my wrist as we walked in the street last week, said, "Daddy, you smell of you."

Cheerio, I must be going.

Father, six years dead, would have been horrified by my skulking off. Such an abandonment would have seemed undignified at the very least. Susan used to go to him when we were fighting and he would take her side, phoning me and saying, "Don't be cruel, boy." He said she was "all in one." She had everything I could want. Dad left his own mother at twenty-one and never saw her again. He didn't approve of leaving, and he liked to be chivalrous. He didn't see that the women could take care of themselves. The man had the power and had to be protective.

Father believed, too, in loyalty. For him to be accused of disloyalty would have been like being called a thief. But what would he have been loyal to? After all, when required, one can always find something to attach one's stubborn faith to. Probably he would have been loyal to the idea of loyalty itself, for fear that without it the world would have been robbed of compassion, and oneself exposed.

Father was a civil servant who later worked as a clerk at Scotland Yard, for the police. In the mornings, and at weekends, he wrote novels. He must have completed five or six. A couple of them were admired by publishers, but none of them got into print. They weren't very bad and they weren't very good. He never gave up; it was all he ever wanted to do. The book on his bedside table had, on the cover, a picture of a middle-aged writer sitting on a pile of books, a portable typewriter on his knees. It was *Call It Experience* by Erskine Caldwell. Under the author's name it said, "Reveals the secrets of a great writer's private life and literary success." The writer did look experienced; he had been around, but he was ready to go on. He was tough. That's what a writer was.

Failure strengthened Father's resolve. He was both brave and foolish, I'd say. He wanted me to be a doctor, and I did consider it, but probably only because I was an admirer of Chekhov and Father liked Somerest Maugham. In the end Dad told me it was hopeless to take up something that wasn't going to provide me with pleasure for the rest of my life. He was wise in that way. I was adept and successful a couple of years after I left university. I could do it; I just could. Whether it was a knack or trick or talent, I didn't know. It puzzled both of us. Art is easy for those who can do it, and impossible for those who can't.

What did Father's life show me? That life is a struggle, and that struggle gets you nowhere and is neither recognized nor rewarded. There is little pleasure in marriage; it involves considerable endurance, like doing a job one hates. You can't leave and you can't enjoy it. Both he and Mother were frustrated, neither being able to find a way to get what they wanted, whatever that was. Nevertheless they were loyal and faithful to one another. Disloyal and unfaithful to themselves. Or do I misunderstand?

I run my hand down the CDs piled on every available surface. Classical, of all periods, with dark Beethoven my God; jazz, mostly of the fifties; blues, rock-'n'-roll and pop, with the emphasis on the mid-sixties and early seventies. A lot of punk. It was the hatred, I think, that appealed. It is great music but you wouldn't want to listen to it.

Victor doesn't have much music over there, and few books. He only had the Bible in his house, and no one read it, not even the Song of Solomon. Now I accompany him to record shops and he flips through the CDs. "Who's this? What's this?" he goes.

He has a lovely helplessness, and has caught my enthusiasm. I took him to see my friend who has a shop. He bought a sky-blue suit which certainly shocks but does not outrage, except in certain low dives. He has tinted his hair. He might resemble a badger, and I did balk at the earring. But I keep my mirth down, and would say: any advance in wisdom requires a good dose of shamelessness.

Separation wouldn't have occurred to a lower-middle-class couple in the fifties. My parents remained in the same house all their lives. Mother was only partially there. Most of the day she sat, inert and obese, in her chair. She hardly spoke—except to dispute; she never touched anyone, and often wept, hating herself and all of us: a lump of living death. She wouldn't wash; there were cobwebs in all the rooms; the plates and cutlery were greasy. We hardly changed our clothes. All effort was a trouble and she lived on the edge of panic, as if everything was about to break down. Occasionally there were reminders of life, a smile or joke, even a conversation. But these were rare, and she was gone. For a long time I had the strange feeling that she reminded me of someone I used to know.

She was aware of it, in some way.

"Selfish," she called herself, because her mind hurt so much she could only think of herself. She didn't know how to enjoy other people, the world, or her own body. I was afraid to approach her, since with such a mother you never knew whether she would send you away or put out her arms for a kiss. My existence was a disturbance. Being a burden, or interruption. I couldn't ask her for anything. But if she didn't like me, I did cause her to worry. And I worried about her worrying. Anxiety handcuffed us to one another. At least we had something in common.

When I was nominated for the Oscar and I rang to tell her, she said, "Will you have to go all that way to America? It's a long way."

"Thanks for the concern," I said.

When we were older money was short. Father refused to look for another job and he wouldn't move to a different part of the country. Nothing was allowed to happen until he "made it." Mother was forced to find employment. She was a school dinner lady; she worked in factories and offices; she worked in a shop. I think the compulsion and other people were better for her than sitting at home.

The day I started to live with my sad girlfriend in London, I went home to pick up my things. I imagined it would be the first and last time I would leave home. I didn't know I'd be making a habit of it. My parents sat in separate armchairs, watching me carry out my records. What was there left for them to do? Hadn't I rendered them irrelevant?

But when my brother and I left, our parents started going to art galleries, to the cinema, for walks and on long holidays. They took a new interest in one another, and couldn't get enough of life. Victor says that once the lights on a love have dimmed, you can never illuminate them again, any more than you can reheat a soufflé. But my parents went through the darkness and discovered a new intimacy.

Can't you, then, apply yourself? Susan often accuses me of lack of application. It was what my teachers said, that I didn't concentrate. But I *was* concentrating. I believe the mind is always concentrated—on something that interests it. Skirts and jokes and cricket and pop, in my case. Despite ourselves, we know what we like, and our errors and distracted excursions are illuminations. Perhaps only the unsought is worthwhile—like Nina's face and the caresses of her long fingers.

Not loving Susan I insist on seeing as a weakness, as my failure and my responsibility. But what is the point of leaving if this failure reproduces itself with every woman? Suppose it is like an illness that you give to everyone you meet? Wouldn't I have to keep a bag permanently packed by any door I had taken refuge behind?

I don't want to think of that.

My bags sits on the floor.

I will be needing pens and paper on my journey. I won't want to forfeit any important emotion. I will pursue my feelings like a detective, looking for clues to the crime, writing as I read myself within. I want an absolute honesty that doesn't merely involve saying how awful one is. How do I like to write? With a soft pencil and a hard dick—not the other way round.

I like paper of all kinds: creamy, white, yellow; thick, thin, lined, plain. In my cupboard I have at least fifty notebooks, each of which, at the time of purchase, filled me with the excitement of what might be said, of new thoughts discovered. Each has a sheet of white blotting paper between the leaves, and all are blank apart from the first page, on which I have usually written something like, "In this notebook I will write whatever comes into my mind, and after a time I will see a picture of myself emerge, made up of significant fragments . . ." And then—nothing. I freeze, as one does when things are getting illegitimately interesting.

I have tried devoting each notebook to a different subject: books I'm reading, thoughts on politics, problems I have with Mother, Susan, present lovers, etc. But as I begin, I become busy washing my weeping fountain pens, refilling them, testing the nibs and wondering why the flow isn't regular. There are few more exquisite instruments than a fountain pen as it glides over good paper, like a finger over young skin.

But somehow I am made for ferocious, uncontrolled scribbling on scrap paper with old Biros and stubby soft pencils.

For our homework, as kids, we would sometimes be asked to write, "What I did today." Now I feel like compiling a list: the things I didn't do today. The things I haven't done in life.

I think of the people I know (later I might write their names in a suitable notebook) and wonder which of them knows how to live well. If living is an art it is a strange one, an art of everything, and particularly of spirited pleasure. Its developed form would involve a number of qualities sewn together: intelligence, charm, good fortune, unforced virtue, along with wisdom, taste, knowledge, understanding, and the recognition of anguish and conflict as part of life. Wealth wouldn't be essential, but the intelligence to accumulate it where necessary might be. The people I can think of who live with talent are the ones who have free lives, conceiving of great schemes and seeing them fulfilled. They are, too, the best company.

Victor and I were in our favourite bar the other day, watching football on television. He said, "When I think of how my wife and I stayed together all those barren and arduous nights and years, I cannot understand it at all. Perhaps it was a kind of mad idealism. I had made a promise that I had to fulfil at all costs. But why? The world couldn't possibly recover from the end of my marriage. My faith in everything would be shattered. I believed in it without knowing how much I believed in it. It was blind, foolish obedience and submission. Probably it was the only kind of religious faith I've had. I used to think I had some radicalism in me, but I couldn't smash the thing that bound me the most. Smash it? I couldn't even see it!"

Dear God, teach me to be careless.

Come on. Forward.

What do runaways wear? This is important. I should make a list, as Susan has taught me. At Victor's there will be no proper place for my clothes. I am quite fastidious about such things. It would be better to leave most of them here. But if Susan has any flair she will slash my Vivienne Westwood jacket. It would be dispiriting if my departure went unnoticed—a measure of delirium is essential. As for shoes, I can't take many pairs, but I will require something both stylish and comfortable to give myself confidence.

I have several suits, each of which I favour at different times and like to wear out to lunch, an event I look forward to all morning, since it is the first time in the day that I become aware of other people. This week I fancy the double-breasted four-button pinstripe. The trousers are tapered, with flat front pockets. I wear them with dark blue suede loafers. It's not boxy but wearing it makes me feel magisterial. I am convinced I will be served first in shops and that I can talk down to people. I will need it for all the bars and restaurants I will be visiting with Victor, to offset his sky-blue number. But I can't go round like that every day. I will need other clothes too.

I bought a brown checked suit the other day, a light, summer thing, to cheer myself up. It has to be altered and they won't send it over for a few days. I bought shirts too, but I can't remember how many or in what colours. I can't stay here just for that; I will have to ring the shop and get the stuff diverted. I can't even wear it yet. And by the time the weather has turned warmer, I will have been gone a while.

I remove my signed photograph of John Lennon from the wall and slip it into the empty bag. That is something to take. A handful of CDs too. Alfred Brendel or Emil Gilels? Marvin Gaye or Otis Redding? Perhaps I should remind myself that I am absconding, not appearing on *Desert Island Discs*. Yet I still can't hear the beginning of "Stray Cat Blues" without wanting to hitchhike to Spain with a teenager. I am, too, more likely to listen to Hot Rats than I am to read Sartre, Camus, Ionesco, Beckett and the other poets of solitude and dread that restored me as a young man. Probably it is the human condition that we are ultimately isolated, and will die alone. But tonight, standing here, I want so much to reach out that I could punch through the window.

Patience is a virtue only in children and the imprisoned. Neither Susan nor I are impulsive. In the middle-class way, while others were frolicking and wasting—how I envied any prolonged dissipation!—we both planned and contained our frivolity in order to get all we have. I had a teacher who used to say that every extra year of education adds five thousand pounds to your income for life. I have been able to rise at five, leave the house and get to my desk by five-forty-five. I have excelled at relinquishing things I liked—it isn't any fun giving up things that are not fun. When unnerved I start seeking pleasures to relinquish. But Victor—or is it his therapist, it is easy to confuse those conspirators these days—says toleration can become a bad habit. Yes, I will defer deferral. I am getting on with it. I want it now!

I have been drinking. I will put down the beer bottle, after this swig.

How little directness there is, when you look around! We have to make things distinct by indirection. What a redundant and fearful dance it all is, as if our feelings are weapons that could kill, and words are their bullets. I will go upstairs, sit on the edge of the bed, and tell Susan firmly and truthfully that I am going to leave. I can't stay here another night. What's the point? How absurd to think that this is something one could prepare for! There is only the unknown and my coming to terms with it. I will pack, kiss the children, and go! It will be done and I will be away.

Yes!

My children hunt through their toy boxes, chucking aside the once-cherished to drag out what they need to keep themselves interested. I am the same with books, music, pictures, newspapers. Can we do this with people? That would be considered shallow. We must treat other people as if they were real. But are they?

Yet what makes me think I should have what I want? Surely you can't constantly be replacing people who don't provide what you need? There must be other opportunities for sustenance—in pictures, books, dance—even within. Yet all these forms are enraptured by love and desire, and are created from them.

Susan, who is four years younger than me, thinks we live in a selfish age. She talks of a Thatcherism of the soul that imagines that people are not dependent on one another. In love, these days, it is a free market; browse and buy, pick and choose, rent and reject, as you like. There's no sexual and social security; everyone has to take care of themselves, or not. Fulfilment, self-expression and "creativity" are the only values.

Susan would say that we require other social forms. What are they? Probably the unpleasant ones: duty, sacrifice, obligation to others, self-discipline.

When she says such things I wonder if we haven't been a particularly privileged and spoilt generation. Between the deprivation of the post-war slump, and the cruelties of the eighties, we were the children of innocent consumerism and the inheritors of the freedoms won by our seditious elders in the late sixties. We had a free, superior and somewhat lazy education. Then we went on the dole for five years in order to pursue our self-righteous politics, before starting work in the media and making a lot of money. We weren't much restrained by morality or religion. Music, dancing and conscienceless fucking were our totems. We boasted that we were the freest there'd ever been.

Like the hippies we disdained materialism. Yet we were less frivolous than the original "heads." If we dropped out to become carpenters and gardeners it was because we wanted to share the experience of the working class. We were an earnest and moral generation, with severe politics. We were the last generation to defend communism. I knew people who holidayed in Albania; apparently the beaches are exquisite. An acquaintance supported the Soviet Union on the day they invaded Afghanistan.

We were dismissive and contemptuous of Thatcherism, but so captivated by our own ideological obsessions that we couldn't see its appeal. Which isn't to say we didn't fight it. There was the miners' strike, and the battles at Wapping. We were left enervated and confused. Soon we didn't know what we believed. Some remained on the left; others retreated into sexual politics; some became Thatcherites. We were the kind of people who held the Labour Party back.

Still, I never understood the elevation of greed as a political credo. Why would anyone want to base a political programme on bottomless dissatisfaction and the impossibility of happiness? Perhaps that was its appeal: the promise of luxury that in fact promoted endless work.

My friends and I talk of culture, the state of our minds, and work. But rarely, now, of what could be; there are adjustments but not revolution. There have been enough revolutions. If Marx had been our begetter, the ideologue of the century's first half, Freud was our new father, as we turned inwards. Certainly, the world in which we negotiate our days at work, in love, in our hobbies, in sport—is one of other people, described, these days, in language derived from analysis. Most of my friends seem to spend most of their time on their backs, sleeping, fucking, or having therapy and talking about their "relationships" on the phone.

The women, I think, were fortunate to go in two directions at once, into themselves and out into the history world. They examined their lives more than we did; they experimented; the interesting ones changed more than we did. What is left? The freedoms Nina takes for granted, a free girl swinging about the city. All is absorbed.

I never married Susan. She asked me several times, in a number of moods, hoping, I suppose, to move or amuse me with one or other of them. It might have been her liking for weddings that put me off, and her fondness for chiffon and those thick cardboard invitations with embossed writing. Certainly I enjoyed making her the only unmarried woman in her group of friends from university. She learned that her love involved sacrifice. Anyhow, I still took it for granted that not marrying was a necessary rebellion. The family seemed no more than a machine for the suppression and distortion of free individuals. We could make our own original and flexible arrangements.

I have been told the reasons for the institution of permanent marriage—its being a sacrament, an oath, a promise, all that. Or a profound and irrevocable commitment to the principle as much as to the person. But I can't quite remember the force and the detail of the argument. Does anyone?

Asif will know. He is an intellectual. But even he doesn't dangle his tongue in his wife's hole on principle.

I asked Nina to marry me.

"I can't," she said.

"I won't ask again."

"Yes, ask," she said. "Ask."

Victor says marrying is too expensive. The women take all your money.

Not that Nina ever asked for anything. She was too proud and scared of change for that. "I don't want to be one of those well-fed women," she'd say. "Not yet," I'd reply.

If I offered to give or lend her money, she looked horrified, as if everything, suddenly being made so easy, was devalued. Scarcity was part of her life, including love. Sometimes too much of everything is as bad as too little.

You pick up other people's feelings. Mother wanted to leave. She would stay; she would always have to stay. Women of her time had no money of their own and nowhere to go. They did, after all, have televisions and fridges. Inside she was on the run—from me; from all of us. Children stop you living. That's what her unhappiness told us. It's them or you.

Mother won't say much about my leaving. She is a little scared of me now, having angered me too much. But she will say that it is bad for the children. Odd how the needs of children seem so often to coincide exactly with the opinions of their parents.

Not only does Susan work until seven, but she attends dinner parties, goes to the cinema and theatre, and sits on boards. She may be exhausted but she's involved. After I'm gone there will be devastation. A lone middle-aged woman with kids doesn't have much cachet, and Susan is always aware of her status. Successful and well-off, I was considered a catch, once. I was offered a lot of work, particularly from America. I wasn't precious about what I did; not precious enough, probably. But talent is always at a premium; everything else requires it. In certain moods she has been proud of me. A man can give a woman gravity and light. Perhaps she would rather have a busted, broken-backed relationship than nothing at all. At least there is someone to empty the dustbin. She will, unfortunately, become the recipient of sympathy. At dinner parties divorced men will be placed next to her. In the end, she will get by without me. In my view she'll be better off that way, though she can't see it yet. And I, without her?

Recently I have been tempted by a dream of self-sufficiency: a small flat, a cat, books, TV, music, a dope plant, friends to dinner; a museum on Sunday, followed by a bus ride to the end of the route with one of my sons. Alone but not lonely. I was living alone before I got back together with Susan. The first boy was conceived out of isolation, you could say, a few months after Father died. Yes; I understand the temptations of self-sufficiency, the idea that we can secure everything we need within, that our own caresses are as lovely as another's. But I don't want to be so seduced again. I will throw myself on others, going all the way, not hovering on the fringe of life.

Victor's flat is in a fashionable, bohemian part of town. There will be plenty of bars and restaurants to go to in the evenings. But he keeps most of his possessions in suitcases, and his washing in a pile in the corner with a damp towel on top. The only food in the kitchen is a loaf of bread, a rancid pat of butter, and several pots of jam, pilfered from hotels. To keep himself going Victor scoffs vitamin pills with his beer.

Victor has a disturbed mind, at times. His head booms like an ancient cavern filled with deadly creatures. I have considered it a sign of intense life to be so tormented. Victor yearns for quality of life, by which he means a quality of feeling, not things. But would you want to live with someone like that? Three times a week he weeps at his therapist's. Five years and no sign of a cure. His therapist has told him to express himself. They offer such advice without considering the public. Who says self-expression improves your mental health? Look at the artists: art therapy every day. You'd think they'd be the sanest people around, Van Gogh, Rothko and all.

Victor gets competitive; men do. He wants what I have, and he wants to be like me. It's painful being him, but he asks for too much, and sometimes hates me for being myself.

★   ★   ★

I turn out the lights and find myself climbing the stairs to the bedroom. What am I doing? If this is my last night here, if these are, indeed, the final hours, hadn't I better get packed and ready? Soon I will be dead. Is it really the last night? No, no, no, never. Not really. I was only entertaining myself. Perhaps I will take a chance. That's a good idea. If she is awake . . . what? Yes; I will talk to her a little—after all, she has guided me out of confusion before. Then I will sleep, and continue as usual next morning. I will be glad to have endured this instructive and heavy discontent, but will have done nothing excessive.

I leave the light on in the hall. I step into the room.

I can make out your hair in the jumble of blankets and pillows. I stand looking at you.

I wish you were someone else.

Is it too much to want a tender and complete intimacy? Is it too much to want to sleep in someone's willing arms?

It's been weeks since we fucked. I've stopped approaching Susan in that way, to see whether, by any chance, she desires me. I have waited for a flicker of interest, not to mention lust or abandon. I am a dog under the table, hoping for a biscuit. Not a crumb.

Without removing my clothes I lie down. Yellow light streaks the room from the streetlamp opposite. It is a harsh, sickly colour, reminding me of the smell of gas. I look at the ceiling where the roof has been leaking. Someone has to be here to sort it out. Without me looking authoritative, the workmen could take advantage.

In the street there are raised voices. Most nights there is

some kind of altercation. My neighbours punch one another, and worse, at every opportunity. Every couple of months a car is torched.

It's a mixed area: immaculate black women in white smocks, head-scarves and long skirts go to the Farrakhan Centre nearby, the men in lounge suits and little red bow ties. Thin, efficient white boys in short-sleeved Ben Shermans, with short, neat hair, hurry to fights, carrying bags of chips. Black men in tattered shirts and shapeless trousers shamble to the pub on the corner. Smart women in black with briefcases go to and from work. Outside the pubs wait women with pushchairs— the girl-babies with pierced ears—yelling through the open door at their permanently parked men staring up at the TV screen. The supermarkets have guards in ill-fitting uniforms watching you from the top of the aisle as you plump the fruit.

There's little to steal. There's more in my fridge than there is in most of the shops. You wonder why people put up with it. But they've got used to it; they can't see that things could be different. It is not how much that people demand which surprises me, but how little.

It is not a safe area, and in the morning I am going. Victor's wife, I remember, rang him urgently after he left, to say there had been an attempted burglary. He was surprised, on returning home, to see the windows had been broken—from the inside.

Now I am warm and getting dozy. The bed is comfortable. The house is silent; the children sheltered, healthy and asleep. She made a lovely meal. Having finished the wine, I have been contentedly swilling my brandy in the glass she bought me.

In India they don't seem to put the same emphasis on romantic love. Couples copulate when necessary and get on with their separate lives. In Lahore my uncle lives in one part of the house with his sons, three brothers, male friends, and anyone else who feels like staying a couple of years. My aunt, the daughters, female servants, and the children, live in another part. They meet, at times, but there is no funny business.

Perhaps it is a fine idea to have the women close but not too close. Presumably, over there they suppress their desire, but I am of a generation that believes in the necessity of satisfying oneself.

Maybe; but I have lost my relish for living. I am apathetic and most of the time want nothing, except to understand why there hasn't been more happiness here. Is it like this for everyone? Is this all you get? Is this the most there could be?

In the morning I will be gone.

It is my yearning for more life that has done this, and we are yearning creatures, a bag of insistent wants. Sense says one needn't follow every impulse, pursuing every woman one fancies. But one can, I guess, run after some of them, never knowing in advance what glory one might find.

Susan stirs.

Which scientist was it said bodies never meet? I stroke her back. I am convinced she can feel my thoughts, can feel me wanting her. If she wakes up, puts out her arms and says she loves me, I will sink back into the pillow and never leave. But she has never done such a thing; nor me to her. In fact, sensing my fingers on her, she moves away, pulling up the covers.

Why then don't I shake her awake and force her to look at me? Have I tried hard enough? Why should I imagine that I am easy to get along with? Perhaps, all this time, she has been making a heroic effort to get along with a morose, over-sensitive, self-absorbed fool. She said the other day, "Imagine the strain of living with someone who doesn't speak for hours, and then says vaguely, 'Have you ever thought of joining a cult?'" She has also complained about my scratching my arse almost continuously in bed so that it is a constant background noise, like the sound of crickets in a movie set in a hot place. There is no doubt that I have an aversion to shopping, housework, washing. Somehow I expect all that to be done without my having thought about it.

Nina, I remember, said I am inflexible. She called me a tyrant. Yes; my feelings are strong, my wishes imposing. Perhaps that is why I have had long periods, years in fact, of imposed indifference, as if nothing mattered. The dismissive shrug in a café was my most eloquent gesture. I was detached, having learned to be cold; intact, no one could touch me, particularly the women I let fall in love with me. I wanted them; I got them; I lost interest. I never rang back, or explained. Whenever I was with a woman, I considered leaving her. I didn't want what I wanted. I found their passion repellent, or it amused me. How foolish they were to let themselves feel so much!

Now I can hardly bear the strength of what I feel. Some nights I could bang my head on the wall, particularly when I've lain here with Susan, knowing that my girlfriend—whichever one, but usually Nina—was out in the city. Perhaps she was missing me; probably she was with some young man. Aching at what I was excluded from, hating myself for my inability to live as I wanted, I have got up, dressed and left the house, walking a starlit misery until exhausted. I have returned to find that one of the kids has shit himself or vomited in his sleep.

Now, like Oliver Twist, I am asking for more.

In a few minutes I will wake her up and tell her some of these things.

How Nina tantalizes. She is aloof, feline, graceful. Everything she does has grace; some call it style. Others will say she knows who she is, and likes being herself. Her doubts don't undermine her, but they do make her inaccessible at times. I must be in love with her. I have yet to find out why.

So?

When did the realization really happen? When did it occur to me to leave? I can remember passing the critical point during one of my meandering conversations with Victor in the bar we go to. I thought, looking at all the free people ordering drinks, what's to stop me getting out and never coming back? But the idea was too cruel and subversive. Immediately I was filled with self-disgust, and saw myself from the back, running, a picture of all the other cowardly men who had fled.

That was eight or nine months ago. Nina and I would meet hurriedly before I had to be home with Susan. If there's nothing more likely to make you feel abandoned, desolate and left out than sexual betrayal, perhaps the only way not to feel it, is to feel nothing for the woman. It seemed a kind of freedom to encourage Nina to see other men, to have her tell me about them and for me to laugh at them.

"How many have you seen this week? And what did the last one do to you?"

"He kissed me."

"And you let him?"

"Yes."

"And then he puts his hands on you. And you, no doubt, put these hands that I'm kissing now on him. And—"

The more she told me, the more beautiful she looked. The more I removed myself, the more I hoped she would pursue me. Yes, I wanted her to follow me as I turned away, but I was also afraid of her feeling discouraged.

I have wavered, vacillated and searched myself for a reason to stay. But once the devil voice of temptation had spoken it wouldn't retract. Yet still I waited! For what? To be absolutely sure. "Nothing's gonna change my world," Lennon sang.

At home I made myself powerless and impotent. I could barely walk. What reason was there for putting one foot in front of the other? At night, when Susan was asleep, I couldn't turn on the lights; in the dark I wore sunglasses and hoped to fall over. Nina saw me shrivelling. If I was powerless I would be innocent. I couldn't damage anyone; blameless, I couldn't encourage retribution. I wished to be wishless!

*   *   *

For a year Nina visited me every two or three weeks at the flat I was using as an office. It was a roomy place, owned by an actor who was working in America. She was living in Brighton, where all runaways and lost individualists end up, teaching English to foreigners, always a last resort for the directionless. I met her—or picked her up; I was in that kind of mood one Sunday afternoon, feeling magnetic or "on"—in a theatre café in London. It was a place I never normally visited, except that a photographer friend had an exhibition there. She was with another girl and as I looked at them I recalled Casanova's advice that it is easier to pick up two women at once than one on her own. After many smiles and a few words, I left. She came after me.

"Join me for tea," I said.

"When?"

"How about in an hour?"

She stayed all evening. In a hurry for love after all this time, I behaved foolishly and, if I remember rightly, spent some time on my knees. She came back the next day.

She was a girl then, looking for someone to take the pressure off. She had run away from home when her mother's boyfriend smashed through the glass in the front door with his hands, and she was forced to hide in a cupboard. She was an unhappy and changeable girl, who often lost herself in inexplicable moods. She had never much been cared for, and kept herself apart. She needed to think she could get by without anyone.

When I first met her, she wore cheap, light, hippie clothes, and hadn't cut her hair. She still blushed and turned away her face. When she spoke it was in a voice so soft I could hardly make her out.

"What?"

"What is your situation?" she said.

"As regards what?"

"Everything."

"Ah. My situation."

"Yes. Will you tell me?"

"I will tell you."

Unavailability can be so liberating. I asked to kiss her. She had to walk round the block to think about it. I waited by the window.

"Yes," she said. "Yes, I will."

Soon we were exchanging the most intimate caresses while eschewing personal questions. In those days my favoured form of contact was the anonymous. Who could blame me for being afraid of the pulsation of feeling?

She said that I studied her constantly. She liked me looking at her.

I've never known a woman who wanted so much to be wanted, or a woman who was more afraid of it. I've never known anyone make more arrivals and departures, not only on the same day, but within the same hour. I preferred her not to go out, and soon blamed her for having any life apart from me, which I considered an infidelity. This is what she shoved into her bag each time she left: hairgrips, slides and combs; little wooden boxes containing cheap Indian jewellery and hash; lip balm, nipple cream; tapes of the sound of the sea or perhaps of dolphins, birds or whales; camomile tea; a stuffed giraffe; postcards and photographs of cats; under-wear, and other bits of the odd equipment necessary to mobile girls, as well as a certain amount of my wardrobe, including shirts, socks and my loafers.

Then, on her long legs, accompanied by a handful of good intentions and a head full of whims, she would make for the door as if pursued.

It made me fret about what it was out there she found so exciting—until I began to wonder about what it was in here that she found over-exciting. I learned that the more she loved me, the more she had to remind herself that she was sepa-rate. Understanding that nearly did me in as, from the win-dow, I waved and watched her go. But at least I saw it.

I had just started to write a new film about an ageing and fragile couple whose children have grown up and done well. The parents go to visit them, only to find their marriages are breaking up. I was excited by the idea and talked about it a lot so as to have her understand what I was trying to do every day.

She would lie on the floor beside my desk and watch me work. She said she envied my having something important to do every morning; something that absorbed everything; something to live for. My sense of purpose made her feel left out. She didn't believe I envied the fact that she woke up in the morning and wondered what she felt like doing that day. Would it be the dancing, pottery or a walk? She went to par-ties on the beach and in warehouses; she'd go any distance for a rave. She played guitar and sang in a group that I went to see. She dedicated all the songs to me. Not yet having acquired the glassy indifference of busy women in the city, she talked to people on the street and felt responsible for them. Her friends were dope heads in old clothes with woolly hats pulled down to their eyes. They were indolent and lacked the spark—like her and not like her. She drifted between boys. When she left them they suggested she considered herself too good for them. Too good for everyone but me.

I lay over her one afternoon. I had kicked off my slippers, and we had thrown the duvet down on the patio. She liked to make love outside, and I didn't mind, provided I didn't get a draught between my legs. The TV was on low. England were playing the West Indies. I was looking at her in awe and puzzlement, unable to understand how I could have such feelings for a girl I didn't know.

She used to say, "You're so neat and gentle, with a soft voice. I've never met anyone who so much wanted the best for me. You know how to speak to people. You make them feel they can tell you the deepest things." She seemed to trust me, as if she knew implicitly that she was safe, and that I would not let her down. But I did. In a strange way, she seemed to expect that, too. At least, then, she knew where she was.

There were mirrors in the bedroom we used. One afternoon, as I lay on the bed to wait for her, I caught a glimpse of myself. My body was thick and hairy, my stomach round, as if I'd swallowed a ball; my little prick stuck out merrily. I could have tied a pink bow on it. In celebration of Wimbledon, I had prepared a handful of strawberries beside the bed, which

I intended to slot between her buttocks and guzzle with cream. I watched myself lean over, pick up a bottle of cold champagne and press it against my balls, before swigging from the bottle. She came into the room in high heels, a suspender belt, my mac, and the pearl earrings I'd bought her. I waved at myself in the mirror! How happy I looked, as if all my epiphanies had come at once!

I can't say I wasn't happy at that time. I liked to compliment myself on having everything in balance. I was also adapting a book for an American studio. I knew they would have the script rewritten, just so they would know they had been thorough. I was used to that and reckoned they'd try a couple more writers on it, before coming back to me. I had a tolerable partner and delightful children, as well as the perfect mistress who, when she became pouty and sulky, I could dismiss. I may have a hypocrite heart, but my vanity was satisfied. As satisfactions go, that is ample.

One day she said, "If you want me, here I am, you can have me."

"Thank you," I said and added, some time later, not wanting to take yes for answer, "Do you mean it?"

She seemed surprised and reminded me that the third time I met her, when she enquired after "my situation" I had said to her, "You can do whatever you want with me. I am at your disposal." And, apparently, I added, "Don't think that I don't love you, because I do."

I do.

*　　*　　*

74

Could I have done more with Susan? I mean, can I do more?

How little, when you think about it, can you will into being. Of what my parents and teachers tried to force on me as a child, little remains except a memory of abhorrence. I was never one of those kids who'd do things because they were compelled. All of me, along with the age, stood against compulsion. Such individualism has got me into trouble. You can, of course, will things for a while, but if you are alive you will rebel. You can protect and encourage the most delicate gifts—love, affection, creativity, sexual desire, inspiration—but you cannot requisition them. You cannot will love, but only ask why you have put it aside for the time being.

Susan and I cannot make one another happy. But the failure scars one, until it seems inevitable that such failure will attend all one's endeavours—if it is indeed happiness that one wants, rather than success, say, or sanctuary. My robust instinct, therefore, wasn't to give up but to persevere.

Susan had obviously been discussing our troubles with a friend. Therapy was recommended, as it always is to the minutely distressed. It saves friends the bother of attending to you. I refused to go. I imagined I needed my turmoil. I knew, too, that I didn't want to love Susan, but for some reason didn't want the clarity of that fact to devastate us both.

She made the appointment as briskly as always, giving the unexceptionable excuse that it was for the sake of the children.

I sat in the car feeling like a child being taken to the doctor by an impatient mother.

*　　*　　*

A few weeks before this, Susan and I visited a couple who had been married nearly a year. On the way I expounded my cheerful theory that people marry when they're at their most desperate, that the need for a certificate is a sure sign of an attenuated affection.

That night I noticed that the husband made a particular, loose-wristed gesture, using both hands when explaining something. I noticed this because it was obvious the wife detested the movement. She even said, while we were there, "Can't you stop doing that?" In the car on the way home Susan and I laid bets on how long the marriage would last. We laughed for the first time in ages, and I wondered how much recognition there was in our mirth.

These days I think often of the couples I know or have met, and consider which of them is in love. There are some. It is tangible, you can see it between them, and feel the depth of their pleasure. Not long ago, at the kids' open day, I noticed a couple who were not engrossed in one another—they had things to do. But they were continuously aware of one another. Then, as their child ran about, and she thought no one was looking, she couldn't wait any longer, and she thrust her hand into her husband's hair and he kissed her.

No wonder everyone wants it—as if they have known such love before and can barely remember it, yet are compelled ever after to seek it as the single thing worth living for.

Without love, most of life remains concealed. Nothing is as fascinating as love, unfortunately.

I know love is dark work; you have to get your hands dirty. If you hold back, nothing interesting happens. At the same time, you have to find the right distance between people. Too close, and they overwhelm you; too far and they abandon you. How to hold them in the right relation?

It is beguiling how, in good relationships, even after years, formerly undiscovered parts of people are suddenly exposed, as in an archaeological dig. There is much to explore, and understand. With other people you can only turn away, bored.

I want to say: this is just the way things are.

I can't have been at my best the first time Susan and I visited the therapist. Once you know it is over there is no comfort in the present. Everybody was irritating me. I shoved strangers on the street. In the tube I pushed someone down the stairs, hoped to be arrested by the police and charged with possession of an uncontrolled mind. I rushed around the flat where I worked from one thing to another. My doctor, a friend, delighted in telling me about the range of available tranquillizers. But I refused to give him the pleasure of witnessing whether they provided tranquillity.

I was surprised we got to the therapist's at all without removing one another's windpipes with our fingernails. Susan and I passed the journey haranguing one another over the correct duration for the immersion of a teabag. According to her I had no facility for making tea, though I drank it all day, even—quite successfully—adding a little milk, on occasions, and sometimes a slice of lemon. But this was not good enough for Susan. I was hoping that the tea question would not come up with the therapist, at least not immediately: I am leaving because I cannot make her a cup of tea.

I could have poured hot water over her head, and Susan was ready to shove my testicles into boiling water, when we rammed the car into the therapist's drive and ran for her door.

I would imagine that therapy has benefited Victor. It gives him the opportunity to think of himself more than he always did, but less gloomily. He knows something of himself now. Whether he has changed is another matter. I suppose it depends on whether one sees self-knowledge as a benefit, and believes in it as the central purpose of mankind. Also, I have wondered whether there's a new class distinction emerging, between those who can afford to maintain their minds and emotions, cleansing themselves of toxic notions each week— and those who have to live with that which poisons them.

Yet despite my reluctance to go—to be coerced, once more—I had decided to confess all, to offer a few secrets without inhibition, such as they were. I wanted to be good at being helped. All the same, as we entered the room I stumbled, fancying I could hear the howls of pitiable couples trapped together for ever within the walls. I had to rest my face against the toilet wall and resist the idea of escaping through the window and absconding across the Vale of Health.

Susan and I sat side by side and six feet apart opposite a middle-aged and somewhat patronizing woman who had a "concerned," if not pained, look. What a job, the harvesting of misery. She will never want for work.

Susan was soon into her second handkerchief.

The therapist, like me, appeared to sympathize with Susan, particularly when—in the attempt to get things started—I tried to define love as curiosity. I argued that unrest, disquiet, curiosity and the desire for more was at the root of life—you could see it in children. I said I had lost my curiosity about Susan. I said I had no passion to know her soul. She bores me; or I bore myself when I am with her. I said:

"All that matters is the hinge!"

The therapist leaned forward. "What does the hinge mean to you?"

"The hinge?"

"Yes. How does it make you feel?"

I leaned towards her. "The hinge of one's mind! Whether it opens inwards or outwards. Let it be outwards. Let it be—out!"

I fell back in the chair, ashamed of my desire, of all I wanted. That I couldn't want my life with Susan—which should have been enough—was inexplicable and cruel. The therapist, surely seeing the point of the hinge, would help me with this.

The woman, who presumably believed in the ungovernable desires of the unconscious, appeared, nonetheless, to be some kind of rationalist. She replied patiently that relationships did become less passionate. This was to be expected. Enthusiasm would be replaced by other consolations.

Consolations! Mad to learn what they were, I could have kissed those consolations from her lips!

"Yes?" I said.

"Contentment," she murmured.

I leaned forward once more. "Sorry?"

She repeated it: contentment.

She was all for maturity and acceptance. Yes!

Sobbing Susan was nodding.

How I wished I were nodding—with my face between Nina's legs, my hands holding her arse up like a dish I am hungry for, my tongue in all her holes at once—tears, dribble, cunt juice, strawberries! I suck the soup of your love. Soul doctor, therapist—who tickles their tongue in your old hole? I am not ready for the wisdom of misery; I have had that with Mother. I am all for passion, frivolity, childish pleasures! Yes, it is an adolescent cry. I want more. Of what? What have you got?

The therapist insisted we see her later that week.

Susan's fat, red weeping face in that room the second time, as I declare that I don't think things can be repaired. To have made it absolutely clear, I should have given her a backhander or a finger in the eye. Then they would have understood! Instead, the therapist gets up and goes to the shelf where she extracts a book. She tries to get me to read a poem aloud. I glance over it. Seeing it is a bad poem, and being smart, I say I've forgotten my glasses. Ever-obedient Susan has to read it out in a tremulous voice, glancing at me in the old way, as if to say, later we will laugh at this. I keep thinking: I'm paying to hear poetry read aloud. I would pay not to hear this. Not even poetry can help us!

After my morning coffee Susan's blonde head coming through the open window of my flat in west London—a bunch of flowers, a book or a video behind her back. She wasn't working then, ten years ago. When I'd done enough for the day, she'd drive round in her little black car at the end of the morning, something tight around her breasts making them bulge and sway. I'd kiss her and pull her through the window.

We'd drive out to the country.

"Pull up your skirt," I'd say, looking at her as we went, hoping for more. "Higher!"

The morning after the first time, we went out for kippers and fried mushrooms. As we walked she put her arms around me. I remember, most of all, her grip. How she pulled me to her! If only I disliked her entirely, and weren't in love with Nina. What we like: English seaside towns, for instance, even in the winter. Certain jokes; her taste in food and pictures. Long discussions about English mod groups of the sixties.

There were other pleasures; there must have been. Or perhaps they were consolations. However, I cannot hunt for them now in the clutter of the past. Certainly, there are fewer of them than I might hope. Not a lot rushes to mind. I can't say that Susan has ever deliberately let me down or been more gratuitously cruel than necessary with someone as recalcitrant as me. I would give her a good reference.

"I have tried to make things work here!" she cried, yesterday. "Every day I have wanted it to be nice for you!"

In front of her I am ashamed. But the truth is, I cannot amuse or arouse her. And yet, out of all the possible people in the world, we have chosen one another. For what? For a grave and difficult task: to frustrate and punish one another. But why?

I shove her a little, roughly, to see if she will wake up. She stirs, sighs, and sleeps on, oblivious.

How rarely are we really disillusioned! I am not leaving this unhappy Eden only because I dislike it, but because I want to become someone else. The dream, or nightmare, of the happy family, haunts us all; it is one of the few Utopian ideas we have, these days. And so I believe, despite everything—as I told Asif—in love. We begin in love and go to some trouble to remain in that condition for the rest of our lives. Isn't it the condition in which men and women are mostly likely to flourish? People become the most of themselves; sadists are sweeter, bankers more generous, coroners enjoy life, even bookmakers are sympathetic. And out there, tonight, in the shitty humming city, there is, I'm certain, someone to love me.

But then Victor believes that too. For three years he had an affair with a married woman he thought would leave her husband. She was, after all, unhappily married. But she preferred unhappiness to Victor. Was that failure? It ended; but perhaps the quality of a love can't be measured by its duration.

At university in the late sixties, Victor had been a radical. Now he lives in a decent flat and earns a good living. But there has always been one thing he has wanted. To have another chance at an ideal love, to marry the right woman, before it is too late for him to demonstrate his new-found enthusiasm, too late for him to play on the floor with his children—children who, this time, will not fling curses and his clothes out of the window after him. He want to see if he can do it as it is meant to be done. That is all. The same as everyone else; not more, and not less. He needs to know that this most important of things is not beyond him. After all, a lot of people do it and some of them are happy.

Soon, therefore, there were others for Victor. Attractive women; good women. Some were a little zealous, particularly the American who, hardly having been into the bedroom, described to me how she intended to rebuild the flat. But none of them was right. Too old, too kind, too wrapped up in their career, too needy, too this, or too that. I'd meet a woman and think of him. We were all working on it, friends, relatives, even one of his children. Potential loves passed through his room like actresses auditioning for a part yet to be written.

He saw me with Nina, and he loved her. As long as she wasn't his, he could see what she was, and enjoy her. But as soon as the other stuff started with a woman—longing, missing, fearing, hoping—he was off. It was too much. Why can't he do it?

Why can't I?

Perhaps I can.

I don't want to wonder who Nina is with tonight as I lie here remembering how, when I came, she would hold my head and whisper in my ear, "And I love you, and I love you . . ." She would caress my ears and compare them to those of the dog across the road when she was a child. I was flattered. It was a pointer.

I rub myself through my jeans. I wish I had someone to do this. Not everything can be achieved alone. I won't do it here. Susan is offended by my solo efforts. She is of a disapproving generation of women. She thinks she's a feminist but she's just bad-tempered.

Nina encouraged me to masturbate on her back, stomach or feet while she slept. She liked me to do it before she rushed off, to have me on her on the tube.

I want Nina but then I always want Nina when I have an erection. I will test my theory that one should masturbate before considering any woman seriously. That way one discovers if one wants her for sex, or whether there is anything more.

But this involves getting up. Increasingly I find myself adopting unnatural positions in order to move about at all. I have to sit down in order to put on my socks; my sons bring me my shoes, if they're in the mood. Then I have to tie my laces, straighten up, get to my feet, and move forward. Like my sons, when I am finally dressed, I consider it an accomplishment. Often, when I get into bed these days, all I do is remove my trousers. It occurs to me now that that could be the reason Susan finds me less attractive than she used to.

I raise myself quietly and tiptoe away from the sleeping woman.

How weak the arc of my urine is, and how I strain to send a respectable semicircle into the pan. Even when my boys were tiny, and those round little worms, their penises, were no thicker than a cable, the arc of their urine had a magnificent velocity. With me there is always a sticky mess on the floor. Dad had prostate cancer. They stuck metal and plastic instruments through the opening of his prick.

I have started to visit hospitals. I know where they all are now, without the A-to-Z. I think of my acquaintances: a woman I lived with for a week has got a brain tumour; another friend has throat cancer, and a good pal has had a stroke; cancer of the balls is rife. I am invited to more funerals than dinner parties. These are their bodies. I omit their minds for the time being. We are going down already, and before we have acclimatized.

On! Over the sink.

I push down my trousers and look for a suitable lubricant. The last time I did this, when Susan had some friends round for dinner, I used my children's shampoo, and felt as if a wasp had been pushed into my urethra. I should have complained to the manufacturer and had them conduct an experiment on animals. Even masturbation can be a medical minefield.

In the cupboard I find a greenish cream with a sugary smell. I stare at the label but find it difficult to make out the print without my reading glasses. After some examination I see that it is an anti-ageing unguent. God knows how much of our money Susan spends on this pig fat. Catching me once using it as hand cream, she became incensed. Maybe if I apply this every day to my prick it'll become fourteen again.

I stick my penis in it.

A few months ago I spotted someone I recognized in the corridor of a company I was visiting. Who is that, I thought, puzzled. Finally I recognized Susan, dressed in clothes too tight and modish, not to mention the purple nail varnish. She wasn't trying to look young, but hadn't realized how she had changed.

Lately, though, she has become concerned about the deterioration of her body. She said that after the second boy, she knew she would never get her previous face back. She could see herself now only in photographs. She always seems to be smoothing grease into the cracks in her face, and at the weekends she windmills in front of exercise videos, the boys and I sitting on the stairs. "Mummy's getting thinner," one of us will say optimistically. It isn't that she has become unattractive but that she has become middle-aged, and therefore of a different order of life. She receives, unfortunately for her, only serious consideration.

What if I met her now, for the first time, at a party? I

would look at her twice, but not three times. It is likely that I would want to talk to her. Fearing those she can't seduce, she can be over-attentive to certain men, looking at them with what I call the "enraptured gaze," until they wonder why she wants to appeal to their vanity rather than their intelligence. There are women who want to please men, and there are men who like to be pleased. You'd think they'd be enough for one another. But it is the women, I am convinced, who require this attention for themselves, and they soon resent the primacy they've given you.

I should have gone out with her for six months. Or maybe a one-night stand would have been sufficient. But I wasn't ruthless enough, and I didn't know what I wanted.

I begin to rub and pull my prick.

How long will she dislike me? A few months? Years? These partings or abandonments can cut deep. But disliking someone is exhausting; to hate them is to stifle oneself interminably.

Victor's wife still doesn't speak to him. She won't let him in the house but makes him sit outside in the car until the children are ready. It might have something to do with Victor persuading her to suck him off and swallow his come—something she would never previously do—the night before he left after fifteen years. By then he could only hate her. Ever since, she has sustained the loathing and bequeathed it to the children, as if her sanity depended on it.

Could I tolerate being disliked? Perhaps, somehow, we have an Arcadian fantasy that there will be a time when everyone will finally agree, that there will be no dissent, dissonance or strife. But one of the virtues of being a parent, I can see, is the ability not to mind being disliked by one's children. At times I hated Father. I would scream at him, even when he returned from the hospital after open-heart surgery. I put laxative in his cereal so he'd shit himself on the train. I hate my children, at times, as they must hate me. You don't stop loving someone just because you hate them.

Susan can be a virulent combatant, with a sharp tongue I've enjoyed. Unfortunately, her bitterness is too urgent to be witty; she lacks detachment. But her crude blows can hit the target. Nevertheless one soon tires of it. I am looking forward to the day when I won't give a damn what she says, when the spell will be broken.

What is it I require? A kind indifference, and some interesting underwear. As Scott Fitzgerald wrote, "So we beat on . . ."

I sort through the laundry basket and extract a pair of her knickers, pulling them from her tights and laying them on the sink. Here we go. No; the grey knickers lack the *je-ne-sais-quoi*. Victor says I can become too self-depriving. The white might just do the trick. But perhaps the black with the lace trim have more dash. When it comes to self-abuse, I am an aesthete.

Is this an act of love or hate, or both?

I wish I had something to look at. Mind you, pinned to the wall is a postcard of the Matisse *Odalisque in Striped Pantaloons*. She is voluptuous, better than the best pornography. But life is the best pornography, I find.

Soon I am running through my library of stimulating scenes. Which one will I replay—the time in Berlin, or the middle-aged Italian who wept? What about the girl who rode her bicycle knickerless? Or perhaps the occasion I was wearing tight cowboy boots and adhesive trousers, and discovered, as the woman lay down for me, that I couldn't remove either my jeans or the boots, even with her pulling at them, and was forced to proceed with them on, in a kind of stumbling bondage.

In the old days it was possible scenes of the future—scenes that might actually occur—which I would use as an aid, rather than this nostalgia. And when, by mistake, I glance into the mirror and see a grey-haired, grimacing, mad-eyed, monkey-like figure with a fist in front of him, and the other hand placed delicately on his side because his back hurts from lifting the children, I know I am more likely to weep than ejaculate.

I was a child once, too.

I will think of Nina.

How often I am sitting in a bar or restaurant, or at a party with friends, and all I want is for her to walk in the door. I am under the impression that at that moment everything will be all right. No one else is as good as she is. There is so much I want to say. Our love is more important than everything else. Yet I am aware how susceptible to illusion we all are. How disturbing it is that our illusions are often our most important beliefs.

I don't think I can keep this up much longer. Before, the mere thought of a woman's body would have me spurting; now this act requires concentration and considerable labour. If there isn't some excitement soon, I'll get cramp or pull a muscle.

Three fingers, up to the knuckle, pushing inside you, stretching into the yielding flesh until it seems like a skin glove. "It feels like a pulse," you say. My hand is a part of you, yet it controls you.

Nina's face; then the way she turns over and offers her arse to me.

That should do it.

Christ. Yes.

I drop Susan's pants into the basket, reminded of D. H. Lawrence's remark that even animals feel sad after ejaculation. I wonder what observation could have led Lawrence to this knowledge. Still, I feel better, as if I wanted to rid myself of desire.

I am washing my hands when I hear a noise. Quickly I close my pants. The bathroom door is pushed open, as if by a ghost. I watch and listen.

From the darkness of the hall a child's luminous dummy bobs into the room, a tiny circle of green light. The boy's eyes are shut as he stands there in his Batman T-shirt, pyjama bottoms and furry slippers, three years old. Actually, he is asleep. He staggers suddenly, and automatically raises his arms as if he has scored a goal. My hands fit under his shoulders, I pull him up along my body, and smell and kiss his hair.

"What are you doing here, my beautiful boy?"

I carry him downstairs, put on a reading light and open the shutters. I lay him on the sofa and pull off his bottoms and soggy nappy. The smell is unpleasantly sharp and familiar at the same time; it is him. He is wilful and keeps trying to turn over, so I place one hand on the middle of his chest and push down, while grasping his ankles with the other as if I am about to hang him upside down from a hook. He thrashes and blinks as I wipe him. Then I shove and push to get the nappy in the right position. It is like trying to change the wheel of a moving car. I am terrified that he will start yelling. At last I replace his pyjama bottoms.

I hope he will do the same for me, one day.

Breathing hard, I sit at the window with him in my arms, whispering and blowing in his ear.

"Have I been good enough to you, little boy?"

I didn't enjoy him much as a baby, dreading the crying and whingeing, the refusal to get dressed, eat or go to sleep, as if my whole purpose was to get him to do things he didn't want to do. I was astonished how whole days would pass when there was no time for anything but him, not even in the evenings, and particularly not at night. Having considered several books on the upbringing of children, usually in the early hours, and often with faeces or vomit on my fingers, once I threw him backwards into his cot, hitting his head. I put brandy in his milk. I booted him hard up the nappy before he was even walking. How can children make us feel so help-less?

Susan cut me out too, keeping the babies and the compe-tence to herself, her female friends and her mother. It has only been in the past few months that I've made myself use-ful. And only recently that I have fallen in love with him, which happened as it did with Nina, as an accumulation of amazement. His outlines became clearer and there seemed more and more to him, as door after door opened on wonder and pleasure, until I was captivated, cheered, moved. His smile; his laughter; his imitations of a cross face, of a funny face, of a sad face, delight me, as do his kindness and concern for me.

Now the boy and I talk ceaselessly. His questions—where does the light go at night, what do spiders eat, why do women have "bosoms," where do people go when they die, and why do they have eyebrows?—are incessant. Where will he get the answers when I'm not here? If I tear myself from the boys, don't I tear them too?

When Victor left home his younger son threw Victor's belongings out of the window before sticking a broken bottle in his arm. He wouldn't have Victor visit him in the hospital. He wouldn't reply to Victor's letters. The other son lived alone in the family house when his mother went away. One night Victor found the boy lying on a sleeping bag in the hall, the only room in the house he used. All the lights in the house had blown or fused. He fed himself by candlelight, eating baked beans from the can. Old newspapers were piled up. The boy was unwashed, his clothes soiled. Surely Victor and his wife had taught the boy to clean himself? But, having had his world broken by his father's assault on happiness, the boy could barely speak or move. Victor is still repairing the damage.

I am leaving this woman alone with two young children. She will have to care for them, predominantly, herself. My presence, however baleful, has perhaps reassured her. Now she will work, buy their clothes, feed them, tend them when they are sick. I'm sure she will ask herself, if she hasn't already, what men are for. Do they serve any useful function these days? They impregnate the women. Later, they might occasionally send money over. What else could fathers be? It wasn't a question Dad had to ask himself. Being a father wasn't a question then. He was there to impose himself, to guide, exert discipline, and enjoy his children. We had to appreciate who he was, and see things as he did. If we grew up to be like him, only better qualified, we would be lucky. He was a good man. He didn't flee, though perhaps he considered it.

I pull the blanket from the back of the sofa and lay it across my son.

Sometimes the boy kicks and punches me, or rakes my face with his nails, and tries to bite me. He calls me "a great big bully." If I scold him, he sobs. If I become angry he stops himself breathing and can only gasp, as if I have taken his life. I feel guilty then, unable to bear the notion that the man he loves most has turned against him. We need one another, bully and boy. If I am away for a few days, travelling or idling somewhere, and I see children of my sons' age on the street or in a restaurant, I feel the panic of separation, and can't understand why I am not with my own sons. On my return I can see how they have changed. I don't want to miss a moment of them. Not only for the sake of their future, but for now, this moment, which is all there is.

It is always them I think of before I fall asleep. And I am leaving.

Yet the children are more agitated than usual when Susan and I are together with them, as if our furies are infectious and they are weeping on our behalf. Perhaps if we continued to live together they would dream of running away. Susan wanted to send the younger boy to "see someone." I said, when the parents go mad, they send their children to psychiatrists.

"It's you who has gone mad," she said. "Your theories are insane."

Cheerio, bitch.

But there is something else I have to face.

When I leave I want her to vanish too. There may be little love, but jealousy remains. I want to live my life but don't want her to live hers. When this is done—and eighteen months, say, have passed, as they surely will—there may be another man in this house. He might be sitting where I am now. My sons, if they have a nightmare, will go to him. Children, who have yet to learn our ways, are notoriously promiscuous in their affection. They'll sit on anyone's knee.

The man will kiss and hold them when they wake up. He might put them to bed and talk to them until they sleep. He might have a northern accent. He might encourage them to support Arsenal. Or perhaps he will become impatient and flick the back of their heads. By then I could be an outsider, sitting in the car waiting for them to come out of the house. And the boy won't remember this night. Neither of them will remember their parents together. They will remember none of this and I will never forget it. She will always know them better than than I will.

Still, I hope she ends up with someone rich. Not that there will be a queue, I hope. Nevertheless, the most grotesque people get laid, and even married. As Joe Orton says, "Marriage excludes no one the freaks roll-call."

The therapist kept saying, you are leaving the children too, don't fool yourself about that. I wanted to shout, no, no, it's her! But we had the children together, which was an assumption of trust and security, that I will break.

At times I feel sorry for the children, having to stay here with her. I can clear out, but they can't.

The boy is sleeping soundly. I love hearing his dreams, and discussing them with him. Susan sneers at my pretentiousness.

I should sleep now. But I would rather not go to bed. There are few things more desolate than undressing in the dark beside a woman who won't wake up for you.

Often, at the thought of going home, blood will rise into my head, pressing into my ears and eyes, until I feel my skull is bulging like an overinflated tyre. I might go to some filthy bar and hold on to a chair, or to someone's house where I could get a grip on the host's wife. One night I arrived late at a dinner party. As usual the women were talking about work and the men about children. I took my place and saw nothing for it but to drink. Things looked up when a middle-aged acquaintance laid his finely coiffured head on the table. His wife, whom he'd left, was refusing to let him see their children, and was, he believed, turning them against him. She was also refusing to sell the house in which his money was tied up. They were going to court. And the acquaintance, with his new young girlfriend at his side, was saying he doubted whether it had been worth it.

The girlfriend replied that he had let the children wreck their romance. It was him she wanted, not the children he'd had with a woman he didn't love. Around the table, other sombre men whose last glimpse of their wives had been at the door of the divorce court, nodded, grumbled and shook their heads. Then the woman got up and left. I should have run after her. My wet-eyed acquaintance said he had given up most of what he had had for her. But when, after a couple of months, they realized that they didn't much like one another, and, in fact, she had tried to tear one of his ears off, there was no way back—no way back to anything solid.

All that for a fuck, I muttered. The other men laughed. But I concluded, having just seen how the little minx fondled the house cat as her lover wept, what a fuck it must have been. A discussion followed, around the table, on the ethics of such a dilemma. But I could only think that there are some fucks for which a person would have their partner and children drown in a freezing sea. My kingdom for a come. Women, I've noticed, are particularly tenacious in this respect. When they want someone there's no stopping them.

My son, there may be a time when I will explain some of these things to you, because there may be a time when I understand them.

*   *   *

Holding the back of his head with one hand, and supporting his back with the other—his eyes are closed and his mouth open—I carry him to bed. But as I am about to lay him down I have a strange feeling. Sometimes you look into a mirror and can't always remember what age you are. Somehow you expect to see a twelve-year-old, or an eighteen-year-old, looking back at you. Now I feel as if I am looking at myself. He is me; I am him; both of us part of one another, but separate in the world. For now it is myself I am carrying in my arms.

I lay him down and cover him up.

I wonder when I will sleep beside him again, if ever. He has a vicious kick and a tendency, at unexpected moments, to vomit in my hair. But he can pat and stroke my face like a lover. His affectionate words and little voice are God's breath to me.

I creep down the stairs. I put my jacket on. I find my keys. I get to the door and open it. I step out of the house. It is dark and cold. The fresh wind sweeps through me. It invigorates me.

Go. You must go.

I am kicking over the traces.

You could go into the dark and fear that you will never emerge.

This must be the death hour, the lowest part of the night. Barely a living thing is moving, including me.

Outside, the dark leaves on the trees flap in the wind like hundreds of long green tongues, the branches knocking at me.

I will roll a joint, if I can. This grass smells obnoxious. Like a damp bonfire, Susan says, particularly if I smoke it without tobacco.

I like watching the plants grow at the back of the garden. When I get home in the evening after a few drinks, and there is nothing for it but to shut the front door, and I know I have to remain under this roof until the morning, as if I am under some kind of house arrest, one of the few things I do like is to go out into the garden. There I spray away at my dope plants, with my youngest boy, packed into his Babygro and felt shoes, tugging and pulling at the hose pipe behind me.

Occasionally I strip off a few leaves, wrap them in newspaper and dry them on the boiler. I have Ecstasy, LSD and an old bottle of amyl nitrate in the fridge. For a while I'd take the "E" every day, starting after breakfast. It made me feel worse, and I knew it. But I didn't stop. I have always preferred to take drugs in the straightest situations, at supper with my parents, for instance. I still do the occasional parent-teacher evening, in my latest favourite suit, on acid. The annual nativity, I find, is always improved by a tab of Purple Haze. It is the secrecy I enjoy, and perhaps the challenge.

Nina used to tease me, saying my attitude towards drugs belonged in another era. It is true that when I was growing up, drugs were fuel for a journey into the self. They also connected me with a more dangerous and defiant world, and even a literary one: De Quincey, Baudelaire, Huxley. For Nina they mean sordidness, prison, and overdoses. It was her fear of needles that had kept her safe, if she is safe.

I've decided to forget the pinstripe suit. It'll get crumpled in my bag and there's nowhere to hang it over there. The Lennon picture is a definite. But I must find a photograph of the children to take with me.

I go to Susan's desk, which is covered in her papers. Hoping to find evidence of some recent betrayal for which I can reproach her and then walk out, I snatch up her wallet and open it. I find only a picture of us with our arms around one another.

In the drawers there are packets of photographs. I select one of my eldest boy a few days old. I am bathing him in the hospital, his head lying in my hand. My face is grave with concentration as I splash his ribs and screwed-up face for the first time. It was Karen I was seeing then. I waved goodbye to Susan in the hospital, picked up the champagne her father had left us, and drank it in bed with Karen. Susan mentioned it the other day.

"I will never forget that you left the hospital without kissing me. Our first child, and you didn't kiss me. Still, at least you love the children. When you go away."

"Go away?"

"Travel. The children ask for you all the time. The first thing they say in the morning is, 'Is Daddy coming home today?'"

I put the photograph in my pocket.

For old times' sake I glance through her journal. It's dusty; she doesn't keep it regularly, but only writes down the things she wants me to read. I glance over the passage in which she wrote, three years ago, of her lover, wondering if she should visit him in Rome. I could see through her lies and told her I would be glad if she went. I was always looking for opportunities to leave her.

I return to my position on the sofa. I will smoke more of this, though it makes me feel I have been handed over for public accusation.

"There you are."

I look up. I look away. I look back again. Susan is at the bottom of the stairs in her white T-shirt and white slippers, her face creased and puffy.

She looks so white I could write on her.

Once, coming home at four, having walked back from some teenage party, I found Mother downstairs in her floor-length stained dressing gown. Scattered on the floor were photographs of her as a young woman. In those old prints she was gawky and keen, with hair as long as mine, sandals, and a flowered dress. She was posed with men who had partings and ties, none of them Father.

Susan must have been watching me staring into space. For how long, I wonder?

I liked taking Nina to restaurants and parties, to openings and exhibitions. I would sit and watch her looking at the pictures. I took pleasure in her pleasure as I led her around London. I wouldn't have gone out otherwise. Our hands were always on one another. Wherever we were, she was my refuge, my pocket of light. But these new pleasures extracted her from a familiar world and pushed her into an intimidating one. I overwhelmed her at times. There was too much of me, I know that. We want love but we don't want to lose ourselves.

Asif was marking papers, surrounded by his alphabetically arranged books on philosophy, education and child development. On his desk were pictures of his wife and children. When he saw me this afternoon at his study door, with Najma standing concernedly behind me, he was alarmed. Perhaps I looked strained, or worse.

"The children are well?" was the first thing he asked.

"Yes, yes."

He was relieved.

We shook hands then.

"And yours?" I say.

"Thank God, yes."

Najma said with a challenge in her eyes, "And Susan?"

"Fine. She's fine."

Asif looked at me enquiringly. I didn't like disturbing his peace. I didn't even know why I had come. I had been walking the streets since morning. Then I hailed a cab and told the driver Asif's address. Perhaps because Victor is a recent convert to hedonism I required the other view.

I said, "Can I speak to you?"

Najma left us reluctantly and Asif exchanged his slippers for his outdoor shoes. I realised that he is getting fuller, and with his waistcoat pulled tight across his stomach, he looks older, more dignified and substantial.

We walked in his garden. I noticed he kept looking up towards the conservatory where Najma was reading in a wicker chair. I fancied she was already condemning me.

I said, "The house is full of poison. Susan wants me to be kind. I can't be kind. We can do nothing for one another. It is a fact. I have decided to leave."

Asif said, "All couples fall out. Even Najma and—"

I said, laughing suddenly, "But I remember."

"What?"

"Over the omelettes at breakfast. Before we went down to the pool—on holiday in Italy last year. Susan and I were civil to one another for hours at a stretch. But you two. The silences. The resentment. You couldn't wait to get to that café where you and I could play table football alone."

"Fair enough. She and I disagree . . . at times." Then he said, "It is easy to turn away too soon. Why be hasty? See what happens. I beg you to wait a year."

"I can't wait another week. In fact I am off in the morning."

"Surely not? But a year is nothing at our age. Is it because of the girl?"

I shrugged. "I don't see her. I've lost her."

"Don't—you are shivering." He put his arm around me. He said, "But you are following her in some way?"

"If I could see the hair on her neck again, I could move outwards from that point. That would be the start, you see, of a new attitude."

"Her hair?"

"Of course."

"It's only that I didn't realize men of our age could get so romantic."

I said, "Asif, no age is excluded from strong feeling."

He snorted. "What a pity you ever met her!"

"Why do you insist on finding this risible?"

"Perhaps I hate to see a man I respect, who is brave and dedicated in some ways—and stubborn in others—blown about by such passions. But I suppose, unlike most people, you can afford to follow your pleasures. And follow them you do."

"Yes. But don't think I don't know that there are more important things to think about—the international political situation, and all."

My sarcasm silences him.

His children run about. They ask for my boys. I say they are at home. Other children's voices rise up from nearby gardens. Kids come to the side gate.

If only I could sit here contentedly in the middle of my life as children seem to in theirs, without constantly worrying about the state of things, tomorrow, next week, next year. But since the age of fourteen, when I conspired against my parents, not fleeing as I intended to, but biding my time and preparing, knowing one day I would be ready, I have required the future as a goal. I've needed something to happen every day that showed a kind of progress or accumulation. I can't bear it when things go slack, when there isn't sufficient intensity. But I would welcome a quiet period. I am hoping for that, in the long run.

He said, "You're very distracted. I know you like to look

after yourself, but you haven't even shaved. Leaving aside your girlfriend's hair for a moment, your own looks as if you've been combing it vertically."

I laugh but say nothing.

After a time he says, "You've made up your mind?"

"I think so."

"I don't want you going to some dismal bedsit. Come here if you want, for a while. I'll put the children in together."

"You are kind, Asif. Thank you. But I couldn't sit here in the middle of your family life after leaving my own."

"It won't be for long."

"Sorry?"

"After a few days' reflection, you'll decide to go back. You are not prepared to miss the children. I don't think you quite realize what it will feel like . . . to leave them. It will hurt them, won't it?"

At that moment my legs almost gave way.

I said, "I know I will have to go through that."

He said, "The new girl you called one of the uneducated educated. Susan is spiky but she is intelligent. I've always enjoyed talking to her. You must, once, have had good reason for choosing her."

"Aren't I allowed to change my mind? If people are rushing away from one another in droves, it is because they are running towards other people."

"All of us yearn for more. We are never satisfied. Wisdom is to know the value of what we have. Every day, if there is some little good fortune, and our children smile at us or for once do what we say, we should consider ourselves lucky."

"I am discouraged. An unhappy relationship can't be a sealed compartment. It seeps into everything else, like a punctured oil can." I looked at him. "You've never considered throwing it all away?"

We both glanced up towards Najma.

"Why do you ask me this?" he said exasperatedly. "Do you think, one day, that I will give a different answer and your view of things will be confirmed?"

"Asif, what view of things?"

"That one doesn't have responsibilities." He sighed and went on, "I'm sorry. I suppose what you are doing is the modern way."

"I would say that there is a new restlessness about."

"Yes, it makes me feel unique for loving the same person continuously for a number of years and not covertly planning an escape. But I do love it here. Every day something is built upon. There is increase. Without it I would be just a man walking down the street with nowhere to go."

"At home, for me, there is no movement."

"With a real love there is little movement. You are going round and round, but further and further. Don't you believe in anything? Or is virtue only a last resort for you?"

What could I say here? Young people are full of tedious belief. Why not me? Not many beliefs come spontaneously to mind. We have reached such a state that after two thousand years of Christian civilisation, if I meet anyone religious— and, thankfully, I do only rarely these days—I consider them to be mentally defective and probably in need of therapy.

I might say: I believe in individualism, in sensualism, and

in creative idleness. I like the human imagination: its delicacy, its brutal aggressive energy, its profundity, its power to transform the material world into art. I like what men and women make. I prefer this to everything else on earth, apart from love and women's bodies, which are at the centre of everything worth living for.

But Asif is intelligent. I don't want to embarrass myself by saying anything too selfish—though I can think of few more selfish institutions than the family. Perhaps I am becoming a committed sceptic.

Probably I am giggling now. I'll speak before he considers me mad.

"I have my opinions," I say. "But they're unimportant. They change every day. It's always something of a relief not to have an opinion, particularly on cultural or political questions. But I tell you, when it comes to this matter, it is an excess of belief that I suffer from."

"Belief in what?"

"In the possibilities of intimacy. In love."

He almost laughed. Then he said, "You've always liked women. You haven't grown out of it."

"But they are likeable. Haven't you noticed?"

"What about someone on the side?"

"You're suggesting that?"

"You travel a lot. You're always in America, turning literature into—"

"Pap."

"There must be opportunities. It might take away the need."

"It does, for a time. But it depends entirely on precisely

what the need is and whether it can be taken care of. Or whether it renews itself, and with how much ferocity. Anyhow, you wouldn't do it."

He said, "Don't forget I am a teacher."

"I know. Why are you saying this?"

"Teaching is difficult, you know. And it is made even more difficult if the children are distressed. In the classroom I see the debris. The fall-out. The broken side of things."

He offered me tea.

I couldn't stay any longer. It was time to get home, bathe my children, see Susan, and pack. I had to make my contribution to the broken side of things.

Victor says, "It was the worst, and also the best thing I have done. For two years after I left I was aware at the back of my mind that something unforgivable had happened. I knew that not far away, people—my wife and children—were suffering as a result of what I had done. However—"

He continues, "You might mock me for the saveloy and chips, and the juicy picked onion in particular. But how many of our friends and acquaintances, having left their partners, would wish to go back to them? How many of them would say, were they able to relive that period, that they wouldn't have left?"

"What's the matter? Are they sick? Are they awake?"

"No," she says.

Susan looks both.

She comes to me from the bottom of the stairs, arms outstretched.

"Hold me. Not like that, as if your arms are tongs. Touch me with your hands."

I remember by eldest son saying, "Why do we have hands?"

I say, "I'm here now."

"Yes. Thank God. Hold me."

I kiss her and move my hands over her. Her T-shirt rides up. Inadvertently, I touch her breast. I reach down. Her public hair is not as luxuriant and soft as Nina's. But if she lets me fuck her here, now, on the floor, I won't leave. I will put my straight shoulder to the wheel and accept my responsibilities for another year. Anyhow, in the morning I'll be too tired. I will get a kipper out of the freezer, scoff a big breakfast and breathe a sigh of relief. I like a happy ending.

She says, "I had a bad dream—that you weren't here. Then I woke up and you weren't there. You're not going to leave, are you?"

"What makes you say that?"

"I don't know, I don't know."

"It's okay," I say. "Calm down, I'll massage you."

"No, thank you. You don't know how to do it. You are too rough."

"I see." I say, "It's not as if you ever touch me."

"Are you surprised?" She says quietly, "You're not, are you?"

* * *

Lying I don't recommend. Except in certain circumstances.

Susan, if you knew me you would spit in my face. I have lied to you and betrayed you every day. But if I hadn't enjoyed those women I wouldn't have stayed so long. Lying protects all of us; it keeps the important going. It is a kindness to lie. If I'd been good all those years, who'd have been impressed? God? A world without lying would be impossible; a world in which lying wasn't deprecated is also impossible. Unfortunately, lying makes us feel omnipotent. It creates a terrible loneliness. Here, tonight, I feel cut off from you and from everyone. Truth telling, therefore, has to be an ultimate value, until it clashes with another ultimate value, pleasure, at which point, to state the obvious, there is conflict.

She begins to wake up.

"What are you doing down here? Why aren't you in bed?"

"I had things to do."

"At this time?"

"I couldn't sleep."

"Why? What's bothering you? Usually you're barely awake." Her eyes sweep my face. "You smell of cigarettes and that awful dope. Your hair's wet. Did you go out? Where did you go? Who did you see?"

Her fingers are on my cheek.

"Ouch."

"What is that? What's happened to your face? Wait—"

She goes to the light switch and, as she moves, so sleepy is she that she stumbles and falls against the table.

Let me catch you.

* * *

Tonight the streets smell of urine. Lorries are parked outside the supermarkets; men push metal containers through the side doors. Young people are out, going somewhere.

Seven years ago, when Susan and I separated for a year and I could be excited by strangers, I knew these bars, knew girls who sold jewellery in the market, people in bands, travelling kids. I had time for the unexpected.

Tonight, having changed the boy's nappy, returned him to his bed and driven to this bar without knowing why, all I see are dozens of ageing young people in improbable and cheap clothes, pressed together. I know no one. My current friends I meet only by arrangement, making appointments with them as one would with a dentist. And Victor, five years older than me, was never going to be in such a place, though, to his credit, he has taken up dancing. He goes to clubs, sometimes alone, where he starts a peculiar, independent, Terpsichorean movement. Soon a space opens up around him. I'm not sure if this is because of his individual style or because people think he's an AWOL policeman.

"I don't mind being a fool," he says. "But stylish young people can be very snobbish."

Outside the bar there are dudes in knee-length thick coats, baggy trousers and boat-like trainers. Funny how drug dealers always stand around doing nothing for ages, before suddenly walking quickly. Tonight I wonder if they have all, simultaneously, been afflicted with head pain, as they clutch their skulls as if posing for Munch's *The Scream,* while speaking into mobile phones. Once, I would have asked the price of this or that drug. Now I consider what will happen to them, and wonder why they have wasted their money on such clothes. But then they would think that I lacked distinction.

I did see someone I knew in the bar. A kid no longer a kid who, at one time, I had seen every day for a few weeks. In my socialist phase I would listen to the misfortunes of such a boy at length, and condemn the society that had made him suffer. He had been lively and smart and full of stories about his adventures on the street, but injured within, making his bravado more poignant. In the bar he stood up against me, wheedling and demanding a thousand pounds to go and live on an Indian Reservation.

I listened to him before saying, "You'd think they'd have enough problems without you."

I try to push past him but he holds on to my hand.

"You can afford to help another human being," he goes, putting on his most pathetic look. "Out of the kindness of your—"

I interrupt him, "I'll give you the money if you tell me this one thing. Where is your father? Why aren't you at home with him?"

He looks at me.

I say, "Answer me!"

"What have you been taking?"

He wheels away.

Out on the street I could easily start gesticulating and

yelling, for I believe some of these men don't know their fathers. Where have all the fathers gone? Once the fathers went to war and returned, if they did return, unrecognizable. Yet still the fathers flee and return, if they return at all, unrecognizable. Do they think about their children? What better things do they have to do? Is it when their women become mothers that they flee? What is it about the mothers that makes it so essential that they be left? Where are the fathers hiding and what are they doing?

Someone must know. I must ask one of them. I must ask myself.

I run to my car. Tonight there is one other place I must visit.

Victor was always kissing Nina and putting his arm around her. He patronized her but, seeing how awkward he is, she took care not to scare him.

One night at his place Victor had some new drugs. When he had become lost in some unknown place, Nina and I started to make love. Victor got into bed with us. How I regret what I wanted to do—which was reduce her in my mind. If she weren't special, my feeling for her wouldn't be as strong.

"Why did you do it?" I asked him.

"You were laughing. You were enjoying yourselves."

I did know how to please her. I would cook for her; I would bathe and massage her while she listened to music. I swore I could love, protect and support her.

She trusted me but was becoming discouraged.

She told Victor, "He keeps leaving me. Every time I get used to him again, he goes home, or worse, on holiday. I am losing hope. I feel suffocated. I don't even know what I am waiting for."

She told me she couldn't see me for a while. She needed to distance herself. I had Victor keep an eye on her, ring her every day and keep me alive in her thoughts. One day, in a truculent and spiteful mood, I asked him if he would go out with her if I weren't around.

I think they saw each other for a couple of weeks. I didn't enquire, and I didn't talk to him as I was away with Susan and the children. Then he rang and told me that she'd asked him not to get in touch any more. He and I resumed our friendship. We didn't speak about Nina. I thought I would soon forget her.

"I went to a bar for a drink. It was crowded. I decided to have a stroll. Then I saw a club and went in and walked about."

"You just saw a club."

I say, "Yes, a line of people on the street."

"What made you go in?"

"I don't know. I think it was the kind of thing I would have enjoyed, before."

Susan says, "It's not like you to be spontaneous. Where is your shirt? Weren't you wearing a shirt earlier?"

"God, yes, I was," I say. "How easy it is to lose things!"

She stares at me.

*   *   *

Having not found Victor in the bar, and the streets seeming more violent than I remember them, I drive to the house where she had a room. I went there several times a few months ago, when she moved to London, to be near me, as she admitted. Her fantasy, she said, was of living around the corner.

The kitchen was always crowded with young people either recovering from some dissipation or preparing for it. I remember her bed on the floor; an Indian coverlet; poetry books; tapes, and the numerous candles that make Christmas so exciting for young women.

"I don't know why I'm living here," she said, as I dragged myself away from one bed in order to return to another. "I should be with you. Can't you stay for ever, or at least tonight?"

I looked at her, naked on the bed, as white as a grain of rice.

"How I wish I could."

"You see, I don't think I can bear this for much longer."

"Won't you wait for me?"

"I don't know."

Tonight I loiter outside, though there is nothing to see through the window. At last I ring the bell. A young man comes to the door. I ask him if he remembers me. He does, though with so little enthusiasm that I wonder if he was one of the people who advised Nina against me.

"Does she still live here?"

He looks at me suspiciously.

He says, "She was away for a time."

"She was?"

"She came back."

"She did? She came back? Could I see her? Is she in?"

"No."

I refrain from slapping him.

At last he informs me that he thinks she has gone to a club nearby.

"Who with?" I say.

"A friend."

"Where is it?"

Sighing, he tells me, as if I should know such things.

I drive down there and stand in line for an hour, terrified they are not going to let me in. As I near the doormen, I remove my shirt in the hope that this will make me seem more contemporary. I conceal it behind a hedge across the road, so I am wearing a T-shirt and jacket.

Inside it is like a disco, only dark, practically black, without the flashing lights that so entertained me as a teenager.

One problem: if she were here I wouldn't be able to see her.

For most of my life, until tonight, I have been young. For most of my life, there were people to look up to, who seemed to know what was going on. Where are they? These days, apart from when I am with Susan, I know who I am. When necessary I can gather myself together and maintain some dignity. But tonight I'm losing it.

Igniting my lighter, I push through the crowd, as if I am exploring a cave.

People are wearing outdoor coats buttoned up to the throat, with pulled-down hats. There's no doubt, British kids are innate meritocrats, and satirists. You can be sure they're always up to something. But tonight it is depressing to see young people so drugged and stupefied. I want to ask why, as if I can't remember. Three years ago, for six months I took cocaine all night every day. It was luck and ambition that kept me clean in the end. Were we such undemanding zombies, and did we believe that being young was a virtue in itself? Undoubtedly. Do my taxes subsidize their indulgence? Probably. Did my father walk uncomprehendingly about such places looking for a young woman to hurl himself at?

I fear for my sons, but it is essential that I leave them tomorrow.

I think I have become the adults in *The Catcher in the Rye.*

Why do I envy these people? In the late sixties and seventies I did feel that I belonged to something, to other young people, and to some sort of oppositional movement. The earnestness I disliked; I was too awkward to join things. But there is something I miss: losing oneself, yes, in a larger cause.

As I press my lighter into the faces I begin to dread the thought of seeing her. What if she is with a young man? What if she despises me now? These faces are young. I must have been insane to fall for such a part-woman. What is wrong with maturity? Think of the conversations I could have—about literature and bitterness—with a forty-year-old! Victor has mentioned an interesting optician with her own shop. People say it is the soul not the body that counts!

I know a place where I could meet some middle-aged women, if they are up so late! Once I level out they will be grateful for my company! They are a larger cause!

I will seek some out!

I begin to make for the door, wherever it is, with some urgency. This is typical of me—to be so close to something, and then flee.

I catch sight of a woman dancing on her own. Surely it is her? I move towards her. No; it is not my love. I can't make out much, but get the impression this woman won't mind if I approach her. Apparently the drugs they take make them friendly, as if they could not manage it otherwise. Perhaps they should give them to all young people. Surely, in such a mood, they won't care if you dance like a crashing helicopter? I want to learn to expect to be received kindly by people.

I shout in the woman's ear and she comes with me to the bar. I can't hear much of what she says. But I imagine going home with her. If she says yes, I will go. A strange room; her things; odd places I have ended up in the past, lost in the city, waiting to see what will turn up. From there, in the morning, I will leave for Victor's without going home.

I was hit then. It seemed to be from behind, and it was a man. It might have been when I examined the ring through the woman's eyebrow by the flame of my lighter. She would have interested Victor.

Susan sits down beside me.

"Don't touch it, it's only where I got punched," I say.

"Were you aggressive?"

"Why it happened, I don't know. It is just what young people like to do. It'll be okay by tomorrow."

"What is this?" she asks.

"A signed photograph of John Lennon."

"Why was it on the stairs?"

I look at her in puzzlement. "Was it? I think I was looking for a better place to hang it."

"In the middle of the night?"

"It seemed to be the right time."

"It's cracked now," she says. "Look at the glass." She says, "Your poor face. Do you want me to bathe you?"

I look at her and say, "There is someone I'm interested in. But she's gone away. That's the truth, I'm afraid."

"You? There's someone interested in you?"

"It surprises you?"

"Well, yes."

"I am surprised that you are surprised."

She is crying.

"Is she going to take you away from me?"

"I shouldn't think so, now."

I open my mouth. I am about to speak.

"What is it?" she says.

"No. Nothing," I say. "Come along."

In the bathroom she bathes me. Then I lead her back to bed, my hand on her arm.

We lie there, back to back.

★   ★   ★

What could be more dreadful than daylight? She is dressing at the end of the bed. The children are bouncing on the mattress. The younger one tries to open my eyelids with his fingers. The other pours apple juice in my ear, wondering whether it will exit through the other. He has the makings of a scientist.

Susan goes downstairs with them.

I turn on to my back, as I do every morning, and think, what do I have to do today? What obligations do I have? What pleasures might there be? Then I remember and shut my eyes.

After a time the front door bangs and the house goes silent. The silence increases, enveloping everything in an ominous softness.

I get up and go down the stairs, but a noise makes me hesitate at the bend. I can see that in the hall Susan is leaving for work, putting her short coat on and pushing her bicycle to the door.

"Will you get something for later? See you at supper time!" she calls out, shutting the door behind her.

Without eating, drinking or thinking excessively, I do everything as quickly as I can. I shave and get some decent clothes on. Moving about the house, I discover my boys' night clothes flung on the floor. I pick them up, smell them, and fold them on their beds.

When the weather is warm, Susan puts talcum powder in her shoes and when she removes them her footprints remain on the floor, traces of her on the carpet, which stop suddenly, like a trail gone cold.

Soon I am zipping up my bag.

Standing up, I scribble a note. "Dear Susan, I have left this house and won't be coming back. I'm sorry to say that I don't think we can make one another happy. I will speak to you tomorrow." That is it. Then I notice she has left a note asking me to pick up her dry cleaning. Cursing, I hurry round the corner to fetch her clothes, and leave them in the bedroom.

I wonder, then, where to place my note. The table in the living room is crowded with flowers, presents, cards. Last week Susan had a birthday party in a nearby restaurant. There must have been almost thirty guests. In her new denim dress and pretty shoes with flowers sewn on the sides, she rushed at each friend as they came in. There was kissing and hugging and shouted bits of gossip. Soon the floor was strewn with ribbon and wrapping paper. I sat and watched her dancing to Tamla Motown records with a school friend. They even danced nostalgically. I recalled a time I was in Venice. She was joining me at the Hôtel des Bains on the Lido, but I didn't know at what time. I had gone downstairs and saw her by accident in the lobby, and she turned and recognized me and her face was full of pleasure.

She's not my type at all, but I'm sure there is something about her I could enjoy. I would like not to see her for a few months, in order to forget her; perhaps, then, I could get a clear view of what she is like, apart from me.

I place the note at the other end of the table, leaning it against a cup. She will not miss it when she comes in. She will sit in that chair over there to read it. I wonder what she will feel then; I wonder what she will do then. The phone is at hand.

I pick up my bag from the centre of the bedroom floor. I walk downstairs and open the front door. Tired but determined, I step outside. It hasn't rained for weeks. The blossom is out. London is in bloom; even I am in bloom, despite everything.

It is a lovely day for leaving.

I shut the door behind me and walk away. I consider going through the park and seeing the boys. But my distracted demeanour would give me away and any questions could cost me the little courage I have. Perhaps I should turn and wave at the house.

I can't say I haven't learned more in this crucible than I've learned anywhere: the education of a heart, slightly cracked, if not broken in places. Whether I will survive the knowledge and put it to good use—whether any of us will—is another matter.

Victor is sitting at the table in his black dressing gown, black socks and slippers, chewing on a piece of toast left on the table from last night, no doubt. But when I come through the door he gets up and kisses me.

"It's done?"

"Yes," I say. "It is done."

Victor watches me and looks jaunty. I notice that the flat has been cleaned. There is not a pickled onion in sight.

I consider unpacking, so as to make it clear to myself that I am staying. But looking around, I cannot see where I will put my things. He will leave for work later, and I will be here alone. I don't feel like going to the office. Perhaps I will go for a walk.

Victor takes my bag and puts it down in the corner. I notice that the coffee is fresh. There are croissants in the oven. I sit down and look at him, a friend. For a while—for how long I don't know—this place will be my home.

I wonder what time Susan will unfold the note and know, and know. She will not be back until the early evening. It is not too late to retrieve it.

"Did you know I'd come?"

"I thought you'd make it—eventually," Victor replies. "Perhaps in a few weeks. It had become inevitable."

"You could tell?"

"How could I not?" Then he says, "Have you told the kids?"

"No."

"That is the hardest."

I bite my lip.

"I'll speak to Susan first," I say. "Then them. I've got a lot to say to them . . . about the whole business of people trying to live together."

He looks at me. He knows this. Still, he is unusually cheerful.

"What's making you smile?" I enquire.

"I have a new interest. We are having lunch in that new place, and then a walk in the park—"

"And then?"

His eyes shine.

He says, "By the way, that girl rang."

"Which girl?"

"Nina. She heard you were looking for her."

I can only think of how good life on earth can be, at times. What grief two people can give one another! And what pleasure!

He says, "I've written her number down in case you've forgotten it."

"Thank you."

He hands me the slip of paper. I pick up the phone and push the buttons; then I replace the receiver.

"Later," I say. "There will be time."

We walked together, lost in our own thoughts. I forget where we were, or even when it was. Then you moved closer, stroked my hair and took my hand; I know you were holding my hand and talking to me softly. Suddenly I had the feeling that everything was as it should be and nothing could add to this happiness or contentment. This was all that there was, and all that could be. The best of everything had accumulated in this moment. It could only have been love.

MIDNIGHT ALL DAY

STRANGERS
WHEN WE MEET

C AN YOU HEAR ME? No; no one can hear me. No one knows I am here.

I can hear them.

I am in a hotel room, sitting forward in a chair, leaning my ear against the wall. In the next room is a couple. They have been talking, amicably enough; their exchanges seem slight but natural. However, their voices are low; attentive though I am, I cannot make out what they are saying.

I recall that when listening through obstructions, a glass can be effective. I tiptoe to the bathroom, fetch a glass, and, holding it against the wall with my head attached, attempt to enhance my hearing. Which way round should the glass go? If people could see me crouched like this! But in here I am alone and everything is spoiled.

This was to be my summer holiday, in a village by the sea. My bag is open on the bed, a book of love poetry and a biography of Rod Stewart on top. Yesterday I went to Kensington High Street and shopped for guidebooks, walking boots, novels, sex toys, drugs, and Al Green tapes for my Walkman. I packed last night and got to bed early. This morning I set my alarm for six and read a little of Stanislavsky's *My Life in Art:* "I have lived a variegated life, during the course of which I have been forced more than once to change my most fundamental ideas . . ."

Later, I ran in Hyde Park and as usual had breakfast in a café with my flatmates, an actress and an actor with whom I was at drama school. "Good luck! Have a great time, you lucky bastard!" they called, as I headed for the station with my bag over my shoulder. They are enthusiastic about everything, as young actors tend to be. Perhaps that is why I prefer older people, like Florence, who is in the next room. Even as a teenager I preferred my friends' parents—usually their mothers—to my friends. It was what people said of their lives that excited me, the details of their description, rather than football or parties.

Just now I returned from the beach, ten minutes walk away, past a row of new bungalows. The sea is lugubrious, almost grey. I trudged beside deserted bathing huts set in scrub land. There was some appropriate beauty in the overcast desolation and drizzle, and the open, empty distances. A handful of men in yellow capes nursed fishing lines on the shore. On a patch of tarmac people were crowded in camper vans, staring out to sea. Otherwise there is no one else there.

I consider all these to be the essential elements for a holiday in England. A couple who need to talk could have the opportunity here.

Bounded by farms and fields of grazing cattle and horses, the hotel is a large cottage with barns to the side, set in flower-filled gardens. There is a dining room, bright as a chandelier with glass and cutlery, where a tie is required— these little snobberies increase the further you are from London. But you can eat the same food in the bar, which is situated (as they said in the hotel guide, which Florence and I studied together) in the basement of the hotel. The rooms are snug, if a little floral, and with an unnecessary abundance of equine motifs. Nevertheless, there is a double bed, a television, and a bathroom one need not fear.

Now there is laughter next door! It is, admittedly, only him, the unconcerned laughter of someone living in a solid, established world. Yet she must have gone to the trouble to say something humorous. Why is she not amusing me? What did Florence say? How long will I be able to bear this?

Suddenly I get up, blunder over the corner of the bed and send the glass flying. Perhaps my cry and the bang will smash their idyll, but why should it?

I doubt whether my lover knows that I have been allocated the next room. Although we arrived in the same car, we did not check in together, since I went to "explore," just as my sisters and I would have done, on holiday with our parents. It is only when I open the door later that I hear her voice and realise we are in adjacent rooms.

I will leave here; I have to. It will not be tonight. The

thought of going home is more than disappointing. What will my flatmates say? We are not best friends; their bemusement I can survive, and I could live in the flat as if I am away, with the curtains drawn, taking no calls, eschewing the pubs and cafés where I do the crossword and write letters asking for work. But if I ring my close friends they will say, Why are you back already? What went wrong? What will I reply? There will be laughter and gossip. The story will be repeated by people who have never met me; it could trail me for years. What could be more beguiling than other people's stymied desire?

Tomorrow I could go on to Devon or Somerset, as Florence and I discussed. We intended to leave it open. Our first time away—in fact our first complete night together—was to be an adventure. We wanted to enjoy one another free of the thought that she would have to return to her husband in a few hours. We would wake up, make love, and exchange dreams over breakfast.

I am not in the mood to decide anything.

They certainly have plenty to say next door: a little unusual, surely, for a couple who have been married five years.

I wipe my eyes, wash my face and go to the door. I will have a few drinks at the bar and order supper. I have inspected the menu and the food looks promising, particularly the puddings, which Florence loves to take a spoon of, push away and say to the waiter, "That's me done!" Perhaps, from across the room, I will have the privilege of watching this.

But I return to my position against this familiar piece of

wall, massage my shin and try to depict what they are doing, as if I am listening to a radio play. Probably they are getting changed. Often, when I am alone with Florence, I turn around and she is naked. She removes her clothes as easily as others slip off their shoes. At twenty-nine her body is supple. I think of her lying naked on my bed reading a script for me, and saying what she thinks, as I fix something to eat. She does the parts in funny voices until I am afraid to take the project seriously. I have a sweater of hers, and some gloves, which she left at my place. Why don't I rap on their door? I am all for surrealism.

They will be in the dining room later. I cannot see why it would occur to him to take her elsewhere tonight. The man will eat opposite his woman, asking her opinion of the sauces, contentedly oblivious of everything else, knowing Florence's lips, jokes, breasts and kindnesses are his. I fear my own madness. Not that I will vault across the table and choke either of them. I will sit with my anger and will not appreciate my food. I will go to bed forlorn, and half-drunk, only to hear them again. The hotel is not full: I can ask for another room. In the bar I saw a woman reading *The Bone People*. There are several young Austrian tourists too, in long socks, studying maps and guide books. What a time we could all have.

But there is an awful compulsion; I need to know how they are together. My ear will always be pressed against this wall.

★　　★　　★

To think that earlier today I was sitting in the train at the station. I had bought wine, sandwiches and, as a surprise, chocolate cake. The sun burned through the window. (It is odd how one imagines that just because the sun is shining in London, it is shining everywhere else.) I had purchased first-class seats, paying for the trip with money earned on a film, playing the lead, a street boy, a drug kid, a thief. They have shown me the rough cut; it is being edited and will have a rock soundtrack. The producer is confident of getting it into the directors' fortnight at Cannes, where, he claims, they are so moneyed and privileged, they adore anything seedy and cruel.

Florence is certainly sharper than my agent. When I first heard about the film from some other actors she told me that when she was an actress she had had supper with the producer a few times. I imagine she was boasting, but she rang him at home, and insisted the director meet me. I sat on her knee with my fingers on her nipple as she made the call. She didn't admit we know one another, but said she has seen me in a play. "He's not only pretty," she said, pinching my cheek. "He has a heartbreaking sadness, and charm."

There were scores of young actors being considered for the part. I recognise most of them, smoking, shuffling and complaining, in the line outside the audition room. I presumed we would be rivals for life but it was to me that the producer said, "It is yours if you want it!"

Waiting for Florence O'Hara on the train made my blood so effervescent that I speculated about whether I could have her in the toilet. I had never attempted such a caper, but she has rarely refused me anything. Or perhaps she could slip her hand under my newspaper. For days I have been imagining what pleasures we might make. We would have a week of one another before I went to Los Angeles for the first time, to Hollywood, to play a small part in an independent American movie.

With two minutes to go—and I was becoming concerned, having already been walking about the station for an hour—I glimpse her framed in the window and almost shouted out. To confirm the fact that we were going on holiday, she was wearing a floppy purple hat. Florence can dress incongruously at times, wearing, say, antique jewellery and a silk top with worn-out, frayed shoes, as if by the time she arrived at her feet she had forgotten what she had done with her head.

Behind her was her husband.

I recognised him from a wedding photograph I saw on the one occasion I popped warily into their flat, to survey their view of Hammersmith Bridge and the river. Florence had suggested I paint the view. Today, for some reason he was seeing her off. She would wave through the window at him—I hoped she would not kiss him—before sinking down next to me.

There is always something suspicious about the need to be alone. The trip had taken some arranging. At first, conspiring in bed, Florence and I thought she should tell her husband she was holidaying with a friend. But intricate lies made Florence's hands perspire. Instead, she ascertained when her husband would be particularly busy at the office, and insisted that she needed to read, walk and think. "Think about what?" he asked, inevitably, as he dressed for work. But, quietly, she could be inflexible, and he likes to be magnanimous.

"All right, my dear," he announced. "Go and be alone and see how much you miss me."

During the week before our departure, Florence and I saw one another twice. She phoned and I caught a taxi outside my front door in Gloucester Road. She put on a head scarf and dark glasses, and slipped out to meet me in one of the many pubs near her flat, along the river. There was an abstraction about her that makes me want her more, and which I assume would be repaired by our holiday together.

Her husband was walking through the train towards me. Despite having left the office for only an hour, he was wearing a cream linen jacket, jeans and old deck shoes, without socks. Fine, I thought, he's so polite he's helping her right into her seat; that's something a twenty-seven-year-old like me could learn from.

He heaved her bag onto the rack and they sat opposite, across the aisle. He glanced indifferently in my direction. She was captivated by the activity on the platform. When he talked she smiled. Meanwhile she was tugging at the skin around her thumbnail until it bled, and she had to find a tissue in her bag. Florence was wearing her wedding ring, something she had never done with me, apart from the first time we met.

With an unmistakable jolt, the train left the station, on its way to our holiday destination with me, my lover and her husband aboard.

I stood up, sat down, tapped myself on the head, searched in my bag and looked around wildly, as if seeking someone to explain the situation to me. Eventually, having watched me eat the chocolate cake—on another occasion she would have licked the crumbs from my lips—Florence left her seat to fetch sandwiches. I went to the toilet where she was waiting outside for me.

"He insisted on coming," she whispered, digging her nails into my arm. "It was yesterday. He gave me no choice. I couldn't resist without making him jealous and suspicious. I had no chance to speak to you."

"He's staying the whole week?"

She looked agitated. "He'll get bored. This kind of thing doesn't interest him."

"What sort of thing?"

"Being on holiday. We usually go somewhere . . . like Italy. Or the Hamptons—"

"Where?"

"Outside New York. I'll encourage him to go home. Will you wait?"

"I can't say," I told her. "You've really made a mess of everything! How could you do such a thing!"

"Rob—"

"You're stupid, stupid!"

"No, no, it's not that!"

She tried to kiss me but I pulled away. She passed her hand between my legs—and I wish she hadn't—before returning to her husband. I walked up and down the train before sitting down. It did not occur to me to sit somewhere else. Blood from her thumb was smeared over my arm and hand.

I had never seen her look this miserable. She is sometimes so nervous she will spill the contents of her bag over the street and have to get on her hands and knees to retrieve her things. Yet she can be brave. On the tube once, three young men started to bait and rob the passengers. While the rest of us were lost in terror, she attacked the robbers with an insane fury that won her a bravery award.

For the rest of the journey she pretended to be asleep. Her husband read a thriller.

At the country station, as I marched off the platform, I saw the hotel had sent a car to pick us up: one car. Before I could enquire about trains back to London, the driver approached me.

"Robert Miles?"

"Yes?"

"This way, please."

The bent countryman led me outside where the air was cool and fresh. The immensity of the sky could have calmed a person. It was for this that Florence and I decided, one afternoon, to get away.

The man opened the car door.

"In you get, sir." I hesitated. He swept dog hairs from the seat. "I'll drive as slowly as I can, and tell you a little about the area."

He deposited my bag in the boot. I had no choice but to get into the car. He shut the door. Florence and her husband were invited to sit in the back. As we drove away the car bulged with our heat and presence. The driver talked to me, and I listened to them.

"I'm glad I decided to come," Florence's husband was saying. "Still, we could have gone up to the House."

"Oh, that place," she sighed.

"Yes, it's like having a third parent. You don't have to keep telling me you don't like it. What made you decide on here?"

I wanted to turn round and say, "I decided—"

"I saw it in a brochure," she said.

"You told me you'd been here as a child."

"Yes, the brochure reminded me. I went to lots of places as a child, with my mother."

"Your mad mother." In the mirror I saw him put his arm around her and lay his hand on her breast.

"Yes," she said.

"Just us now," he said. "I'm so glad I came."

I am hungry.

At last I unstick my ear from the wall, shake my head as if to clear it, go downstairs, and have supper in the bar crowded with the local lushes, who prefer this hotel to the pubs.

I eat with my back to the room, a book in front of me, wondering where Florence and her husband are sitting and what they are saying; like someone sitting in Plato's cave, trying to read the shadows. Halfway through the meal, having resolved to face them at last, I rise suddenly, change my seat and turn around. They are not there.

As I order another drink, the plump girl behind the bar smiles at me. "We thought you were waiting for some lucky person who didn't turn up."

"There's no lucky person, but it's not so bad."

I take my drink and walk about, though I do not know

where I am going. Waitresses tear in and out of the hot dining room, so smart, inhibited and nervous, lacking the London arrogance and beauty. Middle-aged women with painted faces and bright dresses, and satisfied men in suits and ties, who do not question their right to be here—this being their world—are beginning to leave the dining room, holding glasses. For a moment they stand on this piece of earth, as it moves on imperceptibly, and they gurgle and chuckle with happiness.

Optimistically I follow a couple into one of the sitting rooms, where they will have more drinks and coffee. I collapse into a high-backed sofa.

After a time I recognise the voice I am listening to. Florence and her husband have come in and are sitting behind me. They start to play Scrabble. I am close enough to smell her.

"I liked the fish," she is saying. "The vegetables were just right. Not overcooked and not raw."

I have been thinking of how proud I was that I had hooked a married woman.

"Florence," he says. "It's your turn. Are you sure you're concentrating?"

When I started with Florence I wanted to be discreet as well as wanting to show off. I hoped to run into people I knew; I was convinced my friends were gossiping about me. I had never had an adventure like this. If it failed, I would walk away unscathed.

"We don't eat enough fish," she says.

Certainly, I did not think about what her husband might be like, or why she married him. To me she made him irrelevant. It was only us.

He says, "You don't like to kiss me when I've eaten meat."

"No, I don't," she says.

"Kiss me now," he says.

"Let's save it."

"Let's not."

"Archie—"

Her voice sounds forced and dull, as if she is about to weep. How long do I intend to sit here? My mind whirls; I have forgotten who I am. I imagine catastrophes and punishments everywhere. I suppose it was to cure myself of such painful furies that I become depressed so often. When I am depressed I shut everything down, living in a tiny part of myself, in my sexuality or ambition to be an actor. Otherwise, I kill myself off. I have talked to Florence about these things—about "melancholy" as she puts it—and she understands it: the first person I have known who does.

I realise that if I peep around the arm of the sofa I can see Florence from the side, perched on a stool. I move a little; now she is in full view, wearing a tight white top, cream bags and white sandals.

Oddly, I am behaving as if this man has stolen my woman. In fact it is I who have purloined his, and if he finds out, he could easily become annoyed and perhaps violent. But I gaze and gaze at her, at the way she puts her right hand across her face and rests the back of her hand on her cheek with her fingers beneath her eye; a gesture she must have made as a child, and will probably make as an old woman.

If Archie is a ruling presence in our lives, he is an invisible one; and if she behaves a little, let's say, obscurely, at times, it is because she lives behind a wall I can only listen at. She is free during the day but likes to account for where she is. He would have been more than satisfied with, "I spent the afternoon at the Tate," and could endure with less about its Giacomettis. When we separate at the end of each meeting she often becomes agitated and upset.

I assumed that I did not care enough about her to worry about her husband. It never occurred to me that she and I would live together, for instance; we would continue casually until we fell out. Nevertheless, watching her now, I am not ready for that. I want her to want me, and me alone. I must play the lead and not be a mere walk-on.

The barmaid comes and picks up my glass. "Can I get you something else?"

"No thanks," I say in a low voice.

I notice that Florence raises her head a little.

"Did you enjoy your meal?" says the barmaid.

"Yes. Particularly the fish. The vegetables were just right. Not overcooked and not raw." Then I say, "When does the bar close?"

"Thursday!" she says, and laughs.

Without looking at Florence or her husband, I follow her out of the room and lean tiredly across the bar.

"What are you doing down here?" She says this as if she's certain that it is not my kind of place.

"Only relaxing," I say.

She lowers her voice. "We all hate it down here. Relaxing's all there is to do. You'll get plenty of it."

"What do you like to do?"

"We used to play Russian roulette with cars. Driving across crossroads, hoping that nothing is coming the other way. That sort of thing."

"What's your name?"

"Martha."

She puts my drink down. I tell her my room number.

"That's all right," she says. Martha leans towards me. "Listen—" she says.

"Yes?"

Florence's husband sits heavily on the stool beside me and shifts about on it, as if he is trying to screw it into the floor. I scuttle along a little.

He turns to me. "All right if I sit down?"

"Why not?"

He orders a cigar. "And a brandy," he says to Martha. He looks at me before I can turn my back. "Anything for you?"

I start to get up. "I'm just off."

"Something I said?" He says, "I saw you in the train."

"Really? Oh yes. Was that your wife?"

"Of course."

"Is she going to join us?"

"How do I know? Do you want me to ring the room?"

"I don't want you to do anything."

"Have a brandy." He lays his hand on my shoulder. "I say, barmaid—a brandy for this young man!"

"Right," I say. "Right."

"Do you like brandy?" she says to me, kindly.

"Very much," I say.

He drags his tie off and stuffs it in his jacket pocket.

141

"Sit down," he says. "We're on bloody holiday. Let's make the most of it! Can I ask your name?"

I met Florence nearly a year ago in a screening room, where we were the only people viewing a film made by a mutual friend. She lay almost on her back in the wide seat, groaning, laughing and snorting throughout the film. At the end— before the end, in fact—she started talking about the performances. I invited her for a drink. After leaving university, she was an actress for a couple of years. "It was a cattle-market, darling. Couldn't stand being compared to other people."

Yet a few days after we met, she was sitting crosslegged on the floor in my place, as my flatmates wrote down the names of casting directors she suggested they contact. She fitted easily into my world of agents, auditions, scripts, and the confusion of young people whose life hangs on chance, looks, and the ability to bear large amounts of uncertainty. It was not only that she liked the semi-student life, the dope smoking, the confused promiscuity and exhibitionism, but that she seemed to envy and miss it.

"If only I could stay," she would say theatrically, at the door.

"Stay then," I shout from the top of the stairs.

"Not yet."

"When?"

"You enjoy yourself! Live all you can!"

Our "affair" began without being announced. She rang me—I rarely phoned her; she asked to see me—"at ten past five, in the Scarsdale!" and I would be there with ten minutes to spare. Certainly, I had nothing else to do but attend actors' workshops, and read plays and the biographies of actors. Sometimes we went to bed. Sexually she will say and do anything, with the enthusiasm of someone dancing or running. I am not always certain she is entirely there; sometimes I have to remind her she is not giving a solo performance.

Often we go to the theatre in the afternoon, and to a pub to discuss the writing, acting and direction. She takes me to see peculiar European theatre groups that use grotesquerie, masks and gibberish; she introduces me to dance and performance art. When she kisses me goodbye and goes home, or out to meet her husband, I see actresses, girls who work in TV, students, au pairs. They keep me from feeling too much for Florence. There was one night of alcohol and grief, when I wept and hated her inaccessibility. I have not had a suitable girlfriend for more than two years. The last woman I lived with became only my friend; the relationship lacked velocity and a future. My life does tend towards stasis, which Florence recognises.

I had been finding it difficult to break with my background in South London. The men I grew up with were tough and loud-mouthed, bragging of their ignorance and crudity. They believed aggression was their most necessary tool. On leaving school they became villains and thieves. In their twenties, when they had children, they turned to car dealing, building or "security." They continued to go to football matches, drank heavily, and pursued teenage longings, ideals to which they had become addicted. What I want to do—act—represents an inexplicable ambition that intimidates them and, by its nature, will leave them behind. I am not saying that there are not any working-class actors. I hope to play many parts. I want to transform myself until I become unrecognisable. But I will not become an actor for whom being working class is "an act." No cops or criminals in TV series for me.

In the pub with these friends I try to retain the accent and attitudes of my past, but I have emerged from the anonymous world and they are contemptuous and provocative. "Give us a speech, Larry. To buy a drink or not to buy a drink!" they chant, pulling at my expensive shirt. I am about to get into a fight over divergent ideas of who I should be. I begin to consider them cowardly, living only little lives, full of bold talk, but doing nothing and going nowhere. It is not until later that Florence teaches me that part of being successful is the ability to bear envy and plain dislike.

I am not educated. If she notices it, Florence never comments on my ignorance. She can be light-headed and frivolous herself; once she shopped for two days. Nevertheless, she sits me down in front of the most exacting films. Bergman's *Cries and Whispers,* for instance, she thinks it necessary we both absorb through repetition; it is as if she is singing along with the film, or, in the case of that work, moaning. She does not categorise these things as art, as I do, but uses them as objects of immediate application.

Almost as soon as I met Florence, she altered the direction of my life. The Royal Shakespeare Company had offered me a two-year contract. I would share a cottage in Stratford. She would sit with me beside the Avon. I had celebrated in Joe

Allens with friends, and my agent was working on the contract.

To celebrate, I took Florence out to lunch to celebrate. I read in a mazagine that the restaurant was one of the smartest in London, but she swung about in her chair. I should have remembered that she dislikes eating—she is as thin and flat-chested as a dancer. Certainly she does not like sitting down for her food surrounded by people she has seen on television and considers pompous and talentless.

"I have to tell you that you must turn the Stratford opportunity down," she said.

"It's every young actor's dream, Florence."

"Rob, don't be such a common little fool. They're too small, too small," she said. "Not only that suit you're wearing, but the parts. Going to the Royal Shakespeare Company will be a waste of time." She flicks my nose with her fingernail.

"Ow."

"You must listen to me."

I did.

My agent was amazed and furious. Without entirely knowing why, I took Florence's advice. Soon I am playing big roles in little places: Biff in *Death of a Salesman*, in Bristol; the lead in a new play in Cheltenham; Romeo in Yorkshire.

With a girlfriend she came on the train to see a preview, and we travelled back together late at night, drinking wine in plastic cups. She anatomised my performance so severely I took notes. "There were a couple of awful moments when you tried to have us laugh at the character you were playing," she said. "I thought, if he does that again I will go to the box office and ask for my money back!"

Criticism, I suppose, reminded me of my dependency on her. Yet, when she was finished, and I was almost finished off, she continued to look at me without any diminishment of desire and love.

It was fine by her if I took small parts on television or in films. I had to get used to the camera so that I could concentrate on movies, "like Gary Oldman and Daniel Day-Lewis." She said she understood what women would like about me on screen, when I could only laugh at such an idea. Also she said that most actors see only moments; I had to learn how to develop a part through the whole film. She told me to learn as much as I could, for when it took off for me, it would happen very quickly. She even suggested that I should direct movies, saying, "If you generate your own work it will give you another kind of pleasure."

Like my friends at drama school, my head was full of schemes and fantasies. I have always been impressed by people who live with deliberation; but ambition, or desire in the world, makes me apprehensive. I am afraid of what I want, of where it might take me, and what it might make others think of me. Yet, as Florence explains, how are cathedrals and banks built, diseases eliminated, dictators crushed, football matches won—without frustration and the longing to overcome it? Often the simplest things have to be explained. Florence fills me with hope, but ensures it is based on the possible.

I have little idea what Florence dreams of and of what

kind of world she inhabits with Archie, who is in "property"; I doubt she is ensnared in some kind of *Doll's House*. In the middle of the city in which I live there is an undisturbed English continuity: they are London "bohemians." It is an expensive indolence and carelessness, but the money for country houses, and for villas in France and the West Indies, for parties, the opera, excursions and weekends away, never runs out. This set has known one another for generations; their parents were friends and lovers in those alcoholic times, the fifties and sixties. Perhaps Florence is lost in something she does not entirely like or understand, but when she calls her husband's world "grown up" I resent the idea that she considers my world childish. My guess is that she is uncomfortable in such an intransigent world but is unable to live according to her own desire.

"Rob," I say.

Florence's husband offers me his beringed hand. I can hardly bear to touch him, and he must find me damp with apprehension.

"Archie O'Hara. Stayed here before?"

"No . . . I just came down . . . to get away."

"From what?"

"You know."

"Yes," he says, indifferently. "Don't I know. That's what we're doing. Getting away."

We sit there and Martha looks at us as if we all know one another. Archie wears a blue jacket, white shirt and yellow corduroys; his face is smooth and well fed. As Florence has chosen to be with him—most of the time—he must, I imagine, have some unusual qualities. Is he completely dissimilar to me, or does he resemble me in ways I cannot see? Perhaps I will learn.

"How long are you staying?" I ask.

He puffs on his cigar and says nothing.

Martha says, "I could tell you where to go and what to look at, if you want."

Archie says, "Thanks, but I've been thinking of getting another country place. I inherited a stately home as they call them these days, with a lot of Japanese photographing me through the windows. Sometimes I feel like sitting there in a dress and tiara. My wife says you can't sit down without farting into the dust of a dozen centuries. So we might have to drive round . . . estate agents and all that."

I say, "Does your wife like the country?"

"London women have fantasies about fields. But she suffers from hay fever. I can't see the point in going to a place where you know no one. But then I can't see the point in anything."

He puts his head back and laughs.

"Are you depressed?"

"You know that, do you?" He sighs. "It's staring everyone in the face, like a slashed throat." He says after a time, "I'm not going to kill myself. But I could, just as well."

"I had it for two years, once."

He squeezes my arm as Florence sometimes does. "Now it's gone?"

I tap the wooden bar. "Yes."

"That's good to hear. You're a happy little man, are you, now?"

I am about to inform him that it is returning, probably as a result of meeting him. But this is despair, not depression. These distinctions are momentous.

We discuss the emptying out; the fear of living; the creation of a wasteland; the denigration of value and meaning. I tell him melancholy was part of my interior scene and that I considered it to be the way the world was, until I stood against it.

I announce, "People make themselves sick when they aren't leading the lives they should be leading."

He bangs the bar. "How banal, but true."

By now the place has almost emptied. Martha collects the glasses, sweeps the floor and wipes down the bar. She continues to put out brandies for us.

She watches us and says, "There isn't much intelligent conversation down here."

"What do you think of meditation?" he says. "Eastern hogwash or truth?"

"It helps my concentration," I say. "I'm an actor."

"There's a lot of actors about. They rather get under one's feet, talking about "centreing" and all that."

I say, "Do you know any actors? Or actresses?"

"Do you count ten breaths or only four," he says, "when meditating?"

"Four," I say. "There's less time to get lost."

"Who taught you?"

Your wife, I am about to say.

"I had a good teacher," I say.

"Where was the class . . . could you tell me?"

"The woman who taught me . . . I met her by chance, one day, in a cinema. She seemed to like me instantly. I liked her liking me. She led me on, you could say."

"Really?" says Martha, leaning across the bar.

"Only then she took my hand and told me, with some sadness, that she was married. I thought that would suit me. Anyhow, she taught me some things."

Martha said, "She didn't tell you she was married?"

"She did, yes. Just before we slept together."

"Moments before?" said Martha. "She sounds like an awful person."

"Why?"

"To do that to you! Do you want her to leave her husband?"

"What for? I don't know. I haven't thought about it."

Archie laughs. "Wait 'til he catches up with you!"

"I hope I'm not keeping you," I say to Archie.

"My wife will be on her REMs by now. I've missed my conjugals for today."

"Does she usually go to sleep at this time?"

"I can't keep that woman out of bed."

"And she reads in bed? Novels?"

"What are you, a librarian?"

I say, "I like basic information about people. The facts, not opinions."

"Yes. That's a basic interest in people. And you still have that?"

"Don't you?"

He thinks about it. "Perhaps you study people because you're an actor."

Martha lights a cigarette. She has become thoughtful. "It's not only that. I know it isn't. It is an excuse for looking. But looking is the thing." She turns to me with a smile.

"That might be right, my dear," Archie says. "Things are rarely only one thing."

For my benefit she shoots him an angry look and I smile at her.

"Better make a move," he says. "Better had."

I want to ask him more. "What does your wife do? Did you ever see her act?"

"Told you she was an actress, did I? Don't remember that. Don't usually say that, as it's not true. Like women, eh?"

"Sorry?"

"Saw how you appreciated my wife, on the train." He gets down from the stool, and staggers. "It's beautiful when I'm sitting down. Better help us upstairs."

He finds my shoulder and connects himself to it. He is heavy and I feel like letting him go. I do not like being so close to him.

"I'll give you a hand," Martha says. "It's not far. You're in the next room to one another."

One on each side, we heave him upstairs. The last few steps he takes with gingerly independence.

At the door he turns. "Guide me into the room. Don't know the layout. Could be pitch dark with only my wife's teeth for light."

Martha takes his key and opens the door for him.

"Goodnight," I say.

I am not accompanying him into the bedroom.

"Hey." He falls into the room.

I wave at Martha.

"Archie," says startled Florence from the darkness within. "Is that you?"

"Who else, dammit? Undress me!"

"Archie—"

"Wife's duty!"

I sink down beside the wall like a gargoyle and think of her tearing at the warm mound of him. Now I have seen him, his voice seems clearer.

I hear him say, "I was just talking to someone—"

"Who?"

"That boy in the next room."

"Which boy?"

"The actor, you fool. He was in the train. Now he's in the hotel!"

"Is he? Why?"

"How do I know?"

He switches the TV on. I would not have done such a thing when she was sleeping. I think of Florence sleeping. I know what her face will be like.

Next morning it is silent next door. I walk along the corridor hoping I will not run into Florence and Archie. Maids are starting to clean the rooms. I pass people on the stairs and say

"Good morning." The hotel smells of furniture polish and fried food.

At the door to the breakfast room I bump into them. We smile at one another, I slide by and secure a table behind a pillar. I open the newspaper and order haddock, tomatoes, mushrooms and fried potatoes.

Last night I dreamed I had a nervous breakdown; that I was walking around a foreign town incapable of considered thought or action, not knowing who I was or where I was going. I wonder whether I want to incapacitate myself rather than seriously consider what I should do. I need to remind myself that such hopelessness will lead to depression. Better to do something. After breakfast I will get the train back to London.

I am thinking that it is likely that I will never see Florence again, when she rushes around the corner.

"What are you doing? What are you intending to do? Oh Rob, tell me."

She is close to me, breathing over me; her hair touches my face, her hand is on mine, and I want her again, but I hate her, and hate myself.

"What are you intending to do?" I ask.

"I will persuade him to leave."

"When?"

"Now. He'll be on the lunch-time train."

"No doubt sitting next to me."

"But we can talk and be together! I'll do anything you want." I look at her doubtfully. She says, "Don't go this morning. Don't do that to me."

For some reason a man I have never seen before, with a lapel badge saying "Manager," is standing beside the table.

"Excuse me," he says.

Florence does not notice him. "I beg you," she says. "Give me a chance." She kisses me. "You promise?"

"Excuse me," the hotel manager says. "The car you ordered is here, sir." I stare at him. He seems to regard us as a couple. "The rental car—suitable for a man and a woman, touring."

"Oh yes," I say.

"Would you both like to look at it now?"

With a wave, Florence goes. Outside, I gaze at the big, four-door family saloon, chosen in a moment of romantic distraction. I sit in it.

After breakfast I drive into Lyme Regis and walk on the Cobb; later I drive to Charmouth, climb up the side of the cliff and look out to sea. It is beginning to feel like being on holiday with your parents when you are too old for it.

I return to the hotel to say goodbye to Florence again. In the conservatory, reading the papers, is Archie, wearing a suit jacket over a T-shirt, brown shorts and black socks and shoes, looking like someone who has dressed for the office but forgotten to put their trousers on.

As I back away, hoping he has not recognised me, and if he does, that he will not quite recall who I am, he says, "Have a good morning?"

In front of him is a half-empty bottle of wine. His face is covered in a fine glacé of sweat.

I tell him where I've been.

"Busy boy," he says.

"And you? You're still around . . . here?"

"We've walked and even read books. I'm terribly, terribly glad I came."

He pours a glass of wine and hands it to me.

I say, "Think you might stay a bit longer?"

"Only if it's going to annoy you."

His wife comes to the other door. She blinks several times, her mouth opens, and then she seems to yawn.

"What's wrong with you?" asks her husband.

"Tired," she whispers. "Think I'll lie down."

He winks at me. "Is that an invitation?"

"Sorry, sorry," she says.

"Why the hell are you apologising? Get a grip, Florrie. I spoke to this young man last night." He jabs his finger at me. "You said this thing . . ." He looks into the distance and massages his temples. "You said . . . if you experienced the desires, the impulses, within you, you would break up what you had created, and live anew. But there would be serious consequences. The word was in my head all night. Consequences. I haven't been able to live out those things. I have tried to put them away, but can't. I've got this image . . . of stuffing a lot of things in a suitcase that can't be closed, that is too small. That is my life. If I lived what I thought . . . it would all blow down . . ."

I realise Florence and I have been looking at one another. Sometimes you look at someone instead of touching them.

He regards me curiously. "What's going on? Have you met my wife?"

"Not really."

My lover and I shake hands.

Archie says, "Florrie, he's been unhappy in love. Married woman and all that. We must cheer him up."

"Is he unhappy?" she says. "Are you sure? People should cheer themselves up. Don't you think, Rob?"

She crooks her finger at me and goes. Her husband ponders his untrue life. As soon as his head re-enters his hands, I am away, racing up the stairs.

My love is lingering in the corridor.

"Come."

She pulls my arm; with shaking hands I unlock my door; she hurries me through my room and into the bathroom. She turns on the shower and the taps, flushes the toilet, and falls into my arms, kissing my face and neck and hair.

I am about to ask her to leave with me. We could collect our things, jump in the car and be on the road before Archie has lifted his head and wiped his eyes. The idea burns in me; if I speak, our lives could change.

"Archie knows."

I pull back so I can see her. "About our exact relation to one another?"

She nods. "He's watching us. Just observing us."

"Why?"

"He wants to be sure, before he makes his move."

"What move?"

"Before he gets us."

"Gets us? How?"

"I don't know. It's torture, Rob."

This thing has indeed made her mad; such paranoia I find

abhorrent. Reality, whatever it is, is the right anchor. Nevertheless, I have been considering the same idea myself. I do not believe it, and yet I do.

"I don't care if he knows," I say. "I'm sick of it."

"But we mustn't give up!"

"What? Why not?"

"There is something between us . . . which is worthwhile."

"I don't know any more, Florrie. Florence."

She looks at me and says, "I love you, Rob."

She has never said this before. We kiss for a long time.

I turn off the taps and go through into the bedroom. She follows me and somehow we fall onto the bed. I pull up her skirt; soon she is on me. Our howls would be known to the county. When I wake up she is gone.

I walk on the beach; there is a strong wind. I put my head back: it is raining into my eyes. I think of Los Angeles, my work, and of what will happen in the next few months. A part of my life seems to be over, and I am waiting for the new.

After supper I am standing in the garden outside the dining room, smoking weed, and breathing in the damp air. I have decided it is too late to return to London tonight. Since waking up I have not spoken to Florence, only glanced into the dining room where she and her husband are seated at a table in the middle. Tonight she is wearing a long purple dress. She has started to look insistent and powerful again, a little diva, with the staff, like ants, moving around only her because they cannot resist. One more night and she will bring the room down with a wave and stride out towards the sea. I know she is going to join me later. It is only a wish, of course, but won't she be wishing too? It is probably our last chance. What will happen then? I have prepared my things and turned the car around.

There is a movement behind me.

"That's nice," she says, breathing in.

I put out my arms and Martha holds me a moment. I offer her the joint. She inhales and hands it back.

"What are you thinking?"

"Next week I'm going to Los Angeles to be in a film."

"Is that true?"

"What about you?"

She lives nearby with her parents. Her father is a psychology lecturer in the local college, an alcoholic with a violent temper who has not been to work for a year. One day he took against London, as if it had personally offended him, and insisted the family move from Kentish Town to the country, cutting them off from everything they knew.

"We always speculate about the people who stay here, me and the kitchen girl." She says, suddenly, "Is something wrong?"

She turns and looks behind. As Martha has been talking, I have seen Florence come out into the garden, watch us for a bit, and throw up her hands like someone told to mime "despair." A flash of purple and she is gone.

"What is it?"

"Tell me what you've been imagining about me," I say.

"But we don't know what you're doing here. Are you going to tell me?"

"Can't you guess?" I say impatiently. "Why do you keep asking me these things?"

She takes offence, but I have some idea of how to get others to talk about themselves. I discover that recently she has had an abortion, her second; that she rides a motorbike; that the young people carry knives, take drugs and copulate as often as they can; and that she wants to get away.

"Is the bar shut?" I ask.

"Yes. I can get you beer if you want."

"Would you like to drink a glass of beer with me?" I ask.

"More than one glass, I hope."

I kiss her on the cheek and tell her to come to my room. "But what will your parents say if you are late home?"

"They don't care. Often I find an empty room and sleep in it. Don't want to go home." She says, "Are you sure it's only beer you want?"

"Whatever you want," I say. "You can get a key."

On the way upstairs I look into the front parlour. In the middle of the floor Florence and Archie are dancing; or rather, he is holding on to her as they heave about. The Scrabble board and all the letters have been knocked on the floor. His head is flopped over her shoulder; in five years he will be bald. Florence notices me and raises a hand, trying not to disturb him.

He calls out, "Hey!"

"Drunk again," I say to her.

"I know what you have been doing. Up to!" he says with leering emphasis.

"When?"

"This afternoon. Siesta. You know."

I look at Florence.

"The walls are thin," he says. "But not quite thin enough. I went upstairs. I had to fetch something from the bathroom. But what an entertainment. Jiggy-jig, jiggy-jig!"

"I'm glad to be an entertainment, you old fucker," I say. "I wish you could be the same for me."

"What was Rob doing this afternoon?" Florence says. "Don't leave me out of the game."

"Ha, ha, ha! You're a dopey little thing who never notices anything!"

"Don't talk to her like that," I say. "Talk to me like that, if you want, and see what you get!"

"Rob," says Florence, soothingly.

Archie slaps Florence on the behind. "Dance, you old corpse!"

I stare at his back. He is too drunk to care that he's being provoked into a fight.

I feel like an intruder and am reminded of the sense I had as a child, when visiting friends' houses, that the furniture, banter and manner of doing things were different from the way we did them at home. The world of Archie and Florence is not mine.

I am waiting for Martha on the bed when I hear Florence and Archie in the corridor opening the door to their room. The door closes; I listen intently, wondering if Archie has passed out and Florence is lying there awake.

The door opens and Martha rattles a bag of beer bottles. We open the windows, lie down on the bed and drink and smoke.

She leans over me. "Do you want one of these?"

I kiss her fist and open it. "I know what it is," I say. "But I've never had one."

"I hadn't till I came down here," she says. "These are good Es."

"Fetch some water from the bathroom."

Meanwhile I remove the chair from its position beside the wall and begin shoving the heavy bed.

"Let's have this . . . over there . . . against the wall," I say when she returns.

Martha starts to help me, an enthusiastic girl, with thick arms.

"Why do you want this?" she asks.

"I think it will be better for our purposes."

"Right," she says. "Right."

A few minutes after we lie down again, undressed this time, there is a knock on the door. We hold one another like scared children, listen and say nothing. There is another knock. Martha doesn't want to lose her job tonight. Then there is no more knocking. We do not even hear footsteps.

When we are breathing again, under the sheets I whisper, "What do you think of the couple next door? Have you talked about them? Are they suited, do you think?"

"I like him," she says.

"What? Really?"

"Makes me laugh. She's beautiful . . . but dangerous. Would you like to fuck her?"

I laugh. "I haven't thought about it."

"Listen," she says, putting her finger to her lips.

Neither of us moves.

"They're doing it. Next door."

"Yes," I say. "They are."

"They're quiet," she says. "I can only hear him."

"He's doing it alone."

"No. There . . . there she is. A little gasp. Can you hear her now? Touch me."

"Wait."

"There . . . there."

"Martha—"

"Please . . ."

I go into the bathroom and wash my face. The drug is starting to work. It seems like speed, which I had taken with my friends in the suburbs. This drug, though, opens another window: it makes me feel more lonely. I return to the room and switch the radio on. It must have been loud. We must have been loud. Martha is ungrudging in her love-making. Later, there is a storm. A supernatural breeze, fresh, strangely still and cool, fans us.

Martha goes downstairs early to make breakfast. At dawn I run along the stony beach until I am exhausted; then I stop, walk a little, and run again, all the while aware of the breaking brightness of the world. I shower, pack and go down for breakfast.

Florence and Archie are at the next table. Archie studies a map; Florence keeps her head down. She does not appear to have combed her hair. When Archie gets up to fetch something and she looks up, her face is like a mask, as if she has vacated her body.

After breakfast, collecting my things, I notice the door to their room has been wedged open by a chair. The maid is working in a room further along the hall. I look in at the unmade bed, go into my room, find Florence's sweater and gloves in my bag, and take them into their room. I stand there. Her shoes are on the floor, her perfume, necklace, and pens on the bedside table. I pull the sweater over my head. It is tight and the sleeves are too short. I put the gloves on, and wiggle my fingers. I lay them on the bed. I take a pair of scissors from her washbag in the bathroom and cut the middle finger from one of the gloves. I replace the severed digit in its original position.

As I bump along the farm track which leads up to the main road, I get out of the car, look down at the hotel on the edge of the sea and consider going back. I hate separations and finality. I am too good at putting up with things, that is my problem.

London seems to be made only of hard materials and the dust that cannot settle on it; everything is angular, particularly the people. I go to my parents' house and lie in bed; after a few days I leave for Los Angeles. There I am just another young actor, but at least one with a job. When I return to London we all leave the flat and I get my own place for the first time.

I have come to like going out for coffee early, with my son in his pushchair, while my wife sleeps. Often I meet other men whose wives need sleep, and at eight o'clock on Sunday morning we have chocolate milkshakes in McDonalds, the only place open in the dismal High Street. We talk about our children, and complain about our women. After, I go to the park, usually alone, in order to be with the boy away from my wife. She and I have quite different ideas about bringing him up; she will not see how important those differences can be to our son. Peaceful moments at home are rare.

It is in the park that I see Florence for the first time since our "holiday." She seems to flash past me, as she flashed past the window in the train, nine years ago. For a moment I consider letting her fall back into my memory, but I am too curious for that. "Florence! Florence!" I call, again, until she turns.

She tells me she has been thinking of me and expecting us to meet, after seeing one of my films on television.

"I have followed your career, Rob," she says, as we look one another over.

She calls her son and he stands with her; she takes his hand. She and Archie have bought a house on the other side of the park.

"I even came to the plays. I know it's not possible, but I wondered if you ever glimpsed me, from the stage."

"No. But I did wonder if you took an interest."

"How could I not?"

I laugh and ask, "How am I?"

"Better, now you do less. You probably know—you don't mind me telling you this?"

I shake my head. "You know me," I say.

"You were an intense actor. You left yourself nowhere to go. I like you still." She hesitates. "Stiller, I mean."

She looks the same but as if a layer of healthy fat has been scraped from her face, revealing the stitching beneath. There is even less of her; she seems a little frail, or fragile. She has always been delicate, but now she moves cautiously.

As we talk I recollect having let her down, but am unable to recall the details. She was active in my mind for the months after our "holiday," but I found the memory to be less tenacious after relating the story to a friend as a tale of a young man's foolishness and misfortune. When he laughed I forgot—there is nothing as forgiving as a joke.

However, I have often wished for Florence's advice and support, particularly when the press took a fascinated interest in me, and started to write untrue stories. In the past few years I have played good parts and been praised and well paid. However, my sense of myself has not caught up with the alteration. I have been keeping myself down, and pushing happiness away. "Success hasn't changed you," people tell me, as if it were a compliment.

When we say goodbye, Florence tells me when she will next be in the park. "Please come," she says. At home I write down the time and date, pushing the note under a pile of papers.

She and I are wary with one another, and make only tentative and polite conversation; however, I enjoy sitting beside her on a bench in the sun, outside the teahouse, while her eight-year-old plays football. He is a hurt, suspicious boy with hair down to his shoulders, which he refuses to have cut. He likes to fight with bigger children and she does not know what to do with him. Without him, perhaps, she would have got away.

At the moment I have few friends and welcome her company. The phone rings constantly but I rarely go out and never invite anyone round, having become almost phobic where other people are concerned. What I imagine about others I cannot say, but the human mind is rarely clear in its sight. Perhaps I feel depleted, having just played the lead in a film.

During the day I record radio plays and audio books. I like learning to use my voice as an instrument. Probably I spend too much time alone, thinking I can give myself everything. My doctor, with whom I drink, is fatuously keen on pills and cheerfulness. He says if I cannot be happy with what I have, I never will be. He would deny the useful facts of human conflict, and wants me to take antidepressants, as if I would rather be paralysed than know my terrible selves.

Having wondered for months why I was waking up every morning feeling sad, I have started therapy. I am aware, partly from my relationship with Florence, that that which cannot be said is the most dangerous concealment. I am only beginning to understand psychoanalytic theory, yet am inspired by the idea that we do not live on a fine point of consciousness but exist in all areas of our being simultaneously, particularly the dreaming. Until I started lying down in Dr Wallace's room, I had never had such extended conversations about the deepest personal matters. To myself I call analysis—two people talking—"the apogee of civilisation." Lying in bed I have begun to go over my affair with Florence. These are more like waking dreams—Coleridge's "flights of lawless speculation"—than considered reflections, as if I am setting myself a subject for the night. Everything returns at this thoughtful age, particularly childhood.

One afternoon in the autumn, after we have met four or five times, it is wet, and Florence and I sit at a table inside the damp teahouse. The only other customers are an elderly couple. Florence's son sits on the floor drawing.

"Can't we get a beer?" Florence says.

"They don't sell it here."

"What a damned country."

"Do you want to go somewhere else?"

She says, "Can you be bothered?"

"Nope."

Earlier I notice the smell of alcohol on her. It is a retreat I recognise; I have started to drink with more purpose myself.

While I am at the counter fetching the tea, I see Florence holding the menu at arm's length; then she brings it closer to her face and moves it away again, seeking the range at which it will be readable. Earlier I noticed a spectacle case in the top of her bag, but had not realised they were reading glasses.

When I sit down, Florence says, "Last night Archie and I went to see your new film. It was discomfiting to sit there looking at you with him."

"Did Archie remember me?"

"At the end I asked him. He remembered the weekend. He said you had more substance to you than most actors. You helped him."

"I hope not."

"I don't know what you two talked about that night, but a few months after your conversation Archie left his job and went into publishing. He accepted a salary cut, but he was determined to find work that didn't depress him. Oddly, he turned out to be very good at it. He's doing well. Like you."

"Me? But that is only because of you." I want to give her credit for teaching me something about self-belief and self-determination. "Without you I wouldn't have got off to a good start . . ."

My thanks make her uncomfortable, as if I am reminding her of a capacity she does not want to know she is wasting.

"But it's your advice I want," she says anxiously. "Be straight, as I was with you. Do you think I can return to acting?"

"Are you seriously considering it?"

"It's the only thing I want for myself."

"Florence, I read with you years ago but I have never seen you on stage. That aside, the theatre is not a profession you can return to at will."

"I've started sending my photograph around," she continues. "I want to play the great parts, the women in Chekhov and Ibsen. I want to howl and rage with passion and fury. Is that funny? Rob, tell me if I'm being a fool. Archie considers it a middle-aged madness."

"I am all for that," I say.

As we part she touches my arm and says, "Rob, I saw you the other day. I don't think you saw me, or did you?"

"But I would have spoken."

"You were shopping in the deli. Was that your wife? The blonde girl—"

"It was someone else. She has a room nearby."

"And you—"

"Florence—"

"I don't want to pry," she says. "But you used to put your hand on my back, to guide me, like that, through crowds . . ."

I do not like being recognised with the girl for fear of it getting in the papers and back to my wife. But I resent having to live a secret life. I am confused.

"I was jealous," she says.

"Were you? But why?"

"I had started to hope . . . that it wasn't too late for you and me. I think I care for you more than I do for anybody. That is rare, isn't it?"

"I've never understood you," I say, irritably. "Why would you marry Archie . . . and then start seeing me?"

It is a question I have never been able to put, fearing she will think I am being critical of her, or that I will have to hear an account of their ultimate compatibility.

She says, "I hate to admit it, but I imagined in some super- stitious way that marriage would solve my problems and make me feel secure." When I laugh she looks at me hard. "This raises a question that we both have to ask."

"What is that?"

She glances at her son and says softly, "Why do you and I go with people who won't give us enough?"

I say nothing for a time. Then follows the joke which is not a joke, but which makes us laugh freely for the first time since we met again. I have been reading an account by a con- temporary author of his break up with his partner. It is relent- less, and, probably because it rings true, has been taken exception to. Playfully I tell Florence that surely divorce is an underestimated pleasure. People speak of the violence of separation, but what of the delight? What could be more refreshing than never having to sleep in the same bed as that rebarbative body, and hear those familiar complaints? Such a moment of deliverance would be one to hug to yourself for ever, like losing one's virginity, or becoming a millionaire.

I stand at the door of the teahouse to watch her walk back across the park, under the trees; she carries a white umbrella, treading so lightly she barely disturbs the rain drops on the grass, her son running ahead of her. I am certain I can hear laughter hanging in the air like an ethereal jinn.

The next time I see her she comes at me quickly, kissing me on both cheeks and saying she wants to tell me something.

We take the kids to a pub with a garden. I have started to like her shaven-headed boy, Ben, having at first not known how to speak to him. "Like a human being," I decide, is the best method. We put my son on a coat on the ground and he bustles about on his hands and bandy legs, nose down, arse sticking out. Ben chases him and hides; the baby's laugh makes us all laugh. Others' pleasure in him increases mine. It has taken a while, but I am getting used to serving and enjoying him, rather than seeing what I want as the important thing.

"Rob, I've got a job," she says. "I wrote to them and went in and auditioned. It's a pub theatre, a basement smelling of beer and damp. There's no money, only a cut of the box office. But it's good work. It is great work!"

She is playing the mother in *The Glass Menagerie*. By coincidence, the pub is at the end of my street. I tell her I am delighted.

"You will come and see me, won't you?"

"But yes."

"I often wonder if you're still upset about that holiday."

We have never discussed it, but now she is in the mood.

"I've thought about it a thousand times. I wish Archie hadn't come."

I laugh. It is too late; how could it matter now? "I mean, I wish I hadn't brought him. Sitting in that stationary train with you scowling was the worst moment of my life. But I had thought I was going mad. I had been looking forward to the holiday. The night before we were to leave, Archie asked again if I wanted him to come. He could feel how troubled I was. As I packed I realised that if we went away together my marriage would shatter. You were about to go to America. Your film would make you successful. Women would want you. I knew you didn't really want me."

This is hard. But I understand that Archie is too self-absorbed to be disturbed by her. He asks for and takes everything. He does not see her as a problem he has to solve, as I do. She has done the sensible thing, finding a man she cannot make mad.

She goes on, "I required Archie's strength and security more than passion—or love. That was love, to me. He asked, too, if I were having an affair."

"To prove that you weren't, you invited him to come."

She puts her hand on my arm. "I'll do anything now. Say the word."

I cannot think of anything I want her to do.

For a few weeks I do not see her. We are both rehearsing. One Saturday, my wife Helen is pushing the kid in a trolley in the supermarket as I wander about with a basket. Florence comes round a corner and we begin talking at once. She is enjoying the rehearsals. The director does not push her far enough—"Rob, I can do much more!"—but he will not be with her on stage, where she feels "queenlike." "Anyhow, we've become friends," she says meaningfully.

Archie does not like her acting; he does not want strangers looking at her, but he is wise enough to let her follow her wishes. She has got an agent; she is seeking more work. She believes she will make it.

After our spouses have packed away their groceries, Archie comes over and we are introduced again. He is large; his hair sticks out, his face is ruddy and his eyebrows look like a patch of corn from which a heavy creature has recently risen. Helen looks across suspiciously. Florence and I are standing close to one another; perhaps one of us is touching the other.

At home I go into my room, hoping Helen will not knock. I suspect she won't ask me who Florence is. She will want to know so much that she won't want to find out.

Without having seen the production, I rouse myself to invite several people from the film and theatre world to see Florence's play. Drinking in the pub beforehand, I can see that to the director's surprise the theatre will be full; he is wondering where all these smart people in deluxe loafers have come from, scattered amongst the customary drinkers with their elbows on the beer-splashed bar, watching football on televi-

sion with their heads craned up, as if looking for an astro-
nomical wonder. I become apprehensive myself, questioning
my confidence in Florence and wondering how much of it is
gratitude for her encouragement of me. Even if I have put
away my judgement, what does it matter? I seem to have
known her for so long that she is not to be evaluated or criti-
cised but is just a fact of my life. The last time we met in the
teahouse she told me that eighteen months ago she had a
benign lump removed from behind her ear. The fear that it
will return has given her a new fervency.

The bell rings. We go through a door marked "Theatre
and Toilets" and gropingly make our way down the steep,
worn stairs into a cellar, converted into a small theatre. The
programme is a single sheet, handed to us by the director as
we go in. The room smells musty, and despite the dark the
place is shoddy; there is a pillar in front of me I could rest my
cheek on. Outside I hear car alarms, and from upstairs the
sound of cheering men. But in this small room the silence is
charged by concentration and the hope of some home-made
magnificence. For the first time in years I am reminded of the
purity and intensity of the theatre.

When I get out at the interval I notice Archie pulling himself up the stairs behind me. At the top, panting, he takes my
arm to steady himself. I buy a drink, and, in order to be alone,
go and stand outside the pub. I am afraid that if my friends,
the "important" people, remain after the interval it is because
I would disapprove if they left; and if they praise Florence to
me, it is only because they would have guessed the ulterior
connection. The depth and passion Florence has on stage is

clear to me. But I know that what an artist finds interesting about their own work, the part they consider original and penetrating, will not necessarily compel an audience, who might not even notice it, but only attend to the story.

Archie's head pokes around the pub door. His eyes find me and he comes out. I notice he has his son, Ben, with him.

"Hallo, Rob, where's Matt?" says Ben.

"Matt's my son," I explain to Archie. "He's in bed, I hope."

"You happen to know one another?" Archie says.

I tug at Ben's baseball cap. "We bump into one another in the park."

"In the teahouse," says the boy. "He and Mummy love to talk." He looks at me. "She would love to act in a film you were in. So would I. I'm going to be an actor. The boys at school think you're the best."

"Thank you." I look at Archie. "Expensive school too, I bet."

He stands there looking away, but his mind is working.

I say to Ben, "What do you think of Mummy in this play?"

"Brilliant."

"What is your true opinion?" says Archie to me. "As a man of the theatre and film?"

"She seems at ease on stage."

"Will she go any further?"

"The more she does it, the better she will get."

"Is that how it works?" he says. "Is that how you made it?"

"Partly. I am talented, too."

He looks at me with hatred and says, "She will do it more, you think?"

"If she is to improve she will have to."

He seems both proud and annoyed, with a cloudy look, as if the familiar world is disappearing into the mist. Until now she has followed him. I wonder whether he will be able to follow her, and whether she will want him to.

I have gone inside and found my friends, when he is at my elbow, interrupting, with something urgent to say.

"I love Florence more and more as time passes," he tells me. "Just wanted you to know that."

"Yes," I say. "Good."

"Right," he says. "Right. See you downstairs."

FOUR BLUE CHAIRS

AFTER A LUNCH OF SOUP, bread and tomato salad, John and Dina go out on to the street. At the bottom of the steps they stop for a moment and he slips his arm through hers as he always does. They have been keen to establish little regularities, to confirm that they are used to doing things together.

Today the sun beats down and the city streets seem deserted, as if everyone but them has gone on holiday. At the moment they feel they are on a kind of holiday themselves.

They would prefer to carry blankets, cushions, the radio and numerous lotions out on to the patio. Weeds push up between the paving stones and cats lie on the creeper at the top of the fence as the couple lie there in the afternoons, reading, drinking fizzy lemonade and thinking over all that has happened.

Except that the store has rung to say the four blue chairs

are ready. Dina and John can't wait for them to be delivered, but must fetch them this afternoon because Henry is coming to supper tonight. They shopped yesterday; of the several meals they have learned to prepare, they will have salmon steaks, broccoli, new potatoes and three-bean salad.

Henry will be their first dinner guest. In fact he will be their first visitor.

John and Dina have been in the rented flat two and a half months already and most of the furniture, if not what they would have chosen themselves, is acceptable, particularly the bookshelves in all the rooms, which they have wiped down with wet cloths. Dina is intending to fetch the rest of her books and her desk, which pleases him. After that, it seems to him, there will be no going back. The wooden table in the kitchen is adequate. Three people could sit comfortably around it to eat, talk and drink. They have two brightly coloured table cloths, which they bought in India.

They have started to put their things on the table, mixed up together. She will set something out, experimentally, and he will look at it as if to say, what's that?, and she watches him; then they look at one another and an agreement is reached, or not. Their pens, for instance, are now in a shaving mug; her vase is next to it; his plaster Buddha appeared on the table this morning and was passed without demur. The picture of the cat was not passed, but she won't remove it at the moment, in order to test him. There are photographs of them together, on the break they took a year ago when they were both still living with their former partners. There are photographs of his children.

At the moment there are only two rotten kitchen chairs.

John has said that Henry, whom she met once before at a dinner given by one of John's friends, will take an interest in the blue chairs with the cane seats. Henry will take an interest in almost anything, if it is presented enthusiastically.

It has only been after some delicate but amiable discussion that they finally agreed to go ahead with Henry. John and Dina like to talk. In fact she gave up her job so they could talk more. Sometimes they do it with their faces pressed together; sometimes with their backs to one another. They go to bed early so they can talk. The one thing they don't like is disagreement. They imagine that if they start disagreeing they will never stop, and that there will be a war. They have had wars and they have almost walked out on one another on several occasions. But it is the disagreements they have had before, with other people, and the fear they will return, that seem to be making them nervous at the moment.

But they have agreed that Henry will be a good choice as a first guest. He lives nearby and he lives alone. He loves being asked out. As he works near Carluccios he will bring exotic cakes. There won't be any silences, difficult or otherwise.

They first saw the blue chairs four days ago. They were looking for an Indian restaurant nearby, and were discussing their ideal Indian menu, how they would choose the dall from this restaurant on King Street, and the bhuna prawn from the takeaway on the Fulham Road, and so on, when they drifted into Habitat. Maybe they were tired or just felt indolent, but in the big store they found themselves sitting in various arm-chairs, on the sofas, at the tables, and even lying in the deckchairs, imagining they were together in this or that place by the sea or in the mountains, occasionally looking at one another, far away across the shop, or closer, side by side, thinking in astonishment, this is him, this is her, the one I've chosen, the one I've wanted all this time, and now it has really started, everything I have wished for is today.

There seemed to be no one in the shop to mind their ruminations. They lost track of time. Then a shop assistant stepped out from behind a pillar. And the four blue wooden chairs, with the cane seats—after much sitting down, stand-ing up and shuffling of their bottoms—were agreed on. There were other chairs they wanted, but it turned out they were not in the sale, and they had to take these cheaper ones. As they left, Dina said she preferred them. He said that if she preferred them, he did too.

Today on the way to the store she insists on buying a small frame and a postcard of a flower to go in it. She says she is intending to put this on the table.

"When Henry's there?" he asks.

"Yes."

During the first weeks of their living together he has found himself balking at the way she does certain things, things he had not noticed during their affair, or hadn't had time to get used to. For instance the way she likes to eat sit-ting on the front steps in the evening. He is too old for bohemianism, but he can't keep saying "No" to everything and he has to sit there with pollution going in his bowl of pasta and the neighbours observing him, and men looking at her. He knows that this is part of the new life he has longed for, and at these times he feels helpless. He can't afford to have it go wrong.

The assistant in the store says he will fetch the chairs and they will be ready downstairs in a few minutes. At last two men bring the chairs out and stand them at the store exit.

John and Dina are surprised to see that the chairs haven't come individually, or with just a little wrapping. They are in two long brown boxes, like a couple of coffins.

John has already said they can carry the chairs to the tube, and then do the same from there to the flat. It isn't far. She thought he was being flippant. She can see now that he was serious.

To show how it must be done, and indeed that it is possible, he gets a good grip on one box, kicks it at the bottom, and shoves it right out of the shop and then along the smooth floor of the shopping centre, past the sweet seller and security guard and the old women sitting on benches.

At the exit he turns and sees her standing in the shop entrance, watching him, laughing. He thinks how lovely she is and what a good time they always have together.

She starts to follow him, pushing her box as he did his.

He continues, thinking that this is how they will do it, they will soon be at the tube station.

But outside the shopping mall, on the hot pavement, the box sticks. You can't shove cardboard along on concrete; it won't go. That morning she suggested they borrow a car. He had said they wouldn't be able to park nearby. Perhaps they would get a taxi. But outside it is a one-way street, going in the wrong direction. He sees that there are no taxis. The boxes wouldn't fit in anyway.

Out there on the street, in the sun, he squats a little. He gets his arms around the box. It is as if he is hugging a tree. Making all kinds of involuntary and regrettable sounds, he lifts it right up. Even if he can't see where he is going, even if his nose is pushed into the cardboard, he is carrying it, he is moving. They are still on their way.

He doesn't get far. Different parts of his body are resisting. He will ache tomorrow. He puts the box down again. In fact he almost drops it. He looks back to see that Dina is touching the corners of her eyes, as if she is crying with laughter. Truly it is a baking afternoon and it was an awful idea to invite Henry over.

He is about to shout back at her, asking her whether she has any better ideas, but watching her, he can see that she does. She is full of better ideas about everything. If only he trusted her rather than himself—thinking he is always right—he would be better off.

She does this remarkable thing.

She lifts her box onto her hip and, holding it by the cardboard flap, starts to walk with it. She walks right past him, stately and upright, like an African woman with a goat on her shoulders, as if this is the most natural thing. Off she goes towards the tube. This, clearly, is how to do it.

He does the same, the whole African woman upright

stance. But after a few steps the flap of the cardboard rips. It rips right across and the box drops to the ground. He can't go on. He doesn't know what to do.

He is embarrassed and thinks people are looking at him and laughing. People are indeed doing this, looking at him with the box, and at the beautiful woman with the other box. And they look back at him and then at her, and they are splitting their sides, as if nothing similar has ever happened to them. He likes to think he doesn't care, that he is strong enough at his age to withstand mockery. But he sees himself, in their eyes, as a foolish little man, with the things he has wanted and hoped for futile and empty, reduced to the ridiculous shoving of this box along the street in the sun.

You might be in love, but whether you can get four chairs home together is another matter.

She comes back to him and stands there. He is looking away and is furious. She says there's only one thing for it.

"All right," he says, an impatient man trying to be patient. "Let's get on with it."

"Take it easy," she says. "Calm down."

"I'm trying to," he replies.

"Squat down," she says.

"What?"

"Squat down."

"Here?"

"Yes. Where do you think?"

He squats down with his arms out and she grips the box in the tree-hugging pose and tips it and lays it across his hands and on top of his head. With this weight pushing down into his skull he attempts to stand, as Olympic weight lifters do, using their knees. Unlike those Olympic heroes he finds himself pitching forward. People in the vicinity are no longer laughing. They are alarmed and shouting warnings and scattering. He is staggering about with the box on his head, a drunken Atlas, and she is dancing around him, saying, "Steady, steady." Not only that, he is about to hurl the chairs into the traffic.

A man passing by sets the box down for them.

"Thank you," says Dina.

She looks at John.

"Thank you," says John sullenly.

He stands there, breathing hard. There is sweat on his upper lip. His whole face is damp. His hair is wet and his skull itching. He is not in good shape. He could die soon, suddenly, as his father did.

Without looking at her, he picks up the box in the tree-hugging stance and takes it a few yards, shuffling. He puts it down and picks it up again. He covers a few more yards. She follows.

Once they are on the tube he suspects they will be all right. It is only one stop. But when they have got out of the train they find that getting the boxes along the station is almost impossible. The tree-hugging stance is getting too difficult. They carry one box between them up the stairs, and then return for the other. She is quiet now; he can see she is tiring, and is bored with this idiocy.

At the entrance to the station she asks the newspaper seller if they can leave one of the boxes with him. They can carry one home together and return for the other. The man agrees.

She stands in front of John with her arms at her side and her hands stuck out like a couple of rabbit ears, into which shape the box is then placed. As they walk he watches her in her green sleeveless top with a collar, the sling of her bag crossing her shoulder, and the back of her long neck.

He thinks that if they have to put the box down everything will fail. But although they stop three times, she is concentrating, they both are, and they don't put the box down.

They reach the bottom of the steps to the house. At last they stand the box upright, in the cool hall, and sigh with relief. They return for the other box. They have found a method. They carry it out efficiently.

When it is done he rubs and kisses her sore hands. She looks away.

Without speaking they pull the blue chairs with the cane seats from the boxes and throw the wrapping in the corner. They put the chairs round the table and look at them. They sit on them. They place themselves in this position and that. They put their feet up on them. They change the table cloth.

"This is good," he says.

She sits down and puts her elbows on the table, looking down at the table cloth. She is crying. He touches her hair.

He goes to the shop for some lemonade and when he gets back she has taken off her shoes and is lying flat out on the kitchen floor.

"I'm tired now," she says.

He makes her a drink and places it on the floor. He lies

down beside her with his hands under his head. After a time she turns to him and strokes his arm.

"Are you OK?" he says.

She smiles at him. "Yes."

Soon they will open the wine and start to make supper; soon Henry will arrive and they will eat and talk.

They will go to bed and in the morning at breakfast time, when they put the butter and jam and marmalade out, the four blue chairs will be there, around the table of their love.

THAT WAS THEN

WE ARE UNERRING in our choice of lovers, particularly when we require the wrong person. There is an instinct, magnet or aerial which seeks the unsuitable. The wrong person is, of course, right for something—to punish, bully or humiliate us, let us down, leave us for dead, or, worst of all, give us the impression that they are not inappropriate, but almost right, thus hanging us in love's limbo. Not just anyone can do this.

All morning he had wondered whether Natasha would try to kill him.

He was not sure what she wanted, but it would not be a regular conversation. After four years of silence, she had suddenly become unusually persistent, writing to him several times at home and at his agent's. When he sent a note to say there was no point in their meeting she rang him twice at his new house and finally spoke to Lolly, his wife, who was so concerned she opened the door to his room and said, "Is she trying to get you back?"

He turned slowly. "It's not that, I shouldn't think."

"Will you see her?"

"No."

"Will you tell her not to ring again?"

"Yes."

"Good," said Lolly. "Good."

Natasha was drinking coffee at a table outside the café, wearing black, but not leather at least; probably she was the only such sombre, self-conscious person in the park. He had arrived early, but in order to be late had taken his coffee and newspaper to the conservatory, where he had considered the flowerbeds and wished for his son. Soon they would be having conversations and Nick would have less need of other people.

He had phoned Natasha unexpectedly that morning to give her the time and the place to meet, the grounds of an eighteenth-century Palladian villa in West London. He was apprehensive, but could not deny that he was curious to see where they both now were. He calculated that he hadn't actually seen her for five years.

It had been a dull summer and the schools had been open for two weeks. But a day like this, with the sun suddenly breaking through, reminded him of the seasons and of change. On the lawn that sloped down to the pond, people were in short-sleeves and sunglasses. Young couples lay on one another. As it was a middle-class area, families sat on blankets with elaborate picnics; corks were pulled from wine bottles, cotton napkins handed out and children called back from rummaging for conkers in the leaves and long grass.

He had got up and headed towards Natasha with determination, but the soft focus of the light mist and the alternate caresses of autumn heat and chill put him in an unexpectedly sensual mood. This renewed love of existence was like a low erotic charge. He came regularly to this park with his wife and baby and if, today, they were not with him, he could mark their absence by considering how meagre things were without them. At night, when he joined his woman in bed— she wore blue pyjamas, and his son, thrashing in his cot at the end of the room, a blue-striped, short-sleeved Babygro, resembling an Edwardian bathing costume—he knew, at last, that there was nowhere else he would prefer to be.

What he wanted was to have a surreptitious look at Natasha, but he thought she had spotted him. It would be undignified to dodge about.

With his eyes fixed on her, he strode out of the bushes and across the tarmac apron in front of the café, weaving in and out of the tables where dogs, children on bicycles and adults with trays were crowded together, irritable waitresses tripping through. Natasha glanced up and started on the work of taking him in. She even rose, and stood on tiptoe. If he was looking to see how she had aged, she was doing the same to him.

She kissed him on the cheek. "You've cut your hair."

"I've gone grey, haven't I?" he said. "Or was I grey before?"

Before he could draw back, her fingers were in his hair.

"Behind the ear, there used to be a few white hairs," she said. "Now—there's a black one. Why don't you dye it?"

He noticed her hair was still what they called "rock 'n' roll black."

He said, "Why would I bother?"

She laughed. "Don't tell me you're no longer vain. Look at you in your shiny dark blue raincoat. How much did those shoes cost?"

"I have a son now, Natty."

"I know that, Daddio," she said. She tapped her big silver ring on the table, given to her as a teenager by a Hell's Angel boyfriend.

"You like fatherhood?"

He looked away at the tables piled with the Sunday papers, plates and cups, and children's toys. He heard the names of expensive schools, like a saint's roll-call. He remembered, as a child, his parents urging him to be polite, and wished for the time when good manners protected you from the excesses of intimacy, when honesty was not romanticised.

He said, "My boy's a fleshy thing. There's plenty of him to kiss. I don't think we've ever seen his neck. But he has a bubbly mouth and a beard of saliva. I bring him here in his white hat—when he cries he goes red and looks like an outraged chef."

"Is that why you made me come all this way? I couldn't find this bloody place."

He said, "I thought it would amuse you to know . . . In May 1966 the Beatles made promotional films here, for 'Rain' and 'Paperback Writer.'"

"I see," she said. "That's it?"

"Well, yes."

He and Natasha had liked pop of the sixties and seventies; in her flat they had lain on oriental cushions drinking mint tea, among other exotic interests, playing and discussing records.

Before he met her, he had been a pop journalist for several years, writing about fashion, music and the laboured politics that accompanied them. Then he became almost respectable, as the arts correspondent for an old-fashioned daily broadsheet. On this paper it amused the journalists to think of him as young, contradictory and promiscuous. He was hired to be contrary and outrageous.

In fact, at night, he was working to show them how tangled he was. Not telling anyone, he wrote, with urgent persistence, an uninhibited memoir of his father. The book spoke of his own childhood terrors, as well as his father's vanity and tenderness. The last chapter was concerned with what men, and fathers, could become, having been released, as women were two decades earlier, from some of their conventional expectations. Before publication, he was afraid of being mocked; it was an honest book, an earnest one, even.

The memoir was acclaimed and won awards. It was said that men hadn't exposed themselves in such a way before. He gave up journalism to write a novel about young men working on a pop magazine, which was made into a popular film. He lived in San Francisco and New York, taught "creative writing," and rewrote unmade movies. He had got out. He was envied; he even envied himself. People spoke about him, as he had talked of pop stars, once. He met Natasha and things went awry.

She said, "You still listen to all that?"

"How many times can you hear "I Wanna Hold Your Hand" and "She Loves You"? And the new stuff means nothing to me."

She said, "All those symphonies and concertos sound the same."

"At least they can play," he said.

"The musicians are only reading the notes. It's not music, it's map-reading."

"How many of us can do that? It's better that people don't foist their original attempts on the public. Don't forget for years I went to gigs every night. It's funny, I couldn't wait to get home and play something quiet by the Isley Brothers."

He laughed and waved at a man. "How was your holiday?" someone called. "And the builders?"

"These people recognise you," she said. "I suppose they are the sort to read. Insomnia would be their only problem."

He laughed and put his face up to the sun. "They know me as the man with the only infant in the park who wears a leather jacket."

She let him sit, but they were both waiting.

She leaned forward. "After trying to avoid me, what made you want to see me today?"

"Lolly—you spoke to her on the phone—has gone to look at a place we've bought in Wiltshire."

"You've joined the aristocracy?"

"Not a wet-dog-and-bad-pictures country house. A London house in a field. For the first time in ages I had a spare afternoon." He said, "What is it you want?"

"It wasn't to bother you, though it must have seemed like

that." She looked at him with concentration and sincerity. "Do you want a fag?"

"I've given up."

She lit her cigarette and said, "I don't want to be eradicated from your life—cancelled, wiped out."

He sighed. "I was thinking the other day that I would never like my parents again, not in the way I did. There are no real reasons for anything, we just fall in and out of love with things—thank God."

"I would accept that, if you hadn't written about me."

"Did I?"

"In your second novel, published two and a half years ago." She looked at him but he said nothing. "Nick, I believed, at the time we were seeing one another—two years before—we were living some kind of life together in privacy."

"Living together?"

"You slept at my place, and me at yours. Didn't we see each other every day? Didn't we think about one another quite a lot?"

"Yes," he said. "We did do that."

She said, "Nick, you used my sexual stuff. What I like up my cunt."

He lowered his voice. "The Croatian version of the book has come out. It has been translated into ten languages. Who's going to recognise your hairy flaps or my broth of a stomach and withered buttocks?"

"I do. Isn't that enough?"

"Who says it's your cunt? Sometimes a cunt—"

She rubbed her face with her hand. "Don't start. The cunt

in the book is called ME—Middle England. Those who enter it, of whom there seem to be an unnecessary number, and pretty grotesque they are too, are known as Middle Englanders. We—"

"It was always my joke."

"Our joke."

"All right."

"I thought it would stop disturbing me. But it didn't go away. I feel abused by you, Nick."

"That wouldn't be the origin of that feeling."

"No, as you pointed out in the book, when my father was away lecturing, my mother did unwelcome things to me."

He said, "Most of the women I've met have been sexually abused. If some women are afraid of men, or hate them, isn't it going to start there?"

She wasn't listening. She had plenty to say; he let her continue.

She said, "When I saw you the first time I was impressed. Writers are supposed to feel and know. They're wise, with enough honesty, bravery and conscience for us all. Now I'm upset that you saw me as you did. Upset you wrote it down. Would you say anything, expose anyone, provided it served your purpose? If you only believe in your own advantage you would have to agree that that is a miserable place to have ended up." She picked up her cigarettes and threw them down. "Why didn't you make the woman strong?"

"Who is strong? Hitler? Florence Nightingale? Thatcher? She wishes to be strong, impervious to human perplexity. Wouldn't that be more accurate?"

He tried to look at her evenly. She had never come at him like this. She had been confused and tolerant and afraid of losing him. They had parted suddenly, abruptly. But for over a year they had spoken on the phone several times a day, and seen one another in the most excessive situations. He had often wondered why they had not been able to continue; he had even considered seeing her again, if she wanted to. They had got along.

If Natasha was clumsy and felt that her elbows protruded; if she walked with her feet turned out, despite having tried to correct this during her childhood, she brought this to his attention. If she was quick and well read, whatever she knew was inadequate. There was always a spot, blemish, new line, sagging eyelid or patch of dry skin on her cheek which it was impossible for her not to draw attention to. She lacked confidence, to say the least, but had attacks of impassioned self-belief, gaiety and determination which she later condemned. After laughing loudly she clapped her hand over her open mouth. But she wouldn't be suppressed; when she had a fear or phobia, she made a note of it, and fought. Perhaps when she was in her fifties she would reach a cooler equilibrium.

As he looked, her outline seemed to blur. It wasn't only that past and present were merging to form a new picture of her, it was that a third person was sitting with them. This had happened before. Natasha had seemed to place between them another woman, a fiction, who resembled Natasha but was her denial and her Platonic ideal. This Natasha, the pop star, was cool, certain, smart. Photographed in a different light, in better clothes, good at ballet, cooking and conversation, this figure dragged Natasha along to better things, while undermining and mocking her. They had both fallen in love with this desirable prevailing woman who haunted them as a living presence, but would never let them possess her. Compared with her, Natasha could only fail. They had had to find others—strangers—to witness and worship the ideal Natasha; and, when the illusion failed, like a cinema projector breaking down, they had to get rid of them.

"You wrote a bit," he said. "You know how diverse and complex the sources of inspiration are."

"I still write," she said. "Despite your laughing at me."

"It was justice you were interested in, and how to live. Literature makes no recommendations. It's not a guidebook but you did learn that the imagination lifts something up and takes it somewhere else, altering it as it flies. The original idea is only an excuse."

She pretended to choke. "The magic carpet of your imagination didn't fly you very far, baby. Why did you take parts of me and put them in a book? Nick, you were savage about me. I've asked people about this."

"They agree with you?" She nodded. He said, "What are you doing these days?"

"I finished my training. Now I work as a therapist. I have credit card debts up to here. They took the car. Once you start sinking you really go fast. You couldn't—" She shook her head. "No, no. I'm not going to degrade myself."

"Not more than you usually like to," he said.

"No. That's right. Hey. Look."

She threw her cigarette down and pushed up her sleeve.

Drawing a breath, she pushed. There was an appreciable swelling. "I've been going to the gym."

He wondered if she required him to squeeze the muscle. "Popeye's been eating her spinach," he said.

"It makes me feel good," she said.

"That's all that matters."

"I've got into young men."

"Good."

He noticed that her ears were pierced in several places. Perhaps she had violated herself all over. It would be like going to bed with a cactus. He wouldn't mention it. The less he said, the sooner it would be over. He saw he was only there to listen. However, something came to him.

"My mind hasn't entirely gone," he said. "But these days I do pick up a book and have no memory of what I read yesterday. However, I was labouring through a seven-hundred-page biography of someone I liked. It bulged with facts. Almost the only part I found irresistible was the subject's sciatica and slipped disc—you know how it is at our age. In the end I had no idea what the man might be like. Everything personal and human was missing. Then I thought: where else could you get the complexity and detail of inner motion except in fiction? It's the closest we can get to how we are inside."

She looked away. "I've never had a vocation."

"Why don't you go to Spain?"

"What? Vocation, I said."

"Why does a vocation matter?"

"I want to find something to be good at. One of my patients is a skinhead, sexually abused by his mother and sister. I don't think he can even read his own tattoos. It is not me he's hating and sapping as he sits there saying 'cunt, cunt, cunt.' Why am I compelled to help this bastard? Nick, you're omnipotent and self-sufficient in that little room with your special pens that no one's allowed to touch, the coffee that only you can make, music where you can reach it, postcards of famous paintings pinned in front of you. Is it the same?"

"Exactly."

"You were always retreating to that womb or hiding place. What made me cross was how you placed the madness out-side yourself—in me, the half-addicted, promiscuous, self-devouring crazy girl. Isn't that misogyny?"

He looked startled. "I'm not sure."

"You made yourself, Nick, you see, before things got . . . a little mad. You weren't privileged, like some of those show-off scribblers. I remember you sitting with your favourite novels, underlining sentences. The lists of words pinned up by your shaving mirror—words to learn, words to use. You'd write out the same sentence again and again, in different ways. I can't imagine a woman being so methodical and will-driven. You want to be highly considered. Only I wish you hadn't taken a sneaky and spiteful revenge against me."

He said, "It's never going to be frictionless between men and women as long they want things from one another—and they have to want things, that's a relationship."

"Sophistry!"

"Reality!"

She said, "Self-deception!"

He got up. It wouldn't take him long to get home. He

could carry a low chair out into his new garden, on which they had recently spent a lot of money, and read and doze. Six men had come through the side door with plants, trees and paving stones; he and Lolly couldn't wait for nature. It wasn't his money, or even Lolly's, but her American father's. He wondered if he knew what married but dependent women must feel, when what you had wasn't earned or deserved. Humiliation wasn't quite what he felt, but there was resentment.

He had met Natasha one Mayday at a private party at the Institute of Contemporary Arts, just down from Buckingham Palace, in sight of Big Ben. He would always drink and smoke grass before leaving his flat—in order to get out at all; and he was chuckling to himself at the available ironies. Apart from the Soviet invasion of Hungary, there couldn't have been a worse time for socialism. Certainly no one he knew was admitting to being on the hard left, or to having supported the Soviet Union. "I was always more of an anarchist than a Party man," Nick heard as he squeezed through the crowd to the drinks table. A voice replied, "I was only ever a Eurocommunist." He himself announced, "I was never much of a joiner." His more imaginative left-wing acquaintances had gone to Berlin to witness the collapse of the Wall, "to be at the centre of history," as one of them put it. "For the first time," Nick had commented.

It was easy to sneer. What did he know? It was only now that he was starting to read history, having become intrigued by the fact that people not unlike him had, only a few decades before, been possessed by the fatal seriousness of murderous, mind-gripping ideologies. He'd only believed in pop. Its frivolity and anger was merely subversive; it delivered no bananas. If asked for his views, he'd be afraid to give them. But he was capable of description.

Like him, Natasha usually only worked in the morning, teaching, or working on these theses. They both liked aspects of London, not the theatre, cinema or restaurants but the rougher places that resembled a Colin McInnes novel. Nick had come to know wealthy and well-known people; he was invited for cocktails and launches, lunches and charity dinners, but it was too prim to be his everyday world. He started to meet Natasha at two o'clock in a big deserted pub in Notting Hill. They'd eat, have their first drinks, talk about everything and nod at the old Rastas who still seemed permanently installed in these pubs. They would buy drugs from young dealers from the nearby estates and hear their plans for robberies. Notting Hill was wealthy and the houses magnificent, but it had yet to become aware of it. The pubs were still neglected, with damp carpets and dusty oak bars covered in cigarette burns, about to be turned into shiny places crammed with people who looked as though they appeared on television, though they only worked in it.

He and Natasha would take cocaine or Ecstasy, or some LSD, or all three—and retire for the afternoon to her basement nearby. When it got dark they pulled one another from bed, applied their eye-shadow in adjacent mirrors, and stepped out in their high heels.

Now she took his hand. "You can't walk out on me!" She tugged him back into his seat.

He said, "You can't pull me!"

"Don't forget the flowers you came at me with!" she said. "The passion! The hikes through the city at night and breakfast in the morning! And conversation, conversation! Didn't we put our chairs side by side and go through your work! Have you forgotten how easily you lost hope in those days and how I repeatedly sent you back to your desk? Everyone you knew wanted to be a proper writer. None of them would do it, but you thought, why shouldn't I? Didn't I help you?"

"Yes you did, Natasha! Thank you!"

"You didn't put it in the book, did you? You put all that other stuff in!"

"It didn't fit!"

"Oh Nick, couldn't you have made it fit?" She was looking at him. "Why are you laughing at me?"

"There's no way out of this conversation. Why don't we walk a little?"

"Can we?"

"Why not?"

"I keep thinking you're going to go away. Have you got time?"

"Yes."

"My sweet and sour man I called you. D'you remember?" She seemed to relax. "A fluent, creative life, turning ordinary tedium and painful feeling into art. The satisfactions of a self-sufficient child, playing alone. That's what I want. That's why people envy artists."

"Vocation," he said. "Sounds like the name of someone."

"Yes. A guide. Someone who knows. I don't want to sound religious, because it isn't that."

"A guiding figure. A man."

She sighed. "Probably."

He said, "I was thinking . . . how our generation loved Monroe, Hendrix, Cobain, even. Somehow we were in love with death. Few of the people we admired could go to bed without choking on their own vomit. Wasn't that the trouble—with pop, and with us?"

"What d'you mean?"

"We were called a self-indulgent generation. We didn't go to war but we were pretty murderous towards ourselves. Almost everyone I know—or used to."

"But I was just going to—" She reached into her bag and leaned over to him. "Give me your hand," she said. "Go on. I got you something." She passed the object to him. "Now look."

He opened his hand.

On a dreary parade in North Kensington, between a second-hand bookshop and a semi-derelict place hiring out fancy-dress costumes, was a shop where Nick and Natasha went to buy leather and rubberwear. Behind barred windows it was painted black and barely lit, concealing the fact that the many shiny red items were badly made or plain ragged. The assistants, in discreet versions of the available clothes—Nick preferred to call them costumes—were enthusiastic, offering tea and biscuits.

Wrapping themselves in fake-fur coats from charity shops,

Natasha and Nick began going to places where others had similar tastes, seeking new fears and transgressions, of which there were many during this AIDS period. If couples require schemes, they had discovered their purpose. It was possible to be a sexual outlaw as long as there were still people who were innocent. They pressed each other on, playing Virgil to one another, until they no longer knew if they were children or adults, men or women, masters or servants. The transformation into pleasure of the banal, the unpleasant and the plain unappetising was like black magic—poor Don Juan on a treadmill, compelled to make life's electricity for ever.

Nick recalled walking one night onto the balcony of a vast club, seeking Natasha, and looking down on a pageant of bizarre costumes, feathers, semi-nudity, masks and clothes of all periods, representing every passion, every possible kink and kook, zig and zag. Natasha was among them, waiting for him with some bridled old man who worked in a post office.

Nick wondered if everyone involved liked participating in a secret, as they re-created the mystery which children discover by whispers, that what people want to do with one another is strange, and that the uncovering of this strangeness is itself the excitement. Certainly there were terrifying initiations, over and over. They were the oddest people; he learned that there was little that was straightforward about humanity. But what appeared to frighten them all was the mundane, the familiar, the ordinary.

Like actors unable to stop playing a part, as though they could be on stage for ever, he and Natasha wanted to remain at a dramatic pitch where there was no disappointment, no self-knowledge or development, only a state of constant, narcissistic emergency and a clear white light in the head.

In order to consume their punishment with their pleasure, which some might call a convenience, they were stoned. Nick remembered a friend at school saying—and this was the best advertisement for drugs he'd heard—"If you are stoned you can do anything." Why was living the problem? If he looked around at his friends and acquaintances, how many of them were able to survive unaided? They sought absence until they had become like a generation lost to war. Those who survived were sitting in shell-shocked confessional circles in countryside clinics. He suspected they had left success to fools and mediocrities. By midnight he was rarely able to see in front of him; he and Natasha held one another up, like the vertical arms of a staggering triangle. Sobriety was a terror, though they couldn't remember why, and their heroes, legends, myths, were hopeless incompetents, death-soaked tragic imaginations.

He saw people going to heroin like a fate; imagining you could shun it was arrogant or solemn. Nick had wanted to find like-minded people; he turned them into his jailers. He recalled people in rubber masks, coming at him like executioners. It was arduous work, converting people into objects, when he had not been brought up to it.

Midday one morning he woke up at her place. He rose and lumbered about, reacquainting himself with an unfamiliar object, his body. He had been whipped, badly; his face and hands were grazed, too: he must have fallen somewhere and no one, not even him, had noticed.

Somehow she had gone to work, leaving him a note. "Remember, Remember!" she had scrawled in lipstick.

Remember what? Then it returned. His task was to withdraw three thousand pounds from his bank account, which, apart from his flat, was all he had and buy drugs from a man who sold everything, but only in large amounts. It would save them the trouble of having to score continually. In two hours he would have the drugs; minutes later the cocaine would be working, stealing another day and night of his life. Natasha would return; there was a couple they were to meet later; there would be cages, whips, ice, fire.

There had been the death-laden ways of teachers and employers, and there had been rebellion, drugs, pleasure. No one had shown him what a significant life was and the voices that spoke in his head were not kind.

And yet something occurred to him. He walked out of the flat and kept walking through his pain until he reached the suburbs; at last he fell through fields and fields. He never returned to her place. The rest was a depressing cold abstinence and mourning, sitting at his desk half the day, every day, repeatedly summoning a half-remembered discipline, wishing someone would lash him to the chair. Those characters in Chekhov's plays, forever intoning "work, work, work." How stale a prayer, he thought, as though the world was better off for the slavery in it. But boredom was an antidote to unruly wishes, quelling his suspicion that disobedience was the only energy. He had to teach himself to sit still again.

After a freezing month he rediscovered capability and

audacity. Even the idea of public recognition returned, along with competitiveness, envy, and a little pride. He made her leave him alone, and when they met again, tentatively, his fear of any addiction, which had saved him, but which was also the fear of relying on anyone—some addictions are called love—meant he could not like her any more. What could they do together? It wouldn't have happened to the ideal, desirable Natasha.

She had pressed a small envelope into his palm.

"There."

He glanced down.

She said, "You'd be making a mistake to think it was the other things I liked, when it was our talks and your company. You're sweet, Nick, and strangely polite at times. I can't put that together with all you've done to me." She touched his hand. "Go on."

"Now?"

"Then we'll walk."

In the park toilet a boy stood in a cubicle with his trousers down, bent over. His father wiped him, helping him with his belt, zip and buttons. Nick went into the next cubicle and closed the door. He would open the envelope, have a look for old times' sake, and return it. She had had the day she had wanted.

His hands were shaking. He held it in his palm, before opening it. A gram of fine grains, untouched. Heavenly sand. His credit card was in his back pocket.

He returned to her.

He said, "I took the parts of you I needed to make my book. It wasn't a fair or final judgement but a practical transformation, in order to say something. Someone in a piece of fiction is a dream figure . . . picked from one context and thrust into another, to serve some purpose. A tiny portion of them is used."

She nodded but had lost interest.

They walked by the pond, the cascade and the cricket pitch. Children played on felled logs; people sketched and painted; on pedestals, the heads of Roman emperors looked on. Nick and Natasha stepped from patches of vivid sunlight into cooler tunnels. The warm currents had turned chilly. As the sky darkened, the clouds turned crimson. Parents called to their children.

She started to cry.

"Nick, will you take me out of here?"

"If you want."

"Please."

She put her dark glasses on and he led her past dawdling families to the gate.

In his car she wiped her face.

"All those respectable white voices behind high walls. The wealth, the cleanliness, the hope. I was getting agoraphobic. It all makes me sick with regret."

She was trembling. He had forgotten how her turmoil disturbed him. He was becoming impatient. He wanted to be at home when Lolly got back. He had to prepare the food. Some friends were coming by, with their new baby.

She said, "Aren't we going to have a drink? Is this the way? Where are we now?"

"Look," he said.

He was driving beside a row of tall, authoritative stucco houses with pillars and steps. Big family cars sat in the drives. Across the narrow road was a green; overlooked by big trees there were tennis courts and a children's playground. During the week children in crisp uniforms were dropped off and picked up from school; in the afternoons Philippino and East European nannies would sit with their charges in the playground. This was where he lived now, though he couldn't admit it.

"We are thinking of moving here," he said. "What do you think?"

"There's no point asking me," she said. "Everything has become very conventional. You're either in or you're out. I'm with the out—with the weird, the impossible, the victimised and the broken. It's the only place to be."

"Why turn habit into principle?"

"I don't know. Nick, take me to one of the old places. We've got time, haven't we? Are you bored by me?"

"Not yet."

"I'm so glad."

He drove to one of their pubs, with several small rooms, blackened ceilings, benches and big round tables. He ordered oysters and Guinness.

As he sat down he said embarrassedly, "Have you got any more of that stuff?"

"If you kiss me," she said.

"Come on," he said.

"No," she said, putting her face close to his. "Pay for what you want!"

He pushed his face into her warm mouth.

She passed him the envelope. "If you don't leave some I'll kill you."

"Don't worry," he said.

"I will," she said. "Because I know what saved you— greed." She was looking at him. "My place? Don't look at your watch. Just for a little bit, eh?"

He could tell from the flat that she hadn't gone crazy. The furniture wasn't frayed or stained; there were flowers, a big expensive sofa with books on nutrition balanced on the arm. The records were no longer on the floor. She had CDs now, in racks, alphabetical. As usual there were music papers and magazines on the table. She went to put on a CD. He hoped it wouldn't be anything he knew.

He went into the bedroom. It was as dark as ever, but he knew where the light switches were. Looking at the familiar Indian wall-hangings, he sank onto the mattress to pull off his shoes. He flung his clothes onto the bare, unvarnished floorboards, covered in threadbare rugs. The smell of her bed he knew. He could reach the opened bottles of wine and the ashtray. He swigged some sour red and reached for the pillows.

She almost fell on him; she knew he liked her weight, and to be pinned down. He closed his eyes. When she tied him quickly and expertly, he remembered the frisson of fear, the helplessness, and the pleasure coming from some rarely lit place. He struggled, giggled, screamed.

When he awoke she was sitting across the room at her table in her black silk dressing gown, surrounded by papers, unguents, tins, boxes, with her hands in front of her, like a pianist looking for a tune. She turned and smiled. The door to the cupboard in which she kept her "dressing up" things was open.

"Untie me."

"In a while. Tomorrow, maybe."

"Natasha—"

"Look." She opened her dressing gown and sat over him. How salty she was. "Here. If you don't behave I'll read to you from your own work."

He looked up to see her lips pursed in concentration. At last she released him. They were both pleased, a job well done. He started to move quickly in the bed as some inner necessity and accompanying fury led him to desire satisfaction. There was a man he had to meet in a pub, a greedy, unbalanced man with, no doubt, a talent for rapid mathematics. But Nick couldn't find his clothes amongst the flimsy things flung over the bed.

As it was cold he pulled his clothes on under the sheets as usual. But they smelt musty, as if he'd been wearing them for several days. He turned his sweater inside out.

She pulled him up, holding him in her arms. He lit a cigarette. "Natty, I'm off to get the stuff."

She nodded. "Good. Got the money?"

He patted his pocket. "You'll be here when I get back?"

"Oh yes," she said.

He went out into the living room and shook himself, as if he would wake up.

She followed him and said, "What's up?"

"I'm marked," he said, pulling his sleeves up. "Christ. Look! My wrists."

"So you are," she said. "A marked man. They'll fade."

"Not tonight."

She said, "I hope I'm pregnant. It's the right time of the month."

"That would be a nuisance to me."

"Not to me," she said. "It would be a good memento. A decent souvenir."

He said. "You don't know what you're saying."

"Yes I do. Would you like me to let you know?"

"No."

"That's up to you."

He said, "I'd forgotten how drugs make the dullest stuff tolerable. I hope everything goes well for you."

He went out into the street. He was walking quickly but to where he didn't know. He had emptied his mind out; there were good things but not to hand. If only the drug would stop working. At last he remembered his car and returned for it. He drove fast but carefully. Lolly would have finished at the house. She would be on her way back, singing to the boy in the car. He hoped she was safe. He thought of the pleasure on his wife's face when she saw him, and the way his son turned to his voice. There was much he had to teach the boy. He thought that pleasures erase themselves as they occur—

you can never remember your last cigarette. If happiness accumulates it is not because it remains in the bloodstream but because it is the bloodstream.

He unlocked the house. He still hadn't become used to the size and brightness of the kitchen, nor to the silence, unusual for London. The freezer was a room in itself. He took the food out and put it on the table. Now he had to get to the supermarket to pick up the champagne.

On the way out he opened the door to his study. He hadn't been to his desk for a few days. He wanted to think there were other things he liked more, that he wasn't possessed by it. He went in and quickly scribbled some notes. He couldn't write now but after supper he would go to bed with his wife and son; when they were asleep he'd get up to work.

Sitting outside in the car, he examined his sore wrists. He pulled his shirt-sleeves down. Before, he'd never cover them; he knew some men and many women who would show off their hacked, scarred or cut arms, as important marks.

There was something he wished he'd said to Natasha as he left—he had looked back and seen her face at the window, watching him go up the steps. "There are worlds and worlds and worlds inside you." But perhaps it wouldn't mean anything to her.

GIRL

T HEY GOT ON AT Victoria Station and sat together, kissing lightly. As the train pulled away, she took out her
Nietzsche tome and began to read. Turning to the man at her
side she became amused by his face, which she studied continually. Removing her gloves she picked shaving cream from
his ears, sleep from his eyes and crumbs from his mouth,
while laughing to herself. The combination of his vanity,
mixed with unconscious naivety, usually charmed her.

Nicole hadn't wanted to visit her mother after all this time
but Majid, her older lover—it sounded trite calling him her
"boyfriend"—had persuaded her to. He was curious about
everything to do with her; it was part of love. He said it
would be good for her to "re-connect"; she was stronger
now. However, during the past year, when Nicole had
refused to speak to her, and had ensured her mother didn't
have her address, she had suppressed many tormenting

thoughts from the past; ghosts she dreaded returning as a result of this trip.

Couldn't Majid sense how uneasy she was? Probably he could. She had never had anyone listen to her so attentively or take her so seriously, as if he wanted to occupy every part of her. He had the strongest will of anyone she'd known, apart from her father. He was used to having things his own way, and often disregarded what she wanted. He was afraid she would run away.

He had never met her mother. She might be incoherent, or in one of her furies, or worse. As it was, her mother had cancelled the proposed visit three times, once in a drunken voice that was on the point of becoming spiteful. Nicole didn't want Majid to think that she—half her mother's age—would resemble her at fifty. He had recently told Nicole that he considered her to be, in some sense, "dark." Nicole was worried that her mother would find Majid also dark, but in the other sense.

Almost as soon as it left the station, their commuter train crossed the sparkling winter river. It would pass through the suburbs and then the countryside, arriving after two hours at a seaside town. Fortunately, theirs wasn't a long journey, and next week, they were going to Rome; in January he was taking her to India. He wanted her to see Calcutta. He wouldn't travel alone any more. His pleasure was only in her.

Holding hands they looked out at Victorian schools and small garages located under railway arches. There were frozen football pitches, allotments, and the backs of industrial estates where cork tiles and bathroom fittings were manufactured, as well as carpet warehouses and metalwork shops. When the landscape grew more open, railway tracks stretched in every direction, a fan of possibilities. Majid said that passing through the outskirts of London reminded him what an old country Britain was, and how manifestly dilapidated.

She dropped her hand in his lap and stroked him as he took everything in, commenting on what he saw. He looked handsome in his silk shirt, scarf and raincoat. She dressed for him, too, and couldn't go into a shop without wondering what would please him. A few days before, she'd had her dark hair cut into a bob that skimmed the fur collar of the over-coat she was wearing with knee-length motorcycle boots. At her side was the shoulder bag in which she carried her vita-min pills, journal and lip salve, and the mirror which had con-vinced her that her eyelids were developing new folds and lines as they shrivelled up. That morning she'd plucked her first grey hair from her head, and placed it inside a book. Yet she still had spots, one on her cheek and one on her upper lip. Before they left, Majid had made her conceal them with make-up, which she never wore.

"In case we run into anyone I know," he said.

He was well connected, but she was sure he wouldn't know anyone where they were going. Yet she had obeyed.

She forced herself back to the book. Not long after they met, eighteen months ago, he remarked, "You've been to uni-versity but things must have changed since my day." It was true she didn't know certain words: "confound," "pejorative," "empirical." In the house they now shared, he had thousands of books and was familiar with all the writers, composers and painters. As he pointed out, she hadn't heard of Gauguin.

Sometimes when he was talking to his friends she had no idea what they were discussing, and became convinced that if her ignorance didn't trouble him it was because he valued only her youth.

Certainly he considered conversation a pleasure. There had recently occurred an instructive incident when they dropped in for tea on the mother of her best friend. This woman, a sociology lecturer, had known Nicole from the age of thirteen, and probably continued to think of her as poignantly deprived. Nicole thought of her as cool, experienced and, above all, knowledgeable. Five years ago, when one of her mother's boyfriends had beaten up Nicole's brother, this woman had taken Nicole in for a few weeks. Nicole had sat numbly in her flat, surrounded by walls of books and pictures. All of it, apart from the occasional piece of soothing music, seemed vain and irrelevant.

Visiting with Majid she had, by midnight, only succeeded in detaching his hand from the woman's. Nicole had then to get him to leave, or at least relinquish the bottle of whisky. Meanwhile the woman was confessing her most grievous passions and telling Majid that she'd seen him address a demonstration in the seventies. A man like him, she cried, required a substantial woman! It was only when she went to fetch her poetry, which she intended to read to him, that Nicole could get the grip on his hair she needed to extract him.

By providing her with the conversations she'd longed for, he had walked in and seduced her best friend's mother! Nicole had felt extraneous. Not that he had noticed. Pushing him out of there, she was reminded of the time, around the age of fourteen, she'd had to get her mother out of a neighbour's house, dragging her across the road, her legs gone, and the whole street watching.

He laughed whenever she recalled the occasion, but it troubled her. It wasn't the learning that mattered. Majid had spent much of his youth reading, and lately had wondered what adventures he had been keeping himself from. He claimed that books could get in the way of what was important between people. But she couldn't sit, or read or write, or do nothing, without seeking company, never having been taught the benefits of solitude. The compromise they reached was this: when she read he would lie beside her, watching her eyes, sighing as her fingers turned a page.

No; his complaint was that she couldn't convert feelings into words and expected him to understand her by clairvoyance.

Experience had taught her to keep her mouth shut. She'd spent her childhood among rough people that it amused Majid to hear about, as if they were cartoon characters. But they had been menacing. Hearing some distinction in your voice, they would suspect you of ambition and therefore of the desire to leave them behind. For this you would be envied, derided, hated; London was considered "fake" and the people there duplicitous. Considering this, she'd realised that every day for most of her life she had been physically and emotionally afraid. Even now she couldn't soften unless she was in bed with Majid, fearing that if she wasn't vigilant, she would be sent back home on the train.

She turned a few pages of the book, took his arm and snuggled into him. They were together, and loved one another. But there were unaccustomed fears. As Majid reminded her when they argued, he had relinquished his home, wife and children for her. That morning, when he had gone to see the children and to talk about their schooling, she'd become distraught waiting for him, convinced he was sleeping with his wife and would return to her. It was deranging, wanting someone so much. How could you ever get enough of them? Maybe it was easier not to want at all. When one of the kids was unwell, he had stayed the night at his former house. He wanted to be a good father, he explained, adding in a brusque tone that she'd had no experience of that.

She had gone out in her white dress and not come home. She had enjoyed going to clubs and parties, staying out all night and sleeping anywhere. She had scores of acquaintances who it was awkward introducing to Majid, as he had little to say to them. "Young people aren't interesting in themselves any more," he said, sententiously.

He maintained that it was she who was drawing away from them. It was true that these friends—who she had seen as free spirits, and who now lay in their squats virtually inert with drugs—lacked imagination, resolution and ardour, and that she found it difficult to tell them of her life, fearing they would resent her. But Majid, once the editor of radical newspapers, could be snobbish. On this occasion he accused her of treating him like a parent or flatmate, and of not understanding she was the first woman he couldn't sleep without. Yet hadn't she waited two years while he was sleeping with someone else? If she recalled the time he went on holiday with his family, informing her the day before, even as he asked her to marry him, she could beat her head against the wall. His young children were beautiful, but in the park people assumed they were hers. They looked like the mother, and connected him with her for ever. Nicole had said she didn't want them coming to the house. She had wanted to punish him, and destroy everything.

Should she leave him? Falling in love was simple; one had only to yield. Digesting another person, however, and sustaining a love, was bloody work, and not a soft job. Feeling and fear rushed through her constantly. If only her mother were sensible and accessible. As for the woman she usually discussed such subjects with—the mother of her best friend—Nicole was too embarrassed to return.

She noticed that the train was slowing down.

"Is this it?" he said.

"'Fraid so."

"Can't we go on to the seaside?"

She replaced her book and put her gloves on.

"Majid, another day."

"Yes, yes, there's time for everything."

He took her arm.

They left the station and joined a suburban area of underpasses, glass office blocks, hurrying crowds, stationary derelicts and stoned young people in flimsy clothing. "Bad America," Majid called it.

They queued twenty minutes for a bus. She wouldn't let him hail a taxi. For some reason she thought it would be condescending. Anyhow, she didn't want to get there too soon.

They sat in the front, at the top of the wide double-decker, as it took them away from the centre. They swept through winding lanes and passed fields. He was surprised the slow, heavy bus ascended the hills at all. This was not the city and not the country; it was not anything but grassy areas, arcades of necessary shops, churches and suburban houses. She pointed out the school she'd attended, shops she'd worked in for a pittance, parks in which she'd waited for various boyfriends.

It was a fearful place for him too. His father had been an Indian politician and when his parents separated he had been brought up by his mother eight miles away. They liked to talk about the fact that he was at university when she was born; that when she was just walking he was living with his first wife; that he might have patted Nicole's head as he passed her on the street. They shared the fantasy that for years he had been waiting for her to grow up.

It was cold when they got down. The wind cut across the open spaces. Already it seemed to be getting dark. They walked further than he'd imagined they would have to, and across muddy patches. He complained that she should have told him to wear different shoes.

He suggested they take something for her mother. He could be very polite. He even said "excuse me" in bed if he made an abrupt movement. They went into a brightly lit supermarket and asked for flowers; there were none. He asked for lapsang souchong teabags, but before the assistant could reply, Nicole pulled him out.

The area was sombre but not grim, though a swastika had

been painted on a fence. Her mother's house was set on a grassy bank, in a sixties estate, with a view of a park. As they approached, Nicole's feet seemed to drag. Finally she halted and opened her coat.

"Put your arms around me." He felt her shivering. She said, "I can't go in unless you say you love me."

"I love you," he said, holding her. "Marry me."

She was kissing his forehead, eyes, mouth. "No one has ever cared for me like you."

He repeated, "Marry me. Say you will, say it."

"Oh I don't know," she replied.

She crossed the garden and tapped on the window. Immediately her mother came to the door. The hall was narrow. The mother kissed her daughter, and then Majid, on the cheek.

"I'm pleased to see you," she said, shyly. She didn't appear to have been drinking. She looked Majid over and said, "Do you want a tour?" She seemed to expect it.

"That would be lovely," he said.

Downstairs the rooms were square, painted white but otherwise bare. The ceilings were low, the carpet thick and green. A brown three-piece suite—each item seemed to resemble a boat—was set in front of the television.

Nicole was eager to take Majid upstairs. She led him through the rooms which had been the setting for the stories she'd told. He tried to imagine the scenes. But the bedrooms that had once been inhabited by lodgers—van drivers, removal men, postmen, labourers—were empty. The wallpaper was gouged and discoloured, the curtains hadn't been washed for a decade, nor the windows cleaned; rotten mattresses were parked against the walls. In the hall the floorboards were bare, with nails sticking out of them. What to her reverberated with remembered life was squalor to him.

As her mother poured juice for them, her hands shook, and it splashed on the table.

"It's very quiet," he said, to the mother. "What do you do with yourself all day?"

She looked perplexed but thought for a few moments.

"I don't really know," she said. "What does anyone do? I used to cook for the men but running around after them got me down."

Nicole got up and went out of the room. There was a silence. Her mother was watching him. He noticed that there appeared to be purplish bruises under her skin.

She said, "Do you care about her?"

He liked the question.

"Very much," he said. "Do you?"

She looked down. She said, "Will you look after her?"

"Yes. I promise."

She nodded. "That's all I wanted to know. I'll make your dinner."

While she cooked, Nicole and Majid waited in the lounge. He said that, like him, she seemed only to sit on the edge of the furniture. She sat back self-consciously. He started to pace about, full of things to say.

Her mother was intelligent and dignified, he said, which must have been where Nicole inherited her grace. But the place, though it wasn't sordid, was desolate.

"Sordid? Desolate? Not so loud! What are you talking about?"

"You said your mother was selfish. That she always put herself, and her men friends in particular, before her children."

"I did say—"

"Well, I had been expecting a woman who cosseted herself. But I've never been in a colder house." He indicated the room. "No mementos, no family photographs, not one picture. Everything personal has been erased. There is nothing she has made, or chosen to reflect—"

"You only do what interests you," Nicole said. "You work, sit on boards, eat, travel and talk. 'Only do what gives you pleasure,' you say to me constantly."

"I'm a sixties kid," he said. "It was a romantic age."

"Majid, the majority can't live such luxurious lives. They never did. Your sixties is a great big myth."

"It isn't the lack of opulence which disturbs me, but the poverty of imagination. It makes me think of what culture means—"

"It means showing off and snobbery—"

"Not that aspect of it. Or the decorative. But as indispensable human expression, as a way of saying, 'Here there is pleasure, desire, life! This is what people have made!'"

He had said before that literature, indeed, all culture, was a celebration of life, if not a declaration of love for things.

"Being here," he continued, "it isn't people's greed and selfishness that surprises me. But how little people ask of life. What meagre demands they make, and the trouble they go to, to curb their hunger for experience."

"It might surprise you," she said, "because you know successful egotistical people who do what they love. But most people don't do much of anything most of the time. They only want to get by another day."

"Is that so?" He thought about this and said that every day he awoke ebulliently and full of schemes. There was a lot he wanted, of the world and of other people. He added, "And of you."

But he understood sterility because despite all the "culture" he and his second wife had shared, his six years with her had been arid. Now he had this love, and he knew it was love because of the bleakness that preceded it, which had enabled him to see what was possible.

She kissed him. "Precious, precious," she said.

She pointed to the bolted door she had mentioned to him. She wanted to go downstairs. But her mother was calling them.

They sat down in the kitchen, where two places had been laid. Nicole and her mother saw him looking at the food.

"Seems a bit funny giving Indian food to an Indian," the mother said. "I didn't know what you eat."

"That's all right," he said.

She added, "I thought you'd be more Indian, like."

He waggled his head. "I'll try to be." There was a silence. He said to her, "It was my birthday yesterday."

"Really?" said the mother.

She and her daughter looked at one another and laughed.

While he and Nicole ate, the mother, who was very thin, sat and smoked. Sometimes she seemed to be watching them and other times fell into a kind of reverie. She was even-tempered and seemed prepared to sit there all day. He found himself seeking the fury in her, but she looked more resigned than anything, reminding him of himself in certain moods: without hope or desire, all curiosity suppressed in the gloom and agitated muddle of her mind.

After a time she said to Nicole, "What are you doing with yourself? How's work?"

"Work? I've given up the job. Didn't I tell you?"

"At the television programme?"

"Yes."

"What for? It was a lovely job!"

Nicole said, "It wore me out for nothing. I'm getting the strength to do what I want, not what I think I ought to do."

"What's that supposed to mean?" her mother said. "You stay in bed all day?"

"We only do that sometimes," Majid murmured.

Her mother said, "I can't believe you gave up such a job! I can't even get work in a shop. They said I wasn't experienced enough. I said, what experience do you need to sell bread rolls?"

In a low voice Nicole talked of what she'd been promising herself—to draw, dance, study philosophy, get healthy. She would follow what interested her. Then she caught his eye, having been reminded of one of the strange theories that puzzled and alarmed her. He maintained that it wasn't teaching she craved, but a teacher, someone to help and guide her; perhaps a kind of husband. She found herself smiling at how he brought everything back to them.

"Must be lovely," her mother said. "Just doing what you want."

"I'll be all right," Nicole said.

After lunch, in the lounge, Nicole pulled the brass bolt and he accompanied her down a dark flight of stairs. This was the basement where she and her brother and sister used to sleep, Nicole wearing a knitted hat and scarf, as her mother would heat only the front room. The damp room opened on to a small garden where the children had to urinate if the bolt was across. Beyond there were fields.

Late at night they would listen to the yells and crashes upstairs. If one of her mother's boyfriends—whichever man it was who had taken her father's place—had neglected to bolt the door, Nicole would put on her overcoat and wellington boots, and creep upstairs. The boots were required because of overturned ashtrays and broken glass. She would ensure her mother hadn't been cut or beaten, and try to persuade everyone to go to bed. One morning there had been indentations in the wall, along with the remains of hair and blood, where her mother's head had been banged against it. A few times the police came.

Majid watched as Nicole went through files containing old school books, magazines, photographs. She opened several sacks and hunted through them for some clothes she wanted to take back to London. This would take some time. He decided to go upstairs and wait for her. As he went, he passed the mother.

He walked about, wondering where in the house, when Nicole was ten, her father had hanged himself. He hadn't been able to ask. He thought of what it would be like to be living an ordinary life, and the next day your husband is self-murdered, leaving you with three children.

On returning he paused at the top of the stairs. They were talking; no—arguing. The mother's voice, soft and contained earlier, had gained a furious edge. The house seemed transparent. He could hear them, just as her mother must have heard him.

"If he's asked you," she was saying. "And if he means it, you should say yes. And if you're jealous of his bloody kids, have some with him. That'll keep him to you. He's well off and brainy, he can have anyone. D'you know what he sees in you, apart from sex?"

"He says he loves me."

"You're not having me on? Does he support you?"

"Yes."

"Really?"

"Yes."

Quietly Majid sat down on the top step. Nicole was struggling to maintain the dignity and sense she'd determined on that morning.

The mother said, "If you stop working you might end up with nothing. Like I did. Better make sure he don't run off with someone younger and prettier."

"Why should he do that?" Nicole said sullenly.

"He's done it already."

"When?"

"Idiot, with you."

"Yes, yes, he has."

"Men are terrible beasts."

"Yes, yes."

Her mother said, "If it's getting you down, you can always stay here . . . for a while." She hesitated. "It won't be like before. I won't bother you."

"I might do that. Can I?"

"You'll always be my baby."

Nicole must have been pulling boxes around; her breathing became heavier.

"Nicole, don't make a mess in my house. It'll be me who'll have to clear everything up. What are you looking for?"

"I had a picture of Father."

"I didn't know you had one."

"Yes." Shortly after, Nicole said, "Here it is."

He imagined them standing together, examining it.

"Before he did it," said the mother, "he said he'd show us, teach us a lesson. And he did."

She sounded as if she were proud of her husband.

Upstairs Nicole packed her clothes in a bag, then went back to find something in a cupboard; after this, there were other things she wanted.

"I must do this," she said, hurrying around.

He realised that she might want to stay, that she might make him go back alone. He put on his coat. In the hall he waited restlessly.

The mother said to him, "You're in a hurry."

"Yes."

"Is there something you have to get home for?"

He nodded. "Lots of things."

"You don't like it here, I can tell."

He said nothing.

To his relief he saw Nicole emerge and put her scarf on. They kissed her mother and walked quickly back where they'd come. The bus arrived; and then they waited for the train, stamping their feet. As it pulled away, she took out her book. He looked at her; there were some things he wanted to ask, but she had put herself beyond his reach.

Near their house they stopped off to buy newspapers and magazines. Then they bought bread, pasta, hummus, yoghurt, wine, water, juice, florentines. They unpacked it on the kitchen table, on which were piled books and CDs, invitations and birthday cards, with his children's toys scattered underneath. It was only then they realised she'd left the bag of clothes somewhere, probably on the train. Tears came to her eyes before she realised the clothes didn't matter; she didn't even want them, and he said she could buy more.

He sat at the table with the papers and asked her what music she was in the mood for, or if she didn't care. She shook her head and went to shower. Then she walked about naked, before spreading a towel on the floor and sitting on it to massage cream into her legs, sighing and humming as she did so. He started to prepare their supper, all the while watching her, which was one of his preferred occupations. Soon they would eat. After, they would take tea and wine to bed; lying there for hours, they would go over everything, knowing they would wake up with one another.

SUCKING STONES

S OMETHING TO look forward to, that was what she
wanted, however meagre. Every evening, when Marcia
drove back from school through the suburban traffic, angry
and listless, with a talking book on the cassette player and her
son sitting in the back, she hoped she might have received a
letter from a publisher or literary agent. Or there might be
one from a theatre, if she had been attempting a play. She did,
sometimes—quite often—receive "encouragement." It cost
nothing to give, but she cherished it.

As she opened the door, and her son Alec ran into the
house to put the TV on, she found on the mat, handwritten
in black ink on impressively formal grey card, a note from the
famous writer, Aurelia Broughton. Marcia read it twice.

"This is exciting," she said to Alec. "You can look at it but
don't touch it." He was a pupil at the school where she
taught seven-year-olds. She read it again. "Those swine in the

writers' group will be very interested. We'd better get going."

Three years ago Marcia had had a story published in a small magazine of new writing. Last year an hour-long play of hers had been given a rehearsed performance in a local arts centre. It had been directed by an earnest, forceful young man who worked in advertising but loved the theatre.

Marcia had been dismayed by how little the actors resembled the people they were based on. One of the men even had a moustache. How carelessly the actors carried the play in a direction she hadn't considered! After, there had been a debate in the bar. Several members of the writers' group had come to support her. The young histrionic faces, handwaving, and passionate interruptions began to exhilarate her. It was her work they were arguing about!

The director took her to one side and said, "You must send this play to the National Theatre! They need new writers."

He had forgotten that Marcia would be forty this year.

A couple of months later, when the play was returned, she didn't open the envelope. She couldn't see how to go on. She did sometimes feel like this, although it was more ominous now. She had been writing for ten years and had never given up hope. Her need for publication, and the pride it would bring, had grown more acute.

Recently she'd been writing in bed, sometimes for fifteen minutes. At other times she lasted only five. In the morning—oh, the wasted will and lost clarity of words in the morning!—she wrote standing up in her overcoat at the dining-room table, her school bag packed, as her son waited at the front door, juggling with tennis balls. This was the most she could do. At other times she wanted, badly, to harm herself. But self-mutilation was an inaccurate language. Scars couldn't speak.

Marcia dropped the card in her bag along with her pens and the formidable sketchbook in which she made notes. She called them the "tools of her love."

While Alec ate his tea, she phoned Sandor, her "boyfriend"—though she had vowed not to speak to him—and told him about the postcard. He paid little attention to her enthusiasm; it wasn't something he understood. But she couldn't be discouraged.

They drove to her mother's, ten minutes away. It was the plain, semi-detached house in which Marcia had grown up, where her mother lived alone.

She let Alec out and handed him his overnight bag.

"Run to the door and ring the bell. I haven't got time to stop."

Marcia drove to the end of the quiet road in which she had ridden her bicycle as a child. She turned the car round and passed the house, hooting and accelerating as her mother hurried to the front gate in her flapping slippers, raising her hand as if to stop the car, with Alec standing behind her.

The members of the writers' group were making tea and arranging their seats in the cold local hall where they met once a week. On other nights Scouts, Air Cadets and Trotskyists used it. Marcia had started the group by advertising in a local paper. Originally it was to be a reading circle; she thought more people would come. At the last minute she changed the "reading" to "writing." Two dozen poems, screenplays and a complete novel dropped through her letter box. It was not only she who wanted to put her side of things.

Twelve of them sat on hard chairs in a circle, and read to one another. During the past two years they had declaimed terrible confessions that elicited only silence and tears; dreams and fantasies; episodes of soap operas and, occasionally, there was some writing of fire and imagination, usually produced by Marcia.

The group was to have no official leader, though Marcia often found herself in that position. She enjoyed the admiration and even the spite and envy, which she considered "literary." She always kept at least one author's biography beside her bed, and was aware that writing was a contact sport. Marcia also liked to talk about writing and how creativity developed, as if it was a mystery that she would grasp one day. She knew that considering the relation between language and feeling, hearing the names of writers, and speaking of their affairs and rotten personal lives, was what she wanted to do.

She also felt it was an indulgence. Life wasn't about doing what you wanted all day. But didn't Aurelia Broughton do that?

The nurses, accountants, bookshop assistants and clerks who comprised the writers' group—all, somehow, thwarted— were doing their best work. Every one of them had the belief, conviction, hope, that they could interest and engage someone else. They wrote when they could, during their lunch break, or in the spent hours late at night. Yet their spavined stories stumbled into an abyss, never leaping the electric distance between people. These "writers" made crass mistakes and were astonished and sour when others in the group pointed them out. She didn't believe she was such a fool; she couldn't believe it. None of them did.

"I grunt, I grunt. I grunt."

Marcia put on her glasses and regarded the young man who had stood up to read, a waiter in the pizza restaurant in the High Street. He had come to the house and played with Alec. He was pretty, if not a little fey. He had a crush on Marcia. For a while, after reading some George Sand, she considered giving him a try. Before, he had cried if asked to read aloud. Marcia regretted persuading him to "share" his work with them. You couldn't tell how someone's prose would sound by the look of them. This boy had been writing a long piece about a waiter in a pizza parlour attempting to give birth to a tapeworm growing inside his body. As the thick grey worm made its interminable muddy progress into the light, via the waiter's rectum—and God had made the world more quickly—Marcia lowered her head and re-read Aurelia Broughton's card.

At school two weeks ago, Marcia had seen in the newspaper that Aurelia Broughton was reading from her latest novel. It was that night. Spontaneously, but aware that she was ravenous for influence, she dropped Alec at her mother's and drove to London. She parked on a yellow line, and obtained the last ticket. The room was full. People who had just left their offices were standing on the stairs. Students sat cross-legged on the floor. There was some random clapping and then a hush when Aurelia went to the lectern. At first she was nervous, but when she realised the audience was supporting her, she seemed to enter a trance; words poured from her.

After, there were many respectful questions from people who knew her work. Marcia wondered why they had come. What had made her come? Not only a longing for poetry and something sustaining. Perhaps, Marcia thought, she could locate the talent in Aurelia by looking at her. Was it in her eyes, hands or general bearing? Was talent intelligence, passion or a gift? Could it be developed? Looking at Aurelia had made Marcia consider the puzzle of why some people could do certain things and not others.

Aurelia had made an interesting remark. Marcia had sometimes thought of her own ability, such as it was, on the model of an old torch battery, as a force with a flickering intensity, which might run down altogether.

However, Aurelia had said, with grandiose finality, "Creativity is like sexual desire. It renews itself day by day." She went on, "I never stop having ideas. They stream from me. I can write for hours. Next morning I can't wait to start again."

Someone in the audience commented, "It's something of an obsession, then."

"No, not an obsession. It is love," said Aurelia.

The audience wanted a life transformed by art.

Marcia joined a queue to have Aurelia sign the costly hardback. The writer was surrounded by publicists and the shop staff, who opened and passed the books to her. Wearing jewellery, expensive clothes, and an extravagant silk scarf, Aurelia smiled and asked Marcia her name, putting an "e" at the end instead of an "a."

Marcia leaned across the table. "I'm a writer, too."

"The more of us the better," Aurelia replied. "Good luck."

"I've written—"

Marcia tried to talk with Aurelia, but there were people behind, pushing forward with pens, questions, pieces of paper. An assistant manoeuvred her out of the way.

The next day, via Aurelia's publisher, Marcia sent her the first chapter of her novel. She enclosed a letter telling of her struggle to understand certain things. Over the years she had tried to contact writers. Many had not replied; others said they were too busy to see her. Now Aurelia had written to invite her for tea. Aurelia would be the first proper writer she had met. She was a woman Marcia would be able to have vital and straightforward conversations with.

Today Marcia shook her head when asked if she had anything to read to the group. After, she didn't go for a drink with the others but left immediately.

As she was getting into her car, the boy who'd written the tapeworm story ran up behind her.

"Marcia, you said nothing. Are you enjoying the piece? Don't be afraid of being ruthless."

He was moving backwards even as he waited for her reply. She had been accused before, in the group, of being dismissive, contemptuous even. It was true that on a couple of occasions she had had to slip outside, she was laughing so much.

He said, "You seemed lost in thought."

"The school," she said. "I'll never get away."

"Sorry. I thought it might have been the worm."

"Worm?"

"The story I read."

She said, "I didn't miss a grunt. It's coming out, isn't it, the piece. Coming out . . . well." She patted him on the shoulder and got into the car. "See you next week, probably."

Her living-room floor was covered in toys. She remembered a friend saying how children forced you to live in squalor. In the corner of the room, the damp wall had started to crumble, leaving a layer of white powder on the carpet. The bookshelves, hammered carelessly into the alcoves by her incompetent husband, sagged in the middle and were pulling out of the bricks.

She wrote and told Aurelia that she was looking forward to seeing her at the appointed time.

With Aurelia's card propped up against Aurelia's novels and stories, Marcia started to write. She would visit Aurelia and take with her a good deal more of the novel. Aurelia was well connected; she could help her get it published.

Next morning Marcia rose at five and wrote in the cold house until seven. That night, when Alec went to bed, she put in another hour. Normally, whenever she had a good idea she would think of a good reason why it wasn't a good idea. Her father's enthusiasm and her mother's helplessness had created a push-me-pull-you creature that succeeded only at remaining in the same place. She bullied herself—why can't you do this, why isn't it better?—until her living part became a crouching, cowed child.

The urgency of preparing something for Aurelia abolished Marcia's doubts. This was how she liked to work; there was only pen, paper, and something urgent proceeding between them.

During the day, even as she yelled at the children or listened to the parents' complaints, Marcia thought often of Aurelia, sometimes with annoyance. Aurelia had asked her to come to her house at four-thirty, a time when Marcia was still at school. As Aurelia lived in West London, a two-hour drive away, Marcia would have to make an excuse and take the day off in order to prepare to see her. These were the kinds of things famous writers never had to think about.

They were standing, a few days later, in the cramped kitchen looking out over the garden in which she, her father and younger brother had played tennis over a tiny net, when Marcia decided to tell her mother the good news.

"Aurelia Broughton wrote to me. You know, the writer. You've heard of her, haven't you?"

"I have heard of her," her mother said.

Mother was small but wide. She wore two knitted jumpers and a heavy cardigan, which made her look even bigger.

Mother said, "I've heard of lots of writers. What does she want from you?"

Alec went into the garden and kicked a ball. Marcia wished her father were alive to do this with him. They all missed having a man around.

"Aurelia liked my work." Marcia felt she had the right to call the writer Aurelia; they would become friends. "She wants to talk about it. It's great, isn't it? She's interested in what I'm doing."

Her mother said, "You'd better lend me one of her books so I can keep up."

"I'm re-reading them myself at the moment."

"Not during the day. You're at school."

"I read at school."

"You never let me join in. I'm pushed to one side. These are the last years of my life—"

Marcia interrupted her. "I'll be needing to write a bit in the next couple of weeks."

This meant her mother would have to keep Alec in the evenings, and for some of the weekend. His father took him on Saturday afternoons, and returned him on Sunday.

Marcia said, "Could he spend Sunday with you?" Her mother assumed her "put-upon" face. "Please."

Mother formed the same expressions today as she had in the past when caring for two children and a husband, and had made it obvious by her suffering that she found her family overwhelming and pleasureless. Depressives certainly had strong wills, killing off sentient life for miles around them.

"I had a little date, but I'll cancel it," said Mother.

"If it's not too much trouble."

Since Marcia's father had died six years ago, Mother had started going to museums and galleries. In the evenings, after a smoked salmon and cream cheese supper, she went often to the theatre and cinema. For the first time since she was young, she had friends with whom she attended lectures and concerts, sailing home in a taxi, spending the money Father had received on retirement. She had even taken up smoking. Mother had grasped that it was a little late for hopelessness.

Marcia didn't want to wait thirty years.

She had, recently, gained a terrible awareness of life. It

might have started when she began meeting men through the dating agency, which had made her feel—well, morbid. Until recently, she had lived as if one day there would be a salve for her wounds; that someone, a parent, lover, benefactor, would pluck her from chaos.

Marcia didn't become a teacher until she was almost thirty. She and her husband had started wanting to smash at one another's faces. She had, literally, kicked him out of bed; he ran into the street wearing pyjamas and slippers. Without him, she had a child, a mortgage and only a nugatory income, working in a bar and writing in the mornings. The first day at teacher training college had been awful. She had believed she would wear scarves like Aurelia Broughton and write with a gold fountain pen.

Marcia collected stories of struggling women who eventually became recognised as artists. She believed in persistence and dedication. If she wasn't a writer, how would she live with herself and what value would she have? When she was a proper writer, her soul would not be hidden; people would know her as she was. To be an artist, to live a singular, self-determined life, and follow the imagination where it led, was to live for oneself, and to be useful. Creativity, the merging of reason and imagination, was life's ultimate fulfilment.

If she passed a bookshop and saw dozens of luridly coloured blockbusters, she knew these bad and, often, young writers were making money. It seemed tragic and unfair that, unlike them, she couldn't go to a shop and buy the furniture, clothes and music she wanted.

"You hate me interfering," Mother said, "but you wouldn't

want to have got to the end of your life and realised you'd wasted your time."

"Like Father?"

"Filling bits of paper with a lot of scribbling the whole evening."

"How can expressing yourself be a waste of time?"

From the age of eight, after seeing Margot Fonteyn dance, Marcia had wanted to be a dancer; or at least her mother had wanted that for her. Marcia had attended an expensive ballet boarding school while Mother, who had never worked, packed boxes in a local factory to pay for it. Marcia left school at sixteen to get work as a dancer, but apart from not being as good as the others, and lacking the necessary vanity and ambition, she was terrified of appearing on stage. Now Mother kept three pairs of Marcia's ballet shoes on the mantelpiece, to remind Marcia of how she had wasted her mother's efforts.

"Alec is always round here," said Mother. "Not that I don't need the company. But it would be good if that writer woman could offer you some guidance about your . . . work. I expect she knows people employed on the journals."

"Are you talking about the newspapers again?"

Mother often suggested that Marcia become a journalist, writing for the *Guardian* Women's Page about stress at work, or child abuse.

Marcia went into the front room. Mother followed her, saying, "You'd make money. You could stay at home and write novels at the same time. It wouldn't be so bad if you were doing something that brought something in."

Marcia had secretly written articles which she had sent to the *Guardian*, the *Mail*, *Cosmopolitan* and other women's magazines. They had been returned. She was an artist, not a journalist. If only mother would understand that they were different.

Marcia paced the room. The wallpaper was vividly striped, and there was only one overhead light. Her brother used to say it was like living inside a Bridget Riley painting. The fat armchair with a pouffe in front of it, on which Mother kept her TV magazines and chocolates, sat there like Mother herself, heavy and immovable. Marcia didn't want to sit down, but couldn't just leave while there were favours she required.

Marcia said, "All I want is for you to help me make a little time for myself."

"What about me?" said Mother. "I haven't even had a cup of tea today. Don't I need time now?"

"You?" said Marcia. "You pity yourself, but I envy you." Her mother's face started to redden. Marcia felt empty but words streamed from her. "Yes! I wish I'd sat at home for twenty years supported by a good man, being a 'housewife.' Think what I'd have written. Washing in the morning, real work in the afternoon, before picking up the kids from school. I wouldn't have wasted a moment . . . not a moment, of all that beautiful free time!"

Mother sank into her chair and put her hand over her face.

"Better find a man then, if you can," she said.

"What does that mean?" said Marcia, hotly.

"Someone who wants to keep you. What's that one's name?"

Marcia murmured, "Sandor. He's not my boyfriend. He's only a man I'm vaguely interested in."

"I wouldn't be interested in any man," said Mother. "Those dirty creatures aren't really interested in you. What does he do?"

"You know what he does."

"Can't you do better for yourself?"

"No, I can't," said Marcia. "I can't."

Her mother loved living alone, and boasted of it constantly. When Marcia was a child six people had lived in the house, and apart from Mother they had all died or left. Mother claimed that alone she could do whatever she wanted, and at whatever time, apart from the small matter of giving and receiving emotional and physical affection, as Marcia liked to point out.

"Who wants a lot of men pawing at you?" was Mother's reply.

"Who doesn't?" Marcia said.

Marcia recalled Father as he sat on the sofa with his pad and pen. He would casually ask Mother to make him a cup of tea. Mother, whatever else she was doing, was expected to fetch it, place it before him, and wait to see if it was to his liking. It was assumed that she was at Father's command. No wonder she had taken loneliness as a philosophy. Marcia would discuss it with Aurelia.

They were three generations of women, living close to one another. Marcia's grandmother, aged ninety-four, also lived alone, in a one-bedroom flat five minutes' walk away. She was lucid and easily amused; her mind worked, but she was bent double with arthritis and prayed for the good Lord to take her. Her husband had died twenty years ago and she had hardly been out since. To Marcia she was like an animal in a cage, starved of the good things. Where were the men? Marcia's grandfather and father had died; her brother, the doctor, had gone to America; her husband had decamped with a neighbour.

Marcia went into the bathroom, took a Valium, kissed Alec, and went to her car.

That night, alone at home, writing and drinking—as desolate and proud as Martha Gellhorn in the desert, she liked to think—she rang Sandor and told him of her mother's indifference and scorn, and the concentrated work she was doing.

"The novel is really moving forward!" she said. "I've never read anything like it. It's so truthful. I can't believe no one will be interested!"

She talked until she felt she were speaking into infinity. Even her therapist, when Marcia could afford to see her, said more.

She had met Sandor in a pub, after the man she was with, picked from a black folder in the dating agency office, had made an excuse and left. What was wrong with her? The man only came up to her chest! One woman in the writing group went out with a different man every week. It was odd, she said, how many of them were married. Sandor wasn't.

After her monologue, she asked Sandor what he was doing.

"The same," he said, and laughed.

"I'll come and see you," she said.

"Why not? I'm always here," he replied.

"Yes, you are," she said.

He laughed again.

She saw him, a fifty-year-old Bulgarian, about once a month. He was a porter in a smart block of flats in Chelsea, and lived in a room in Earl's Court. He considered the job, which he had obtained after drifting around Europe for fifteen years, to be ideal. In his black suit at the desk in the entrance, he buzzed people in, took parcels and accepted flowers, went on errands for the tenants, and re-read his favourite writers, Pascal, Nietzsche, Hegel.

None of the men she had met through the agency had been interested in literature, and not one had been attractive. Sandor had the face of an uncertain priest and the body of the Olympic cyclist that he had been. He was intelligent, well mannered and seductive in several languages. He could, when he was "on," as he put it, beguile women effortlessly. He had slept with more than a thousand women and had never sustained a relationship with any of them. What sort of man had no ex-wife, no children, no family nearby, no lawyers, no debt, no house? She marvelled at her ability to locate melancholy in people. She would have to unfreeze Sandor's dead soul with the blow-torch of her love. Did she have sufficient blow? If only she could find something better to do.

"See you, Sandor," she said.

She swigged wine from the bottle she kept beside her bed. She managed to fall asleep but awoke soon after, burning with uncontrollable furies against her husband, Mother, Sandor, Aurelia. She understood those paintings full of devils and writhing, contorted demons. They did exist, in the mind. Why was there no sweetness within?

She arrived an hour early at Aurelia's house, noted where it was, parked, and walked about the neighbourhood. It was a sunny winter's day. This was a part of London she didn't know. The streets were full of antique shops, organic grocers, and cafés with young men and their babies sitting in the window. People strolled in sunglasses and dark clothes, and gathered in groups on the pavement to gossip. She recognised actors and a film director. She looked in an estate agent's window; a family house cost a million pounds.

She bought apples, vitamins and coffee. She chose a scarf in Agnès b. and paid for it by credit card, successfully averting her eyes from the price, as she had earlier avoided a clash with a mirror in the shop.

At the agreed time Marcia rang Aurelia's bell and waited. A young woman came to the door. She invited Marcia in. Aurelia was finishing her piano lesson.

In the kitchen overlooking the garden, two young women were cooking; in the dining room a long, polished table was being laid with silverware and thick napkins. In the library Marcia examined the dozens of foreign-language editions of Aurelia's novels, stories, essays—the record of a writing life.

There was a sound at the door and a man came in. Aurelia's husband introduced himself.

"Marcia." She adopted her most middle-class voice.

"You must excuse me," the man said. "My office is down the road. I must go to it."

"Are you a writer?"

"I have published a couple of books. But I have conversations for a living. I am a psychoanalyst."

He was a froglike little man, with alert eyes. She wondered if he could see her secrets, and that she had thought he'd become an analyst so that no one had to look at him.

"What a ravishing scarf," he said.

"Thank you."

"Goodbye," he said.

She waited, glancing through the chapters of the novel she had brought to show Aurelia. It seemed, in this ambience, to be execrable stuff.

She caught sight of Aurelia in the hall.

"I'll be with you in one minute," said Aurelia.

Aurelia shut the door on the piano teacher, opened it to the man delivering flowers, talked to someone in Italian on the telephone, inspected the dining room, spoke to the cook, told her assistant she wouldn't be taking any calls, and sat down opposite Marcia.

She poured tea and regarded Marcia for what seemed a long time.

"I quite enjoyed what you sent me," Aurelia said. "That school. It was a window on a world one doesn't know about."

"I've written more," Marcia said. "Here."

She placed the three chapters on the table. Aurelia picked them up and put them down.

"I wish I could write like you," she sighed.

"Sorry?" said Marcia. "Please, do you mean that?"

"My books insist on being long. But one couldn't write an extended piece in that style."

"Why not?" said Marcia. Aurelia looked at her as if she should know without being told. Marcia said, "The thing is, I don't get time for . . . extension." She was beginning to panic. "How do you get down to it?"

"You met Marty," she said. "We have breakfast early. He goes to his office. He starts at seven. Then I just do it. I haven't got any choice, really. Sometimes I write here, or I go to our house in Ferrara. For writers there's rarely anything else but writing."

"Doesn't your mind go everywhere except to the page?" said Marcia. "Do you have some kind of iron discipline? Don't you find ludicrous excuses?"

"Writing is my drug. I go to it easily. My new novel is starting to develop. This is the best part, when you can see that something is beginning. I like to think," Aurelia went on, "that I can make a story out of anything. A murmur, a hint, a gesture . . . turned into another form of life. What could be more satisfying? Can I ask your age?"

"Thirty-seven."

Aurelia said, "You have something to look forward to."

"What do you mean?"

"One's late thirties are a period of disillusionment. The early forties are a lovely age—of re-illusionment. Everything comes together then, you will find, and there is renewed purpose."

Marcia looked at the poster of a film which had been made of one of Aurelia's books.

She said, "Sometimes life is so difficult . . . it is impossible to write. You don't feel actual hopelessness?"

Aurelia shook her head and continued to look at Marcia. Her husband was an analyst; he would have taught her not to be alarmed by weeping.

"It's those blasted men that have kept us down," Marcia said. "When I was young, you were one of the few contemporary writers that women could read."

"We've kept ourselves down," said Aurelia. "Self-contempt, masochism, laziness, stupidity. We're old enough to own up to it now, aren't we?"

"But we are—or at least were—political victims."

"Balls." Aurelia softened her voice and said, "Would you tell me about your life at the school?"

"What sort of thing?"

"The routine. Your day. Pupils. The other teachers."

"The other teachers?"

"Yes."

Aurelia was waiting.

"But they're myopic," Marcia said.

"In what way?"

"Badly educated. Interested only in soap operas."

Aurelia nodded.

Marcia mentioned her mother but Aurelia became impatient. However, when Marcia recounted the occasion when she had suggested the school donate the remains of the Harvest Festival to the elders of the Asian community centre, and a couple of the teachers had refused to give fruit to "Pakis," Aurelia made a note with her gold pen. Marcia had, in fact, told the headmaster about this, but he dismissed it, saying, "I have to run all of this school."

Marcia looked at Aurelia as if to say, "Why do you want to know this?"

"That was helpful," Aurelia said. "I want to write something about a woman who works in a school. Do you know many teachers?"

Marcia's colleagues were teachers but none of her friends were. One friend worked in a building society, another had just had a baby and was at home.

"There must be people at your school I could talk to. What about the headmaster?"

Marcia made a face. Then she remembered something she had read in a newspaper profile of Aurelia. "Don't you have a daughter at school?"

"It's the wrong sort of teacher there."

"Sorry?"

"I was looking for something rougher."

Marcia was embarrassed. She said, "Have you taught writing courses?"

"I did, when I wanted to travel. The students are wretched, of course. Many I would recommend for psychiatric treatment. A lot of people don't want to write, they just want the kudos. They should move on to other objects."

Aurelia got up. As she signed Marcia a copy of her latest novel, she asked for her telephone number at school. Marcia couldn't think of a reason not to give it to her.

Aurelia said, "Thank you for coming to see me. I'll look at your chapters." At the door she said, "Will you come to a party I'm giving? Perhaps we will talk more. An invitation will be sent to you."

From across the road Marcia looked at the lighted house and the activity within, until the shutters were closed.

Marcia waited beside Sandor at his porter's desk until he finished work at seven. They had a drink in the pub where they had met. Sandor went there every evening to watch the sport on cable TV. He didn't ask her why she had suddenly turned up, and didn't mention Aurelia Broughton, though Marcia had rung to say she was coming up to see her. He talked of how he loved London and how liberal it was; no one cared who or what you were. He said that if he ever had a house he would decorate it like the pub they were sitting in. He talked of what he was reading in Hegel, though in such a garbled fashion she had no idea what he was saying or why it interested him. He told her stories of the criminals he'd known and how he'd been used as a getaway driver.

He asked her if she wanted to go to bed. His request was put in the tone of voice that said it was just as fine if she preferred not to. She hesitated only because the house in which he had a room could have been a museum to the 1950s, along with the failure of the two-bar electric fire to make any impression on the block of cold that sat in the room like death. There was also the hag of a landlady who would sit at the end of his bed at midnight.

"Don't worry, I've just given her *Crime and Punishment* to read," Sandor laughed, following Marcia into his room. Books were piled on the floor beside the bed. His washing hung over the back of a chair. All his possessions were here.

Lying down with him, she noticed his loaf of white sliced bread and carton of milk on the chest of drawers.

"Is that all your food?"

"Bread and butter fills me up. Then I read for four or five hours. Nothing bothers me."

"It's not much of a life."

"What?"

"You're not in prison."

He looked at her in surprise, as if it had never occurred to him that he wasn't in prison, and didn't have to make the best of nothing.

He kissed her and she thought of inviting him to her house at the weekend. He was kind. He would entertain Alec. But she might start to rely on him; she would always be asking for more. If anyone requested him to yield, shift or alter, he left them. She might not want him, but she didn't want to be forsaken.

After, she stood up to get dressed, looking at him where he lay with his hand over his eyes. She couldn't spend the night in such a place.

That night, for the first time, she wished Alec weren't in Mother's bed. Marcia slept with her face in his unwashed clothes. In the morning she didn't write. She had lost the desire, which was also her desire for life. What illusory hopes had she invested in Aurelia? Seeing her had robbed Marcia of something. She had emptied herself out, and Aurelia was full. Where would she find the resources, the meaning, to carry on?

Aurelia had asked her to bring someone to the party; another teacher, a "pure" teacher Aurelia had said, meaning not a teacher pretending to be a writer. Maybe Marcia should have said no. But she wanted to leave the door open with Aurelia, to see what might develop. Aurelia might read the three chapters and be excited by them. Anyhow, Marcia wanted to go to the party.

"How did it go with Miss Broughton?" asked her mother the next time Marcia went round. "We've chatted on the phone, but you haven't mentioned it."

"It was fine, just great."

Her mother said, "You're sullen, like a teenager again."

"I don't know what to say."

Mother said, more softly, "What came of it?"

"You should have seen the house. Five bedrooms—at least!"

"You got upstairs?"

"I had to. And three receptions!"

"Three? What do they do in all that space! What would we do with it!"

"Have races!"

"We could—"

"The flowers, Mum! The people working there! I've never known anything like it."

"I bet. Was it on a main road?"

"Just off. But near the shops. They've got everything to hand."

"Buses?" enquired her mother.

"I shouldn't think she goes on a bus."

"No," said Mother. "I wouldn't go on another bus again if I didn't have to. Off-street parking?"

"Yes. Room for two cars, it looked like." Marcia said, "We chatted in her library and got to know one another. She invited me to a party."

"To a party? She didn't invite me?"

"She didn't mention you at all," Marcia said. "And nor did I."

"I'm sure she wouldn't mind if I came with you. I'll get my glad rags on!"

"But why?" said Marcia.

"Just to go out. To meet people. I might interest them."

Before, this would have been a kind of joke, and Mother would have returned to her moroseness. She certainly was getting healthy, if she thought she might interest people.

"I'll think about it," Marcia said.

"I can't wait!" sang her mother. "A party!"

Aurelia rang from her car. The connection wasn't good, but Marcia gathered that Aurelia was "in the neighbourhood" and wanted to "pass by for a cup of tea."

Marcia and Alec were having fish fingers and baked beans. Aurelia must have been close; Marcia had hardly cleared the table, and Alec hadn't finished throwing his toys behind the sofa, when Aurelia's car drew up outside.

At the door she handed Marcia another signed copy of her new novel, came in, and sat down on the edge of the sofa.

"What a beautiful boy," she said of Alec. "Fine hair—almost white."

"And how are you?" said Marcia.

"Tired. I've been doing readings and giving interviews, not only here but in Berlin and Barcelona. The French are making a film about me, and the Americans want me to make a film about my London . . . Sorry," she said. "Am I making you crazy?"

"Of course."

Aurelia sighed. Today she looked shrewd and seemed to vibrate with intensity. She didn't want to talk, or listen, rather. When Marcia told her that her will to work had collapsed, she said, "I wish mine had."

She got up and glanced along the shelves of Marcia's books.

"I like her," said Marcia, naming a woman writer, of about the same age as Aurelia.

"She can't write at all. Apparently she's a rather good amateur sculptor."

"Is that so?" said Marcia. "I liked her last book. Did you read the chapters I gave you?" Aurelia looked blankly at her. Marcia said, "The chapters from my novel. I left them."

"Where?"

"On your table."

"No. No, I didn't."

"Perhaps they're still there."

Marcia guessed Aurelia wanted to see how she lived, that she wasn't looking at her but through her, to the sentences and paragraphs she would make of her. It was an admirable ruthlessness.

At the door Aurelia kissed her on both cheeks.

"See you at the party," she said.

"I'm looking forward to it."

"Don't forget—bring someone pedagogical."

Marcia put Aurelia's novel on the shelf. Aurelia's books were among the rows of books; the books full of stories, the stories full of characters and craft, waiting to be enlivened by someone with a use for them. Or perhaps not.

Mother refused to have Alec to stay. It was the first time she had done this. It was the day before the party.

"But why, why?" said Marcia, on the telephone.

"I realised you weren't taking me to the party, though you didn't bother to actually tell me. I made other arrangements."

"I was never taking you to that party."

"You never take me anywhere."

Marcia was shaking with exasperation. "Mum, I want to live. And I want you to help me."

"I've helped you all my life."

"Sorry? You?"

"Who brought you up? You're educated, you've got—"

Marcia replaced the receiver.

She rang friends and a couple of people in the writers' group, even the boy who'd written about the tapeworm. No one was available to babysit. Half an hour before she needed to leave, the only person left to ask was her husband, who lived nearby. He was surprised and sarcastic. They rarely spoke but, when necessary, dropped notes through one another's doors.

He said he had been intending to spend the evening with his new girlfriend.

"How sweet," said Marcia.

"What do you want me to do?" he said.

"Can't you both come over?"

"Desperate. Must be another new boyfriend. Have you got any crisps . . . and alcohol?"

"Take what you want. You always did."

It was the first time she had let her husband into the house since he had left. If the girlfriend was there he wouldn't, at least, snoop around.

When they arrived, and the girlfriend removed her coat, Maria noticed she was pregnant.

Marcia changed upstairs. She could hear them talking in the living room. Then she heard music.

She was at the door, ready to go. Alec was showing them his new baseball cap.

Her husband held up a record sleeve. "You know, this is my record."

"I'm in a rush," she said.

In the car she thought she must have been mad, but what she was doing was in the service of life. People don't take enough risks, she thought. She didn't, though, have a teacher who might interest Aurelia. However, Aurelia wouldn't turn her away at the door. Marcia had done enough for Aurelia. Had Aurelia done enough for her?

It was Aurelia's husband who let her in and fetched her a

glass of champagne, while Marcia looked around. The party was being held on the ground floor of the house, and Marcia recognised several writers. The other guests seemed to be critics, academics, psychoanalysts and publishers.

The effort of getting there had made her tense. She drank two glasses of champagne quickly and attached herself to Aurelia's husband, the only person, apart from Aurelia, she knew.

"Do you want to be introduced as a teacher, or as a writer?" he said. "Or neither?"

"Neither, at the moment." She took his arm. "Because I am neither one nor the other."

"Keeping your options open, eh?" he said.

He introduced her to several people, and they talked as a group. The main topic was the royal family, a subject she was surprised to hear intellectuals taking an interest in. It was like being at the school.

She liked Aurelia's husband, who nodded and smiled occasionally; she liked being afraid of him. He understood other people and what their wishes were. Nothing would shock him.

He was a little shocked later on, in the conservatory, when she reached up to kiss him. She was saying, "Please, please, only this . . ." when, across the room, she saw the headmaster of her school, and his wife, talking to a female writer.

Aurelia's husband gently detached her.

"I apologise," she said.

"Accepted. I'm flattered."

"Hallo, Marcia," said the headmaster. "I hear you've been very helpful to Aurelia."

She didn't like the headmaster seeing her drunk and embarrassed.

"Yes," she said.

"Aurelia's going to come to the school and see what we do. She's going to talk to the older pupils." He lowered his mouth to her ear. "She has given me a complete set of her books. Signed."

She wanted to say, "They're all signed, you stupid cunt."

She left the house and walked a little. Then she went back and traversed the party. People were leaving. Others were talking intensely. Nobody paid her any attention.

Sandor was lying on his bed with his hand over his eyes. She sat beside him.

"I've come to say I won't be coming so often now. Not that I've ever really come often, except recently. But . . . it will be even less."

He nodded. He was watching her. Sometimes he took in what she said.

She went on, "The reason, if you want to know the reason—"

"Why not?" he said. He sat up. "I'd get you something . . . but, I'm so ashamed, there's nothing here."

"There's never anything here."

"I'll take you out for a drink."

"I've had enough to drink." She said, "Sandor, this is hateful. There's a phrase that kept coming into my mind at the party. I came to tell it to you. Sucking stones. That's it. We look to the old things and to the old places, for sustenance. That's where we found it before. Even when there's nothing there we go on. But we have to find new things, otherwise we are sucking stones. To me, this"—she indicated the room— "is arid, impoverished, dead."

His eyes followed her gesture around the room as she condemned it.

"But I'm trying," he said. "Things are going to look up, I know they are."

She kissed him. "Bye. See you."

She cried in the car. It wasn't his fault. She'd go back another day.

She was late home. Her husband was asleep in his girlfriend's arms, his hand on her stomach. On the floor was an empty bottle of wine and dirty plates; the TV was loud.

She carried the record from the deck, scratched it with her fingernail, and replaced it in its cover. She roused the couple, thanked them, pushed the record under her husband's arm, and got them out.

She started up the stairs but stopped halfway, took another step, and went down again. She returned to the living room and put on her overcoat. She went out onto the small concrete patio behind the house. It was dark and silent. The cold shocked her into wakefulness. She removed her coat. She wanted the cold to punish her.

Early in the morning, during the summer holidays, she sometimes danced out here, with Alec watching her, to parts of Prokofiev's *Romeo and Juliet*.

Now she put the kitchen light on and laid a square of

bricks. She went back into the house and collected her files. She carried them outside and opened them. She burned her stories; she burned the play, and the first few chapters of the novel. There was a lot of it and it made a nice fire. It took a long time. She was shivering and stank of smoke and ash. She swept up. She ran a bath and lay in it until the water was tepid.

Alec had got into her bed and was asleep. She put her notebook on the bedside table. She would keep it with her, using it as a journal. But otherwise she would stop writing for a while; at least six months, to begin with. She was clear that this wasn't masochism or a suicide. Perhaps her dream of writing had been a kind of possession, or addiction. She was aware that you could get addicted to the good things, too. She was making a space. It was an important emptiness, one she would not fill with other intoxications. She might, she knew, turn into her mother, sucking stones at the TV night after night, terrified by excitement.

After a time there might be new things.

A MEETING, AT LAST

M ORGAN'S LOVER'S husband held out his hand.
"Hallo, at last," he said. "I enjoyed watching you standing across the road. I was delighted when, after some consideration, you made up your mind to speak with me. Will you sit down?"

"Morgan," said Morgan.

"Eric."

Morgan nodded, dropped his car keys on the table and sat down on the edge of a chair.

The two men looked at one another.

Eric said, "Are you drinking?"

"In a while—maybe."

Eric called for another bottle. There were two already on the table.

"You don't mind if I do?"

"Feel free."

"I do now."

Eric finished his bottle and replaced it on the table with his fingers around the neck. Morgan saw Eric's thin gold wedding ring. Caroline would always drop hers in a dish on the table in Morgan's hall, and replace it when she left.

Eric had said on the phone, "Is that Morgan?"

"Yes," Morgan replied. "Who—"

The voice went on, "Are you Caroline's boyfriend?"

"But who is this asking?" said Morgan. "Who are you?"

"The man she lives with. Eric. Her husband. Okay?"

"Right. I see."

"Good. You see."

Eric had said "please" on the phone. "Please meet me. Please."

"Why?" Morgan had said. "Why should I?"

"There are some things I need to know."

Eric named a café and the time. It was later that day. He would be there. He would wait.

Morgan rang Caroline. She was in meetings, as Eric must have known. Morgan deliberated all day but it wasn't until the last moment, pacing up and down his front room when he was already late, that he walked out of the house, got in his car and stood across the road from the café.

Although Caroline had described Eric's parents, his inarticulate furies, the way his head hung when he felt low and even, as Morgan laughed, the way he scratched his backside, Eric had been a shadow man, an unfocused dark figure that had lain across their life since they had met. And while Morgan knew things about him that he didn't need to know, he had little idea of what Eric knew of him. He had yet to find out what Caroline might have recently told him. The last few days had been the craziest of Morgan's life.

The waitress brought Eric a beer. Morgan was about to order one for himself but changed his mind and asked for water.

Eric smiled grimly.

"So," he said. "How are you?"

Morgan knew that Eric worked long hours. He came home late and got up after the children had gone to school. Looking at him, Morgan tried to visualise something Caroline had said. As she prepared for work in the morning, he lay in bed in his pyjamas for an hour, saying nothing, but thinking intently with his hands over his eyes, as if he were in pain, and had to work something out.

Caroline left for work as early as she could in order to phone Morgan from the office.

After a couple of months, Morgan requested her not to speak about Eric, and particularly not about their attempts at love-making. But as Morgan's meetings with Caroline were arranged around Eric's absences, he was, inevitably, mentioned.

Morgan said, "What can I do for you?"

"There are things I want to know. I am entitled."

"Are you?"

"Don't I have any rights?"

Morgan knew that seeing this man was not going to be easy. In the car he had tried to prepare, but it was like revising for an exam without having been told the subject.

"All right," Morgan said, to calm him down. "I understand you."

"After all, you have taken my life."

"Sorry?"

"I mean my wife. My wife."

Eric swigged at his bottle. Then he took out a small pot of pills and shook it. It was empty.

"You haven't got any painkillers, have you?"

"No."

Eric wiped his face with a napkin.

He said, "I'm having to take these."

He was upset, no doubt. He would be in shock. Morgan was; Caroline too, of course.

Morgan was aware that she had started with him to cheer herself up. She had two children and a good, if dull, job. Then her best friend took a lover. Caroline met Morgan through work and decided immediately that he had the right credentials. Love and romance suited her. Why hadn't she been dipped in such delight every day? She thought everything else could remain the same, apart from her "treat." But as Morgan liked to say, there were "consequences." In bed, she would call him "Mr. Consequences."

"I'm not moving out of my house," Eric said. "It's my home. You're not intending to take that from me, as well as my wife?"

"Your wife . . . Caroline," Morgan said, restoring her as her own person. "I didn't steal her. I didn't have to persuade her. She gave herself to me."

"She gave herself?" Eric said. "She wanted you? You?"

"That's the truth."

"Do women do that to you?"

Morgan tried to laugh.

"Do they?" Eric said.

"Only her—recently."

Eric stared, waiting for him to continue. But Morgan said nothing, reminding himself that he could walk out at any time, that he didn't have to take anything from this man.

Eric said, "Do you want her?"

"I think so, yes."

"You're not sure? After doing all this, you're not sure?"

"I didn't say that."

"What do you mean then?"

"Nothing."

But perhaps he wasn't sure. He had become used to their arrangement. There were too many hurried phone calls, misunderstood letters, snatched meetings and painful partings. But they had lived within it. They even had a routine. He had received more from Eric's wife—seeing her twice a week— than he had from any other woman. Otherwise, when he wasn't working, he visited art galleries with his daughter; he packed his shoulder bag, took his guide book and walked about parts of the city he'd never seen; he sat by the river and wrote notes about the past. What had he learned through her? A reverence for the world; the ability to see feeling, certain created objects, and other people as important—indeed, invaluable. She had introduced him to the pleasures of carelessness.

Eric said, "I met Caroline when she was twenty-one. She

didn't have a line on her face. Her cheeks were rosy. She was acting in a play at university."

"Was she a good actress? She's good at a lot of things, isn't she? She likes doing things well."

Eric said, "It wasn't long before we developed bad habits."

Morgan asked, "What sort of thing?"

"In our . . . relationship. That's the word everyone uses." Eric said, "We didn't have the skill, the talent, the ability to get out of them. How long have you known her?"

"Two years."

"Two years!"

Morgan was confused. "What did she tell you? Haven't you been discussing it?"

Eric said, "How long do you think will it take me to digest all this?"

Morgan said, "What are you doing?"

He had been watching Eric's hands, wondering whether he would grasp the neck of the bottle. But Eric was hunting through the briefcase he had pulled out from under the table.

"What date? Surely you remember that! Don't you two have anniversaries?" Eric dragged out a large red book. "My journal. Perhaps I made a note that day! The past two years have to be rethought! When you are deceived, every day has another complexion!"

Morgan looked round at the other people in the café.

"I don't like being shouted at," he said. "I'm too tired for that."

"No, no. Sorry."

Eric flipped through the pages of the book. When he saw Morgan watching, he shut the journal.

Eric said in a low voice, "Have you ever been deceived? Has that ever happened to you?"

"I would imagine so," said Morgan.

"How pompous! And do you think that deceiving someone is all right?"

"One might say that there are circumstances which make it inevitable."

Eric said, "It falsifies everything." He went on, "Your demeanour suggests that it doesn't matter, either. Are you that cynical? This is important. Look at the century!"

"Sorry?"

"I work in television news. I know what goes on. Your cruelty is the same thing. Think of the Jews—"

"Come on—"

"That other people don't have feelings! That they don't matter! That you can trample over them!"

"I haven't killed you, Eric."

"I could die of this. I could die."

Morgan nodded. "I understand that."

He remembered one night, when she had to get home, to slip into bed with Eric, Caroline had said, "If only Eric would die . . . just die . . ."

"Peacefully?"

"Quite peacefully."

Eric leaned across the table. "Have you felt rough, then?"

"Yes."

"Over this?"

"Over this." Morgan laughed. "Over everything. But definitely over this."

"Good. Good." Eric said, "Middle age is a lonely time."

"Without a doubt," said Morgan.

"That's interesting. More lonely than any other time, do you think?"

"Yes," said Morgan. "All you lack seems irrevocable."

Eric said, "Between the age of twelve and thirteen my elder brother, whom I adored, committed suicide, my father died of grief, and my grandfather just died. Do you think I still miss them?"

"How could you not?"

Eric drank his beer and thought about this.

"You're right, there's a hole in me." He said, "I wish there were a hole in you."

Morgan said, "She has listened to me. And me to her."

Eric said, "You really pay attention to one another, do you?"

"There's something about being attended to that makes you feel better. I'm never lonely when I'm with her."

"Good."

"I've been determined, this time, not to shut myself off."

"But she's my wife."

There was a pause.

Eric said, "What is it people say these days? It's your problem! It's my problem! Do you believe that? What do you think?"

Morgan had been drinking a lot of whisky and smoking grass, for the first time. He had been at university in the late sixties but had identified with the puritanical left, not the hippies. These days, when he needed to switch off his brain, he noticed how tenacious consciousness was. Perhaps he wanted to shut off his mind because in the past few days he had been considering forgetting Caroline. Forgetting about them all, Caroline, Eric and their kids. Maybe he would, now. Perhaps the secrecy, and her inaccessibility, had kept them all at the right distance.

Morgan realised he had been thinking for some time. He turned to Eric again, who was tapping the bottle with his nail.

"I do like your house," said Eric. "But it's big, for one person."

"My house, did you say? Have you seen it?"

"Yes."

Morgan looked at Eric's eyes. He seemed rather spirited. Morgan almost envied him. Hatred could give you great energy.

Eric said, "You look good in your white shorts and white socks, when you go out running. It always makes me laugh."

"Haven't you got anything better to do than stand outside my house?"

"Haven't you got anything better to do than steal my wife?" Eric pointed his finger at him. "One day, Morgan, perhaps you will wake up and find in the morning that things aren't the way they were last night. That everything you have has been sullied and corrupted in some way. Can you imagine that?"

"All right," said Morgan. "All right, all right."

Eric had knocked his bottle over. He put his napkin on the spilled beer and popped his bottle on top of that.

He said, "Are you intending to take my children away?"

"What? Why should I?"

"I can tell you now, I have had that house altered to my specifications, you know. I have a pergola. I'm not moving out, and I'm not selling it. Actually, to tell the truth"—Eric had a sort of half-grin, half-grimace on his face—"I might be better off without my wife and kids."

"What?" said Morgan. "What did you say?"

Eric raised his eyebrows at him.

"You know what I mean," Eric said.

Morgan's children were with their mother, the girl away at university, the boy at private school. Both of them were doing well. Morgan had met Eric's kids only briefly. He had offered to take them in if Caroline was prepared to be with him. He was ready for that, he thought. He didn't want to shirk the large tasks. But in time one of the kids could, say, become a junkie; the other a teenage prostitute. And Morgan, having fallen for their mother, might find himself burdened. He knew people it had happened to.

Eric said, "My children are going to be pretty angry with you when they find out what you've done to us."

"Yes," said Morgan. "Who could blame them?"

"They're big and expensive. They eat like horses."

"Christ."

Eric said, "Do you know about my job?"

"Not as much as you know about mine, I shouldn't think."

Eric didn't respond, but said, "Funny to think of you two talking about me. I bet you'd lie there wishing I'd have a car crash."

Morgan blinked.

"It's prestigious," Eric said. "In the newsroom, you know. Well paid. Plenty of action, continuous turnover of stories. But it's bland, worthless. I can see that now. And the people burn out. They're exhausted, and on an adrenaline rush at the same time. I've always wanted to take up walking . . . hill-walking, you know, boots and rucksacks. I want to write a novel. And travel, and have adventures. This could be an opportunity."

Morgan wondered at this. Caroline had said that Eric took little interest in the outside world, except through the medium of journalism. The way things looked, smelled, tasted, held no fascination for him; nor did the inner motives of living people. Whereas Morgan and Caroline, dawdling in a bar with their hands playing on one another, loved to discuss the relationships of mutual acquaintances, as if together they might distil the spirit of a working love.

Morgan picked up his car keys. He said, "Sounds good. You'll be fine then, Eric. Best of luck."

"Thanks a bunch."

Eric showed no sign of moving.

He said, "What do you like about her?"

Morgan wanted to shout at him, he wanted to pound on the table in front of him, saying, I love the way she pulls down her clothes, lies on her side and lets me lick and kiss her soft parts, as if I have lifted the dish of life up to my face and burst through it into the wonderland of love for ever!

Eric was tensing up. "What is it?"

"What?"

"You like about her! If you don't know, maybe you would be good enough to leave us alone!"

"Look, Eric," Morgan said, "if you calm yourself a minute, I'll say this. More than a year ago, she said she wanted to be with me. I've been waiting for her." He pointed at Eric. "You've had your time with her. You've had plenty. I would say you've had enough. Now it's my turn."

He got up and walked to the door. It was simple. Then it felt good to be outside. He didn't look back.

Morgan sat in the car and sighed. He started off and stopped at the lights on the corner. He was thinking he would go to the supermarket. Caroline could come round after work and he would cook. He would mix her favourite drink, a whisky mac. She would appreciate being looked after. They could lie down together on the bed.

Eric pulled open the door, got in, and shut the door. Morgan stared at him. The driver behind beeped his horn repeatedly. Morgan drove across the road.

"Do you want me to drop you somewhere?"

"I haven't finished with you," said Eric.

Morgan looked alternately at the road and at Eric. Eric was sitting in his car, in his seat, with his feet on his rubber mat.

Morgan was swearing under his breath.

Eric said, "What are you going to do? Have you decided?"

Morgan drove on. He saw that Eric had picked up a piece of paper from the dashboard. Morgan remembered it was a shopping list that Caroline had made out for him. Eric put it back.

Morgan turned the car round and accelerated.

"We'll go to her office now and discuss it with her. Is that what you want? I'm sure she'll tell you everything you want to know. Otherwise—let me know when you want to get out," said Morgan. "Say when."

Eric just stared ahead.

Morgan thought he had been afraid of happiness, and kept it away; he had been afraid of other people, and had kept them away. He was still afraid, but it was too late for that.

Suddenly he banged the steering wheel and said, "Okay."

"What?" said Eric.

"I've decided," said Morgan. "The answer is yes. Yes to everything! Now you must get out." He stopped the car. "Out, I said!"

Driving away, he watched Eric in the mirror getting smaller and smaller.

MIDNIGHT ALL DAY

IAN LAY BACK in the only chair in the room in Paris, waiting for Marina to finish in the bathroom. She would be some time, since she was applying unguents—seven different ones, she had told him—over most of her body, rubbing them in slowly. She was precious to herself.

He was glad to have a few minutes alone. There had been many important days recently; he suspected that this would be the most important and that his future would turn on it.

For the past few mornings, before they went out for breakfast, he had listened to Schubert's Sonata in B-flat Major, which he had not previously known. Apart from a few pop tapes, it was the only music in Anthony's flat. Ian had pulled it out from under the futon on their first day there.

Now, as he got up to play the CD, he glimpsed himself in the wardrobe mirror and saw himself as a character in a Lucian Freud painting: a middle-aged man in a thin, tan raincoat, ashen-faced, standing beside a dying pot plant, over-weight and with, to his surprise, an absurd expression of hope, or the desire to please, in his eyes. He would have laughed, had he not lost his sense of humour.

He turned the music up. It concealed the voices that came from a nearby children's school. They reminded him of his daughter, who was staying, at the moment, with her grand-mother in London. Ian's wife, Jane, had been taken to hospi-tal. He had to discuss this with Marina, who didn't yet know about it. She did not want to hear about his wife and he did not want to talk about her. But unless he did, his wife would continue to shadow him—both of them—darkening every-thing.

Although Ian had been a pop kid, and overawed by what he imagined classical music meant, he listened avidly to the Schubert sonata, sometimes walking up and down. No mat-ter how often he heard it, he could not remember what came next; what it said to him he did not know, as the piece had no distinct overall mood. He liked the idea of it being music he would never understand; that seemed to be an important part of it. It was a relief, too, that he still had the capacity to be aroused and engrossed, as well as consoled. Some mornings he woke up wanting to hear the piece.

He and Marina had spent ten days in the tiny flat belong-ing to Ian's closest friend and business partner, Anthony, who had a French lover or mistress. On the rue du Louvre, the apartment was well situated for walks, museums and bars, but it was on the sixth floor. Marina found it an increasing strain to mount the narrow, warped wooden stairs. Not that they went out more than once a day. The weather had been fresh and bright, but it was freezing. The flat was cold, apart from where it was too hot, beside the electric fire attached to the wall, where the only armchair stood.

What was between him and Marina? Had they only dreamed one another? He did not know, even now. All he could do was find out by living through to the end every sigh and shout of their stupid, wonderful, selfish love. Then they would both know if they were able to go on.

He had listened to the sonata twice by the time she came in, naked, holding her stomach. She lowered herself onto the futon to dress. He had yearned for days and months and years for her, and now could not remember if they were speaking or not.

"Don't get cold," he said.

"I've got nothing to wear."

Few of her skirts and trousers fitted now she was pregnant. He himself had left London with two pairs of trousers and three shirts, one of which Marina was usually wearing. It had made him feel like a thief to think of removing his clothes from the flat he had shared with his wife, particularly when she was not there. He had fewer possessions now than he had had as a student, twenty years ago.

He said, "We must buy some clothes."

"How much money do we have left?"

"One of the credit cards is still working. At least it was last night."

"How will we pay it off?"

"I'll get a job."

She snorted. "Really?"

Before they left London she had been turned down for a job because she was pregnant.

He said, "Maybe in an off-licence. Why are you laughing?"

"You—so delicate, so proud—selling beers and crisps."

He said, "It's important to me—not to let you down."

"I've always supported myself," she said.

"You can't now."

"Can't I?"

He said, "Anthony might lend me some money. You haven't forgotten that he's coming this afternoon?"

"We can't keep asking him for money."

"I love you," he said.

She looked at him. "That's good."

The previous evening they had walked to a restaurant near the Jardins du Luxembourg, and had talked of how seriously the Parisians took their food. The waiters were professional waiters, rather than students, and the food was substantial and old-fashioned, intended to be eaten rather than looked at. The older people tucked wide napkins into their fronts and the children sat on cushions on their seats.

"This was my dream, when I was a teenager," Marina had said, "to come to Paris to live and work."

"We're living in Paris now," he had replied. "Sort of."

She said, "I didn't imagine it would be like this. In these conditions."

Her bitter remark made him feel he had trapped her; perhaps she felt the same. As they walked back, in silence, he wondered who she was, the layer upon layer of her. They were peeling and scraping, both hoping to find the person underneath, as if it would reveal the only useful truth. But in the end you had to live with all of someone else.

He and Marina had been to Paris, on an invented business trip, over a year ago, but otherwise they had met only intermittently. These ten days were the longest they had been together. She still kept a room in a house with other young people. Her pregnancy made the women envious and confused, and the boys over-curious as to why she kept the father's name a secret.

When Ian left his wife, he and Marina had spent a few nights together in Anthony's London house. Anthony lived alone; the house was large and painted white, with stripped floorboards, the latest style. It was almost bare, apart from several pale, expensive sofas, and resembled a stage set, ready for the actors to start. But Ian felt like a trespasser and told Anthony he had to get away. Five years before, they had started a film production company together. However, Ian had not been to work for almost three months. He had instructed Anthony to freeze his salary and had walked about the city drunk, talking only to the mad and derelict, people who did not know him. If you made yourself desperately sick you had to live in the present; there was nowhere else. But killing yourself was a difficult and time-consuming job and Anthony had made him stop doing it. Ian did not know whether he could go back to work. He had no idea what he was doing. This was partly why Anthony was coming to Paris, to extract a decision from Ian.

Ian could not forget how generous Anthony had been. It

was at his insistence and expense that Ian and Marina had travelled to Paris and stayed in his apartment.

"Go and see whether you two want to be together," he had said. "Stay there as long as you like. Then let me know."

"Everyone's advised me to give her up and go back to Jane. They keep telling me how nice Jane is. I can't do that, but they think I'm a fool . . ."

"Be a fool and to hell with everyone else," Anthony had said.

As Marina dressed now, Ian knew they were close to a permanent break. They had had their time in Paris and the distance between them was considerable. In the past few days she had talked of returning to London, finding a small flat, getting a job, and bringing up the child alone. Many women did that now; it seemed almost a matter of pride. He would be redundant. It was important for her to feel she could get by without him, he saw that. But if their love, from a certain point of view, seemed like a dangerous addiction, he had to persuade her that they had a chance together, even though, half the time, he did not believe it himself. He did not want to fight; everything was going to hell and that was the fate he had to submit to. But a part of him was not ready to submit. Believing in fate was an attempt to believe you had no will of your own and he did not want that, either.

"I'm hungry," she said.

"We'll eat then."

He helped her to her feet.

She said, "I've been feeling dizzy."

"Tell me at any time if you want to sit down, and a chair will be produced."

"Yes. Thank you."

He held her, leaning forward over her stomach.

She said, "I'm so glad you're here."

"I'll always be here, if you want me."

She regarded herself in the mirror. "I look like a penguin."

"Let's set out across the tundra, then," he said.

"Don't mock me."

"I'm sorry if I've offended you."

"Let's not start," she said.

She was anxious, now her breasts were full, her cheeks red, and her arms, legs and thighs sturdy, that he had loved only her slimness and youth. She felt weary, too, and seemed, in her late twenties, to have passed into another period of her life, without wanting to. All she wanted, most of the time, was to lie down. Veins showed through the pale skin of her legs; every evening she asked him to massage her aching ankles. But her skin was clear; her long hair shone. There was no spare flesh on her. She was taut, pressed to the limit; and healthy.

At the bottom of the stairs she was breathless, but they were both glad to be outside.

He liked walking in Paris: the streets lined with galleries, and the shops full of little objects—a city of people concerned with their senses. It seemed quiet, and stifled by good taste, compared to the vulgar rush, fury and expense of London, which had once again become fashionable. The walls of the London newsagents were lined with magazines and papers, full of the profiles of new artists, playwrights, songwriters, actors, dancers, architects—spitting, cynical, unsettling and argumentative in the new British way. Restaurants opened every day, and the chefs were famous. At midnight in Soho and Covent Garden, you had to push through crowds as if you were at a carnival. It was not something Ian could take an interest in until he had a love, and was settled.

As he walked, Ian saw a smartly dressed, middle-aged man coming towards him, holding the hand of a girl about the same age as his daughter. They were talking and laughing. Ian presumed the girl was late for school, and her father was taking her; there was nothing more important for the man to do. Close, encouraging, generous, available—Ian thought of the father he had wanted to be. He knew children needed to be listened to. But these were ideas he would have to revise; he could not, now, be his own father, in another generation. There would be a distance. He imagined his daughter saying, "Dad walked out. He was never there." He would do his best, but it was not the same; he had failed without wanting to.

Ian turned away and waited for Marina to catch up. Her head was bent, as it often was, and she wore a grey woolly hat, with a bobble. Over her long black dress she had on an ankle-length fur-collared overcoat, and trainers. When she was next to him, he took her arm.

He had become accustomed to her size. For days he seemed to forget they were having a child until, at unexpected moments, the terror of how overwhelming it could be seized him, along with the fact that they couldn't escape one another. At the beginning they had talked of an abortion; but neither of them could have lived with such a crude negation of hope. They loved one another, but could they live together? This was the ordeal of his life. If he was unable to make this work, then not only had he broken up his family for nothing, but he was left with nothing—nothing but himself.

He thought of what she had to take on: him grumbling about how awful everything was, and groaning and yelling in his sleep, as if he were inhabited by ghosts; his fears and doubts; his sudden ecstasies; his foolishness, wisdom, experience and naivety; how much he made her laugh and how infuriated she could become. How much there was of other people! If falling in love could only be a glimpse of the other, who was the passion really directed at? They were living an extended, closer look at one another.

In a café nearby, where they had been going every day, she sat down while he stood at the bar to order breakfast. He spoke English in a low voice, as Marina was annoyed that he would not try to speak French. It was almost twenty-five years since he had studied the language, and the effort and his helplessness were humiliating.

He watched as the Parisians came in, knocked their coffee back, devoured a croissant, and hurried off to work. Marina sat with her hands under her stomach. The baby must have been awake, for he—they knew it was a boy—was kicking in her. At times, so thin and stretched had her stomach become, she felt she would split, as if the boy were trying to kick his way out. There were other anxieties—that the baby would be blind or autistic—as well as new pains, flutterings and pulses in her stomach. These were ordinary fears; he had been through this before with another woman, but did not like to remind her.

"You look even more beautiful today," he said, sitting down. "Your eyes are brighter than for a long time."

"I'm surprised," she said.

"Why?"

"It's been so difficult."

"A little, yes," he said. "But it'll get easier."

"Will it?"

Of course he was ambivalent about having another child. He recalled sitting in the flat with Jane, having returned from the hospital with their daughter. He had taken a week off work and realised then how little time he and Jane had spent together over the past five years. Once, their fears had coincided; that had been love, for a while. He saw that they had had to keep themselves apart, for fear of turning into someone they both disliked. He did not want to use her words; she did not want his opinions inside her. The girl was, and remained, particularly in her rages, the expression or reminder of their incompatibility, of a difference they were unable to bridge. He was looking forward to seeing his daughter without Jane.

"What's bothering you today?" Marina said, when they were drinking their coffee. "You stare into the distance for ages. Then you jerk your head around urgently, like a blackbird. I wonder what sort of worm it is you've spotted. But it's nothing, is it?"

"No. Only . . . I've got to talk to Anthony this afternoon . . . and I haven't decided what to say."

"Or what to do."

"That's right."

She said, "You don't want to go back?"

"I don't know." They buttered their croissants in silence. "Things are certainly starting to seem a little aimless here." He said, "Anthony's changed."

"In what way?"

"You don't want me to go on about it, do you?"

She said, "But I love our talks. I love the sound of your voice . . . even if I don't listen to every word."

He told her they had run the company for themselves, for fun. They had never wanted to work excessive hours, or accept projects for the money alone. In the past five years they had made three feature films, one of which had been critically successful and made its money back. They had also produced a number of television documentaries. But recently, without discussing it fully with Ian, Anthony had taken on an expensive American comedy project, to be shot in London, with a petulant and talentless director.

Anthony had made new friends in film and TV. He flew to Manchester United's home matches and sat in the directors' box. He went to New Labour dinners and, Ian presumed, donated money to the Party. He boasted of a new friend who had a trout stream at the end of his garden, though Ian doubted whether Anthony would recognise a trout unless it was served to him on a plate.

In the past twenty years Ian had come to know most of the people in his profession. He was a natural son-type, who liked to listen and admire; he collected mentors. Most of these friends, the majority of whom were from ordinary backgrounds, now lived in ostentatious luxury, like the great industrialists of the nineteenth century. They were the editors of newspapers, film directors, chairmen of publishing houses, heads of TV companies, senior journalists and professors. In their spare time, of which they seemed to have a lot, they became the chairmen of various theatre, film and arts boards. The early fifties in men was a period of frivolity, self-expansion and self-indulgence.

If Ian was perplexed, it was because that generation, ten years ahead of him, had been a cussed, liberated, dissenting lot. Somehow Thatcher had helped them to power. Following her, they had moved to the right and ended up in the centre. Their left politics had ended up as social tolerance and lack of deference. Otherwise, they smoked cigars and were driven to their country houses on Friday afternoons; sitting with friends overlooking their land, while local women worked in the kitchen, they fretted about their knighthoods. They were as thrilled as teenagers when they saw themselves in the newspapers. They wanted to be prefects.

"They've lost their intellectual daring," Ian said.

"There's a bit of you that sees all that as the future," Marina said.

"I'm aware that one has to find new things," he said. "But I don't know what they should be."

He looked at her. He felt ready to bring up the subject of his wife.

"We'll have to go back to London eventually," he said. "Quite soon, probably, and . . . face everything. I want to do that and I don't want to do it."

"Where will we go?" she said. "I've got nothing, your money is in your wife's house, and you haven't got a job."

"Well—"

He believed she trusted him and imagined he might know, despite everything, what he was doing. Looking at her sweet face now, and her long fingers tearing at a croissant, he contemplated her inner dignity. If he thought she was regal, it was not because she was imperious, but because she was still. She never fidgeted; there was nothing unnecessary in anything she did.

They had stopped talking of the future and what they might do to make a life together, as if they had turned into children and wanted to be told. They drifted about Paris, according to some implicit routine, looking at their guidebooks, visiting galleries, museums and parks, going to restaurants in the evening.

If he were to love her, he had to be transformed from a man who could not do this with Jane, to a man who could do it with Marina. And the transformation had to be rapid, before he lost her. If he could not get along with this woman, he couldn't get along with any of them and he was done for.

"Shall we go?" she said.

He helped her into her coat. They crossed the Seine on the wooden bridge with the benches, where they sat facing the Pont Neuf, enjoying the view. He thought, then, that this was a better moment to start to talk about his wife; but he took Marina's arm, and they moved on.

They knew the eager queue outside the Musée d'Orsay would not take long to go down. He was amazed by the thirst of the crowds, to look at good things.

Inside, Marina was walking somewhere when, adjacent to Rodin's "Gates of Hell," Ian found himself standing beside the tower of white stone that was "Balzac." Ian had seen it many times since he was a teenager, but on this occasion it made him suddenly laugh. Surely, Balzac had been a flabby and dishevelled figure, obsessed by money rather than the immortality that Rodin had him gazing towards? As far as Ian could remember, Balzac had hurried through life and received little satisfaction; his ambition had been a little ridiculous—or perhaps, narrow and unreflective. Yet this was a man: someone who had taken action, converting experience into something powerful and sensual.

Rodin had certainly made Balzac a forceful figure. Ian was reminded of how afraid his own timid mother had been of his noise and energy; she was forever telling him to "calm down." His being alive at all seemed to alarm her. With Marina, too, Ian had been afraid of his own furies, of his power, and of the damage he believed that being a man might do, and how it might make her withdraw her love. What evil had marauding men caused in the twentieth century! Hadn't he damaged his wife? And yet, looking at Rodin's idea of Balzac now, he thought: rather a beast than a castrated angel. If the tragedy of the twentieth century had been fascism and communism, the triumph was that both had been defeated. Without guilt we lose our humanity, but if there is too much of it, nothing can be redeemed!

Leaving the Musée d'Orsay he realised how quickly he was walking, and how revived and stimulated he was. Rodin and Balzac had done him good.

As they entered a restaurant, Marina pointed out that the place looked expensive, but he hurried her in, saying, "Let's just eat—and drink!"

She looked at him questioningly, but he wanted to talk, keeping the Rodin in mind like a talisman, or a reminder of some suppressed childhood ecstasy. He could push against the world, and it would survive. He had probably read too much Beckett as a young man. He would have been better off with Joyce.

"I know you don't want to hear about this," he said, "but my wife . . ."

"Yes? What is it?"

He had alarmed her already.

"She is in hospital. She took pills and alcohol . . . and passed out. I believe she did it after I told her about the baby. Our baby. You know."

"Is she dead?"

"Perhaps that would seem like a relief. But no. No." He went on, "It's a terrible thing to do, to others, to our daughter in particular. I was surprised by it, as Jane never seemed to like me. She must be deranged at the moment. She will have to realise that she can't cling to me for ever. I don't want to go on about it. I wanted you to know, that's all."

For a time she was silent.

"I feel sorry for her," she said. She started to weep. "To have lost a love that you thought would continue for ever, and to have to recover from that. How terrible, terrible, terrible!"

"Yes, well—"

She said, "How do I know you won't do the same to me?"

"Sorry?"

"How do I know you won't leave me, as you left her?"

"As if I make a habit of . . . that sort of thing?"

"You've done it once. Perhaps more. How do I know?"

Outrage stopped his mouth. If he spoke he would say terrible things, and they would not understand one another. But he had to keep speaking to her.

She went on, "I fear, constantly, that you will tire of me and go back to her."

"I'll never do that, never. Why should I?"

"You know one another."

He said, "After a certain age everything happens under the sign of eternity, which is probably the best way to do things. I haven't got time now, for vacillation."

"But you are feeble," she said. "You don't fight for yourself. You let people push you around."

"Who?"

"Me. Anthony. Your wife. You were always afraid of her."

"That is true," he said. "I cannot stop wanting to rely on the kindness of others."

"You can't survive on only that." She was not looking at him. "Your weakness confuses people."

"I'm not a fantasy, but a wretched human with weaknesses—and some strengths—like everyone else. But I want to be with you. That I am certain of." He paid the bill. "I need to go for a walk," he said. "I want to think about what I'm going to say to Anthony. I'll see you at the apartment later."

She took his hand. "It would be a shame if your intelligence and wit . . . if your ideas went to waste. Now kiss me."

He went out, leaving her with her notebook. He walked about aimlessly in the cold. Soon he was in the café where he was to meet Anthony, an hour before he was due, drinking beer and coffee.

He thought that Anthony would understand the difficulties one might have with a woman. But as a business partner, Ian was not certain that Anthony would be patient. Ian had behaved recklessly; madly even. Anthony had less use for him now. If Ian had jettisoned his own wife, Anthony might do the same to him.

From inside the café Ian saw Anthony's chauffeur-driven Mercedes. After sending the car away, Anthony checked his hair and brushed himself down. He had a young woman with him, to whom he was giving instructions. She would be his new assistant. Leaving her walking up and down the pavement making calls, Anthony came in.

He was wearing a well-cut dark suit; his hair had been dyed. Anthony was tall and skinny; he drank little. Apart from confusion and an inability to get along with women, he had few vices. Ian had attempted to introduce him to a few. After Anthony's first Ecstasy pill (provided by Ian, who got them from his postman) they took drugs—mostly Ecstasy, along with cocaine, to keep them up; and cannabis, to bring them down—for a year, which was how long it took them to realise that they couldn't resurrect the pleasure they'd had on the first night. Ian now took only tranquillisers.

"Where is she?" Anthony asked, looking about. "How does she look?"

"She's at the apartment. She looks splendid. Only . . . I told her about Jane."

Anthony sat down and ordered an omelette. "A bloody blackmailing nuisance," he murmured.

Ian said, "It was making me mad, the fear of telling her. Can you tell me how Jane is?"

He had asked Anthony to look into it. Anthony would know how to find out.

Anthony said, "There's nothing physically wrong with her. Of course, she's distressed and depressed, but she will survive that. She's coming out of hospital today."

"Do you think I should go and see her?"

"I don't know."

Ian said, "Consciousness is proving a little tenacious at the moment. Where are my tranquillisers?"

"I told the quack they were for me. He wouldn't give me any. Said I'm tranquil enough."

"So you didn't bring any?"

"No."

"Oh, Anthony."

Anthony opened his briefcase and took out a gadget, a little computer, clearing a space for it on the table. "Listen—" He was busy. Ian's recent slow pace wasn't Anthony's. "I need your advice about a director I—we—might use. I think you know him."

While Ian gave his opinion Anthony typed, rather inaccurately, it seemed to Ian; Anthony's fingers seemed too fat for the keys. It was a machine Ian knew he would never understand, just as his mother had decided it was too late to bother with videos and computers. Still, Ian wondered whether he was really the fool he liked to take himself for. His ideas weren't so bad.

He and Anthony switched subjects quickly, as Ian liked to, to football. Ian hadn't been getting the English papers; he wanted the results. Anthony said he'd been to Stamford Bridge to watch Manchester United play Chelsea.

"I'm assuming you want to make me jealous, " Ian said.

"Why don't you come next time?"

"It's true, I miss London."

When he could not sleep, Ian liked to imagine he was being driven in a taxi through London. The route took him through the West End and Trafalgar Square, down the Mall, past Buckingham Palace—with Green Park, lit like a grotto, on the right; through the perils of Hyde Park Corner, then past the Minema (showing an obscure Spanish film), and the windows of Harvey Nichols. If you did not know it, what a liberal and individual place you would think London was! He was becoming tired of the deprivations of this little exile.

He started to wonder whether Marina was asleep, or walking in Paris. It occurred to him that she might have left and gone back to London. He wondered if this was a wish on his part, to end his anxiety at last. But he knew it was not what he wanted. He felt like rushing to the apartment to reassure her.

Ian asked, "How's the American project?"

"Shooting in the summer."

"Really?"

"Of course. It wasn't difficult getting the money, as I told you."

He felt patronised by Anthony, but he was at ease with him too.

Ian said, "I don't know why you didn't make those films I liked."

"You were breaking up. Then you weren't around. Why don't you do them now? There's money for development."

"Marina and I haven't got anywhere to live."

Anthony waved out of the window at his assistant, still walking up and down.

"She'll find you a flat. If you come back to London I'll put you in a hotel from tomorrow and there'll be an apartment from Monday. Right?" Ian said nothing. Anthony said, "You did the right thing by leaving—leaving Jane, and then leaving London."

"Jane kept saying I didn't try hard enough. It's certainly true that I was . . . preoccupied elsewhere, some of the time. But I was with her for six years."

"Long enough, surely, to know whether you want to be with someone. You've done it. It's over. You're free," Anthony said.

Ian liked the way Anthony made it seem straightforward.

"I'm full of regret," Ian said, "for how unhappy I've been so much of the time."

Anthony sighed. "You can't hold on to that unhappiness for ever."

Ian said, "No. I've come to believe in romantic love, too. I feel a fool having fallen for the idea. What's wrong with subli-mation? Rather a Rembrandt than a wank, don't you think?"

"Why not sublimation as well as copulation?" said Anthony. "Look at Picasso." He leaned across the table. "How is it with Marina?"

"It's the ordeal of my life. Cold turkey, psychosis and death—all at once. I've been trying to understand something about myself . . . and what I might be able to do. I'm clearer now. I don't want to give up."

"Why should you? You only have to look at her to see how passionate she is about you. It's funny how blind one can be to such obvious things. Ian, there's a lot happening in the company. I'd like it if you came back. Soon. Monday, say." Anthony was looking at him. "What do you think?"

"You really need to know?"

"Yes."

Ian realised he hadn't talked to Marina about it. Only rarely did he ask her advice. He was used to doing everything alone. If he could solicit her help, if he could learn to turn to her, maybe she would feel more involved. Perhaps love was an exchange of problems.

"I'll ask Marina's advice."

"Good," Anthony said.

Ian wanted to carry on talking but Anthony was late for a meeting. After, he would meet his lover. Ian stood up to go.

"The thing is, I'm a bit short of money at the moment."

"Of course."

Anthony opened his cheque book and wrote a cheque. Then he gave Ian some cash. Outside, Ian was introduced to

Anthony's assistant. He wondered how much she knew of him. Anthony said Ian was returning to work on Monday. When Anthony and the young woman got into the car, Ian waved from the pavement.

As he walked back, Ian thought that he wanted to be at home, in a house he liked, with a woman and children he liked. He wanted to lose himself in the mundane, in unimportant things. Perhaps those things were graspable now. Once he had them, he could think of others, and be useful.

He pushed the key into the lock, got into the building and ran up the stairs. He rang the bell repeatedly. It was cold but he was sweating. He rang again. Then he fiddled with the keys. At last he unlocked the door and went up the hallway. The room was dark. He put the light on. She was lying on the bed. She sat up.

THE UMBRELLA

———

THE MINUTE THEY ARRIVED at the adventure playground, Roger's two sons charged up a long ramp and were soon clinging to the steel netting that hung from a high beam. Satisfied that it would take them some time to extricate themselves, Roger sat on a bench and turned to the sports section of his newspaper. He had always found it relaxing to read reports of football matches he had not seen.

Then it started to rain.

His sons, aged four and five and a half, had refused to put on their coats when he picked them up from the au pair half an hour before. Coats made them look "fat," they claimed, and Roger had had to carry them under his arm.

The older boy was dressed in a thin, tight-fitting green outfit and a cardboard cap with a feather in it: he was either Robin Hood or Peter Pan. The younger wore a plastic holster with two silver guns, a plastic dagger and a sword, blue wellington boots, jeans with the fly open, and a chequered neckerchief which he pulled over his mouth. "Cowboys don't wear raincoats," he said, through a mouthful of cloth.

The boys frequently refused Roger's commands, though he could not say that their stubbornness and pluck annoyed him. It did, however, cause him trouble with his wife, from whom he had separated a year previously. Only that morning she had said on the phone, "You are a weak and inadequate disciplinarian. You only want their favour."

For as long as he could, Roger pretended it was not raining, but when his newspaper began to go soggy and everyone else had left the playground, he called the boys over.

"Damn this rain," he said, as he hustled them into their hooded yellow raincoats.

"Don't swear," said Eddie, the younger boy. "Women think it's naughty."

"Sorry." Roger laughed. "I was thinking I should have got a raincoat as well as the suit."

"You do need a lovely raincoat, Daddy," said Oliver, the oldest.

"My friend would have given me a raincoat, but I liked the suit more."

He had picked up the chocolate-coloured suit from the shop that morning. Since the early seventies, that most extravagant of periods, Roger had fancied himself as a restrained but amateur dandy. One of his best friends was a clothes designer with shops in Europe and Japan. A few years ago this friend, amused by Roger's interest in his business, had invited Roger, during a fashion show at the British

Embassy in Paris, to parade on the catwalk in front of the fashion press, alongside younger and taller men. Roger's friend had given him the chocolate suit for his fortieth birthday, and had insisted he wear it with a blue silk shirt. Roger's sons liked to sleep in their newly acquired clothes, and he understood their enthusiasm. He would not normally wear a suit for the park, but that evening he was going to a publishing party, and then on to his third date with a woman he had been introduced to at a friend's house; a woman he liked.

Roger took the boys' hands and pulled them along.

"We'd better go to the teahouse," he said. "I hope I don't ruin my shoes."

"They're beautiful," said Oliver.

Eddie stopped to bend down and rub his father's loafers. "I'll put my hands over your shoes while you walk," he said.

"That might slow us down a little," Roger said. "Run for it, mates!"

He picked Eddie up, holding him flat in his arms like a baby, with his muddy boots pointing outwards. The three of them hurried across the darkening park.

The teahouse was a wide, low-ceilinged shed, warm, brightly lit and decorated in the black and white colours and flags of Newcastle United. The coffee was good and they had all the newspapers. The place was crowded but Roger spotted a table and sent Oliver over to sit at it.

Roger recognised the mother of a boy in Eddie's nursery, as well as several nannies and au pairs, who seemed to congregate in some part of this park on most days. Three or four of them had come to his house with their charges, when he lived with his wife. If they seemed reticent with him, he doubted whether this was because they were young and simple, but rather that they saw him as an employer, as the boss.

He was aware that he was the only man in the teahouse. The men he ran into with children were either younger than him, or older, on their second families. He wished his children were older, and understood more; he should have had them earlier. He'd both enjoyed and wasted the years before they were born; it had been a long, dissatisfied ease.

A girl in the queue turned to him.

"Thinking again?" she said.

He recognised her voice but had not brought his glasses.

"Hello," he said at last. He called to Eddie, "Hey, it's Lindy." Eddie covered his face with both hands. "You remember her giving you a bath and washing your hair."

"Hey, cowboy," she said.

Lindy had looked after both children when Eddie was born and lived in the house until precipitately deciding to leave. She had told them she wanted to do something else but, instead, had gone to work for a couple nearby.

The last time Roger had run into Lindy, he had overheard her imitating his sons' accents and laughing. They were "posh." He had been shocked by how early these notions of "class" started.

"Haven't seen you for a while," she said.

"I've been travelling."

"Where to?"

"Belfast, Cape Town, Sarajevo."

"Lovely," she said.

"I'm off to the States next week," he said.

"Doing what?"

"Lecturing on human rights. On the development of the notion of the individual . . . of the idea of the separate self." He wanted to say something about Shakespeare and Montaigne, as he had been thinking about them, but realised she would refuse to be curious about the subject. "And on the idea of human rights in the post-war period. All of that kind of thing. I hope there's going to be a TV series."

She said, "I came back from the pub and turned on the TV last week, and there you were, criticising some clever book or other. I didn't understand it."

"Right."

He had always been polite to her, even when he had been unable to wake her up because she had been drinking the previous night. She had seen him unshaven, and in his pyjamas at four in the morning; she had opened doors and found him and his wife abusing one another behind them; she had been at their rented villa in Assisi when his wife tore the cloth from the table with four bowls of pasta on it. She must have heard energetic reconciliations.

"I hope it goes well," she said.

"Thank you."

The boys ordered big doughnuts and juice. The juice spilled over the table and the doughnuts were smeared round their mouths. Roger had to hold his cappuccino out in front of him to stop the boys sticking their grimy fingers in the froth and sucking the chocolate from them. To his relief they joined Lindy's child.

Roger began a conversation with a woman at the next table who had complimented him on his sons. She told him she wanted to write a newspaper article on how difficult some people found it to say "No" to children. You could not charm them, she maintained, as you could people at a cocktail party; they had to know what the limits were. He did not like the idea that she had turned disciplining her child into a manifesto, but he would ask for her phone number before he left. For more than a year he had not gone out socially, fearing that people would see his anguish.

He was extracting his notebook and pen when Lindy called him. He turned round. His sons were at the far end of the teahouse, rolling on top of another, larger, boy, who was wailing, "He's biting me!"

Eddie did bite; he kicked too.

"Boys!" Roger called.

He hurried them into their coats again, whispering furiously for them to shut up. He said goodbye to the woman without getting her phone number. He did not want to appear lecherous.

He had always been proud of the idea that he was a good man who treated people fairly. He did not want to impose himself. The world would be a better place if people considered their actions. Perhaps he had put himself on a pedestal. "You have a high reputation—with yourself!" a friend had said. Everyone was entitled to some pride and vanity. However, this whole business with his wife had stripped him of his moral certainties. There was no just or objective way to resolve competing claims: those of freedom—his freedom—

to live and develop as he liked, against the right of his family to have his dependable presence. But no amount of conscience or morality would make him go back. He had not missed his wife for a moment.

As they were leaving the park, Eddie tore some daffodils from a flowerbed and stuffed them in his pocket. "For Mummy," he explained.

The house was a ten-minute walk away. Holding hands, they ran home through the rain. His wife would be back soon, and he would be off.

It was not until he had taken out his key that he remembered his wife had changed the lock last week. What she had done was illegal: he owned the house; but he had laughed at the idea she thought he would intrude, when he wanted to be as far away as possible.

He told the boys they would have to wait. They sheltered in the little porch where water dripped on their heads. The boys soon tired of standing with him and refused to sing the songs he started. They pulled their hoods down and chased one another up and down the path.

It was dark. People were coming home from work.

The next-door neighbour passed by. "Locked out?" he said.

"'Fraid so."

Oliver said, "Daddy, why can't we go in and watch the cartoons?"

"It's only me she's locked out," he said. "Not you. But you are, of course, with me."

"Why has she locked us out?"

"Why don't you ask her?" he said.

His wife confused and frightened him. But he would greet her civilly, send the children into the house and say goodbye. It was, however, difficult to get cabs in the area; impossible at this time and in this weather. It was a twenty-minute walk to the tube station, across a dripping park where alcoholics and junkies gathered under the trees. His shoes, already wet, would be filthy. At the party he would have to try and remove the worst of the mud in the toilet.

After the violence of separation he had expected a diminishment of interest and of loathing, on her part. He himself had survived the worst of it and anticipated a quietness. Kind indifference had come to seem an important blessing. But as well as refusing to divorce him, she sent him lawyers' letters about the most trivial matters. One letter, he recalled, was entirely about a cheese sandwich he had made for himself when visiting the children. He was ordered to bring his own food in future. He thought of his wife years ago, laughing and putting out her tongue with his semen on it.

"Hey there," she said, coming up the path.

"Mummy!" they called.

"Look at them," he said. "They're soaked through."

"Oh dear."

She unlocked the door and the children ran into the hall. She nodded at him. "You're going out."

"Sorry?"

"You've got a suit on."

He stepped into the hall. "Yes. A little party."

He glanced into his former study, where his books were

packed in boxes on the floor. He had, as yet, nowhere to take them. Beside them were a pair of men's black shoes he had not seen before.

She said to the children, "I'll get your tea." To him she said, "You haven't given them anything to eat, have you?"

"Doughnuts," said Eddie. "I had chocolate."

"I had jam," said Oliver.

She said, "You let them eat that rubbish?"

Eddie pushed the crushed flowers at her. "There you are, Mummy."

"You must not take flowers from the park," she said. "They are for everyone."

"Fuck, fuck, fuck," said Eddie suddenly, with his hand over his mouth.

"Shut up! People don't like it!" said Oliver, and hit Eddie, who started to cry.

"Listen to him," she said to Roger. "You've taught them to use filthy language. You are really hopeless."

"So are you," he said.

In the past few months, preparing his lectures, he had visited some disorderly and murderous places. The hatred he witnessed puzzled him still. It was atavistic but abstract; mostly the people did not know one another. It had made him aware of how people clung to their antipathies, and used them to maintain an important distance, but in the end he failed to understand why this was. After all the political analysis and talk of rights, he had concluded that people had to grasp the necessity of loving one another; and if that was too much, they had to let one another alone. When this still seemed inadequate and banal, he suspected he was on the wrong path, that he was trying to say something about his own difficulties in the guise of intellectual discourse. Why could he not find a more direct method? He had, in fact, considered writing a novel. He had plenty to say, but could not afford the time, unpaid.

He looked out at the street. "It's raining quite hard."

"It's not too bad now."

He said, "You haven't got an umbrella, have you?"

"An umbrella?"

He was becoming impatient. "Yes. An umbrella. You know, you hold it over your head."

She sighed and went back into the house. He presumed she was opening the door to the airing cupboard in the bathroom.

He was standing in the porch, ready to go. She returned empty-handed.

"No. No umbrella," she said.

He said, "There were three there last week."

"Maybe there were."

"Are there not still three umbrellas there?"

"Maybe there are," she said.

"Give me one."

"No."

"Sorry?"

"I'm not giving you one," she said. "If there were a thousand umbrellas there I would not give you one."

He had noticed how persistent his children were; they asked, pleaded, threatened and screamed, until he yielded.

He said, "They are my umbrellas."

"No," she repeated.

"How petty you've become."

"Didn't I give you everything?"

He cleared his throat. "Everything but love."

"I did give you that, actually." She said, "I've rung my friend. He's on his way."

He said, "I don't care. Just give me an umbrella."

She shook her head. She went to shut the door. He put his foot out and she banged the door against his leg. He wanted to rub his shin but could not give her the pleasure.

He said, "Let's try and be rational."

He had hated before, his parents and brother, at certain times. But it was a fury, not a deep, intellectual and emotional hatred like this. He had had psychotherapy; he took tranquillisers, but still he wanted to pulverise his wife. None of the ideas he had about life would make this feeling go away.

"You used to find the rain 'refreshing,'" she sneered.

"It has come to this," he said.

"Here we are then," she said. "Don't start crying about it."

He pushed the door. "I'll get the umbrella."

She pushed the door back at him. "You cannot come in."

"It is my house."

"Not without prior arrangement."

"We arranged it," he said.

"The arrangement's off."

He pushed her.

"Are you assaulting me?" she said.

He looked outside. An alcoholic woman he had had to

remove from the front step on several occasions was standing at the end of the path holding a can of lager.

"I'm watching you," she shouted. "If you touch her you are reported!"

"Watch on!" he shouted back.

He pushed into the house. He placed his hand on his wife's chest and forced her against the wall. She cried out. She did bang her head, but it was, in football jargon, a "dive." The children ran at his legs. He pushed them away.

He went to the airing cupboard, seized an umbrella and made his way to the front door.

As he passed her she snatched it. Her strength surprised him, but he yanked the umbrella back and went to move away. She raised her hand. He thought she would slap him. It would be the first time. But she made a fist. As she punched him in the face she continued to look at him.

He had not been hit since he left school. He had forgotten the physical shock and then the disbelief, the shattering of the feeling that the world was a safe place.

The boys were screaming. Roger had dropped the umbrella. His mouth throbbed; his lip was bleeding. He must have staggered and lost his balance for she was able to push him outside.

He heard the door slam behind him. He could hear the children crying. He walked away, past the alcoholic woman still standing at the end of the path. He turned to look at the lighted house. When they had calmed down, the children would have their bath and get ready for bed. They liked being read to. It was a part of the day he had always enjoyed.

He turned his collar up but knew he would get soaked. He wiped his mouth with his hand. She had landed him quite a hit. He would not be able to find out until later whether it would show. If it did, it would cause interest and amusement at the party, but not to him; not with a date to go to.

He stood in a doorway watching the people hurry past. His trouser legs stuck to his skin. It would not stop raining for a long time. He could not just stand in the same place for hours. The thing to do was not to mind. He started out then, across the Green, in the dark, wet through, but moving forward.

MORNING IN THE
BOWL OF NIGHT

IT HAD BEEN SNOWING.

He got to the house, looked at his watch, saw he was late, and hurried on to a pub he knew at the end of the street. He pushed the door and a barking Alsatian on a chain leapt at him. Young children, one of them badly bruised, chased one another across the slush-wet floor, tripping over the adults' feet. The jukebox was loud, as were the TV and the drinkers' voices. He hadn't been in here for months yet he recognised the same people.

He was backing out when the barman shouted, "Hey, my man Alan. Alan, where you been?" and started to pull him a pint.

Alan took a seat at the bar, lit a cigarette and drank off half his glass. If he finished quickly he might get another pint in him. It would mean he had no money but why would he need money tonight? The last time he had attended a school nativity play and carol service he had been fourteen, and his best friend's father had turned up so soaked in alcohol that he didn't realise his tie had been dunked in red wine and was still dripping. The boys pointed and laughed at him, and his son had been ashamed.

Alan nodded at the barman who placed the second pint beside the first. Alan's son was too young for shame; in fact, Mikey was starting to worship his father.

Alan needed to calm himself. Melanie, his present girl-friend, with whom he'd lived for a year, had pursued him down the street as he'd left the flat, pulling on his hand and begging him not to go. He told her repeatedly that he had promised his son that he would attend the nativity play. "All the daddies will be there," Mikey had said.

"And so will this daddy," Alan had said.

After much shouting, Alan left Melanie standing in the snow. God knows what state she'd be in when he returned home, if she were there at all. Alan worked in the theatre, though not as an actor. Yet today he felt she had cast him as a criminal, a role he wasn't prepared to play.

Alan finished both drinks and got up to go. It would be the first time he, his wife and their son had been out together as a family since he had left, eighteen months ago.

Perhaps it was his fear that had communicated itself to Melanie. He wasn't sure, however, that fear was the right word. On the way over he had been trying to identify the feeling. It wasn't even dread. The solution came to him now as he approached the house. It was grief; a packed, undigested lump of grief in his chest.

The boy was standing on a chair by the window. Seeing his father he jumped up and down, shouting, "Daddy, Daddy, Daddy!" banging on the smudged glass.

It had been a week since Alan had seen Mikey, and he was used to looking for the alteration in him. Yet how peculiar he still found it to visit his own son as if he were dropping by for tea with a relation. What he liked most was taking Mikey out to cafés. Occasionally the boy would slip off his stool and run about to demonstrate how high he could jump, but mostly they sat and made conversation like friends, Mikey asking the most demanding questions.

"You're late," Anne said at the door. "You've been drinking."

She was shaking, and her eyes were fixed and wide. He was familiar with these brief possessions, the sudden fits of rage she had throughout the day, usually when she had to ask for something.

Alan slipped past her. "Pretty Christmas tree," he said.

He crouched down and Mikey ran into his arms. He was wearing tartan trousers and a knitted sweater. He handed Alan a maroon woolly hat. Anne went to get her coat. Alan pulled the hat down over Mikey's face, and then, as the kid struggled and shouted, picked him up and buried his face in his stomach.

Alan had never liked the street, the area or the house. It had some kind of guilty hold over him. When he visited he felt he should go upstairs, get into bed, close his eyes and resume his old life, as if it were his duty and destiny. Anne still blamed him for leaving, though Alan couldn't understand why she didn't see that it had been best for both of them.

"Kiss," said Mikey when Anne joined them. "Kiss together."

"Sorry?"

"Kiss Mummy."

Alan looked at his wife.

She had lost weight, her face coming to a point at her chin for the first time in years. She had been dieting; starving herself, it looked like. Her face was covered in white make-up or powder. Her lips were red. He had never let her wear lipstick, not liking it on his face. She dressed better now, presumably on his money. She hadn't been sleeping at the house often, he knew that. Her mother had been staying there with Mikey, not knowing—or not saying—when she would be back.

He and Anne managed to press their lips together for a moment. Her perfume touched off an electric flash of uncontrollable memories, and he shuddered. He tried to think of the last time they had touched one another. It must have been a couple of months before he left. He remembered thinking then, this will be the last time.

It was dark when they went out. Mikey held their hands as they swung him between them. To Alan's relief he chattered away.

Outside the school the parents, dressed up, were getting out of their cars and passing through the gates in the snow. Alan noticed with surprise how happy the children were and how easily their laughter came, whereas the parents exchanged only the necessary courtesies. Was he a particularly gloomy person? His girlfriend said he was. "If I am, you have made me so," was his reply. He did feel gloomy, certainly. Perhaps it was his age.

Inside it was warm and bright, and even the teachers smiled. Alan chuckled to himself, imagining what other people might think, seeing him with Anne. How unusual it was, these days, to see a husband and wife together. He exchanged a few amiable words with her, for the public show.

The nativity was performed by the eight- and nine-year-olds, with younger children playing shepherds as well as trees and stars. A painted sky suspended between shortened broom handles was held up by two tiny children. The angels had cardboard wings and costumes made from net curtains. Next year Mikey would be old enough to take part.

A few weeks ago the teacher had asked Alan for suggestions as to how the nativity should be done. Alan was the administrator of a small touring theatre group. He loved the emotional intimacy that actors created between them; and he still liked the excitement of the "show," the live connection between his colleagues on stage and those who had left their homes for the honest spectacle. There was some sort of important fear that united them all, which made the theatre different from the cinema. His work was badly paid, of course. Some of the actors he worked with appeared on television; the director was married to a rich woman. Alan, though, had no other income. His girlfriend Melanie was an actress. She was pregnant and soon wouldn't be able to work for a while.

When the nativity started Alan checked his pocket. He had taken a handkerchief out with him, a proper cloth handkerchief given to him, inexplicably, by Anne, years ago. He had not gone out with a pocket handkerchief since his last day at school. But all afternoon he had been afraid the children's voices would make him break down. To cheer himself up he had thought of his father, in church at Christmas—the only time he went—singing as loud as he could, not caring that he was out of tune. They were celebrating, Father said, not making a record for Deutsche Grammophon.

The parents cried and laughed through the nativity, and the younger children, like Alan's son, shouted out joyfully.

Alan compared himself to the people he knew there. At the door he had been greeted by a man who had said, "I could do with a drink, too, but I'm not allowed."

Until the man reminded him that he had fixed Alan's car a couple of times, Alan couldn't think who he was, for he was thin and decrepit, with a shaven head.

"But at least you look well, you look well," the man said, as Alan moved away uncomfortably, only at this stage becoming aware of how ill the man must be.

There was a woman sitting in the adjacent row. Alan had been told by an acquaintance earlier in the year that she had thrown herself naked from a window, smashing her face and breaking her ribs, before being taken to hospital in a straitjacket. Another woman, sitting further along the row, had ignored him, or perhaps she hadn't seen him. But she had walked often with him in the park, as their children played. She had told him she was leaving her husband.

It had been a murderous century, yet here, in this comfortable corner of the earth, by some fluke, most of them had been spared. For that he sang, wondering, all the same, why they were so joyless.

Melanie hadn't been pregnant long, but her body had started to change. She was losing her girlishness. Apart from her thick waist, she felt heavy and claimed she was already forced to walk with a "waddle." She wasn't working at the moment, so it didn't matter that she had to go back to bed in the morning. When they weren't fighting he would sit with her, eating his breakfast.

She had an appointment the next day, for an abortion. He would pick her up the day after. A long time ago he had been involved in two other abortions. The first he had avoided by going away to stay with another woman. Of the second, he remembered only how the woman lay on the floor and wept afterwards. He recalled sitting across the room from her with his eyes closed, counting back from a thousand. The relationships had broken immediately after. His life with Melanie would end, too. It would seem pointless to go on. Why was it important that relationships went on? By tomorrow night his hope would be destroyed. He couldn't go from woman to woman any more.

Their arguments were bitter and their reconciliations no longer sweet. He had locked her out of the flat. She had thrown away a picture his wife had given him. Alan had flung some of her belongings into the street. For weeks they had pounded one another, emerging into the world as if they'd walked out of a fire, their skin blackened, eyes staring, not knowing what had happened. Would they be together for good or only until tomorrow?

Looking sideways at his wife now, over the head of the boy who connected them for ever, Alan knew he couldn't make such a mistake again.

In their better moods, he and Melanie talked to the child in her belly and considered names for her. They had talked of having a child in a few years. But a child wasn't a fridge that you could order when you wanted, or when you could afford it. The child in her belly already had a face.

Outside the school, as the three of them walked away, Alan spotted an abandoned supermarket trolley. Instantly he picked Mikey up, dumped him in it and ran with it along the side of the road. The yells of the delighted boy, crouching in the clattering tray as they skidded around corners and over speed bumps, and Anne's cries as she ran behind, trying to keep up, pierced the early evening dark.

Laughing, breathless and warm, they soon arrived at the house. Anne closed the shutters and switched on the Christmas tree lights. The room had changed since he'd last been there. It contained only her things. There was nothing of him left in it.

She poured Alan a glass of brandy. Mikey gulped down his juice. Anne said he could pick a bar of chocolate from the tree if he shared it with them. As they discussed the nativity Alan noticed that his son seemed wary and uncertain, as if he weren't sure which parent he should go to, sensing he couldn't favour one without displeasing the other.

At last Alan got up to leave.

"Oh, I forgot," Anne said. "I bought some mince pies and brandy butter. I don't know why I bothered, but I did. You still like them, don't you? I'll put them on one plate for you and Mikey to share. Is that okay?"

She went to heat them up. Alan had told Melanie he wouldn't be long. He had to go to her. What a terrifying machine the imagination could be. If it was terrible between them tonight, they might do something irreversible tomorrow. He was afraid her mind might become set.

"You look as if you're in a hurry," Anne said, when she returned.

He said, "I'll finish my drink and have one of these pies, and then I'll be off."

"Will you be coming on Christmas Day?"

He shook his head.

She said, "Not even for an hour? She can't bear to be parted from you, eh?"

"You know how it is."

She looked at him angrily. "How is it that you can't spend time with your own son?"

He couldn't say that Melanie wanted him to be with her on Christmas Day, otherwise she would go away.

Mikey had gone quiet, and was watching them.

She said, "It has lasted a long time, with this woman. For you."

"It's going well, yes. We're having a baby, too."

"I see," she said, after a while.

"I'm quite pleased," he said.

Melanie had told a number of her friends that she was pregnant; she discussed it constantly on the phone. Anne was the first person he had told.

"You could have waited."

"For what?" He said, "Sorry, I couldn't wait. You know how it is."

"Why do you keep saying that?"

"It's a fact. There you are. Live with it."

She said, "I will, thank you." Then she said, "You won't be wanting to see Mikey so much, then."

"Yes I will."

"Why should you?"

He said, "Why shouldn't I?"

"You left us. I only have him. She has everything."

"Who?"

"Your girlfriend."

"Listen," he said. "I'll see you later."

He got up and went out into the hall.

At the door the boy held on to the bottom of Alan's coat. "Stay here for ever and ever amen."

Alan kissed him. "I'll be back soon."

"Sleep in Mummy's bed," said Mikey.

"You can do that for me."

Mikey pressed a piece of chocolate into his hand. "In case you get hungry when I'm asleep." Then he said, "I talk to you when you're not here. I talk to you through the floor."

"And I hear you," said Alan.

His son was in the window, waving and shouting out. He could see his wife, standing back in the room, watching him go.

He left the house and went to the pub. At the bar he ordered a beer with a chaser. It wasn't until the barman put them in front of him that he remembered he had no money.

He apologised and although the barman started to say something, Alan turned and went.

It was cold now. Everything was freezing, the metal of the cars, the sap in the plants, the earth itself. He passed through familiar streets, made unfamiliar by the snow. Many houses were dark; people were starting to go away. As the snow thickened, a rare and unusual silence also fell on the city. He walked faster, swinging his arms inside his coat until he was warm. He thought of the dying man he had met at the door of the school, and of what a terrible thing it was that he hadn't recognised him. He wanted to find the man and say to him, we all grow different and change, every day; it was that, only that. Certainly, no sooner did Alan think he'd understood something of himself than he was changed. That was hope.

From a certain point of view the world was ashes. You could also convert it to dust by burning away all hope, appetite, desire. But to live was, in some sense, to believe in the future. You couldn't keep returning to the same dirty place.

He ran up the steps to the house. The light was on. He knew things would be all right if she were wearing the dressing gown he had given her.

In the kitchen she was heating a quiche and making salad. She looked at him without hostility. Not that she spoke; he didn't either. He watched her, but was determined not go to her. He believed that if he could cut his desire for her out of himself, he could survive. At the same time he knew that without desire there was nothing.

Sitting there, he thought that he had never before realised that life could be so painful. He understood, too, that no amount of drink, drugs or meditation could make things better for good. He recalled a phrase from Socrates he had learned at university: "A good man cannot suffer any evil, either in life or after death." Wittgenstein, commenting on this, talked of feeling "absolutely safe." He would look it up. Maybe there was something in it for him, some final "inner safety."

They changed into their night clothes and at last got into his favourite place, their bed. Opening her dressing gown he put his hand on her stomach and caressed her. For a short while she lay in his arms as he touched her. Then she touched him a little, before turning over and falling asleep.

He started to think of his sleeping son, as he always did at this time, wondering if Mikey had woken up and was talking to him "through the floor." He wanted to go and kiss his son goodnight, as other fathers did. Perhaps he would have another son, and it would be different. He looked around the room. There wasn't enough space for a wardrobe; their clothes were piled at the end of the bed. On a chair next to him, illuminated by a tilting lamp, was a copy of *Great Expectations*, a bottle of massage oil encrusted with greasy dust, his reading glasses, a glass with a splash of wine in it, and a notebook.

His life and mind had been so busy that the idea of sitting in bed to write in his journal, or even to read, seemed an outlandish luxury, the representation of an impossible peace. But also, that kind of solitude seemed too much like waiting for something to start. He had wanted to be disturbed; and he had been.

He knew their resentments went deep and continued to grow. But he and Melanie were afraid rather than wicked. In their own, clumsy way, they were each fighting to preserve themselves. Love could be torn down in a minute, like taking a stick to a spider's web. But love was an admixture; it never came pure. He knew there was sufficient love and tenderness between them; and that no love should go wasted.

THE PENIS

ALFIE WAS HAVING breakfast with his wife at the kitchen table.

He couldn't have slept for more than three hours, having been out the previous night. He was a cutter—a hairdresser—and had to get to work. Once there, as well as having to endure the noise and queues of customers, he had to make conversation all day.

"Did you have a good time last night?" his wife asked.

They had got married a year ago in Las Vegas.

"I think so," he said.

"Where did you go?" She was looking at him. "Don't you know?"

"I can remember the early part of the evening. We all met in the pub. Then there was a club and a lot of people. Later there was a porn film."

"Was it good?"

"It wasn't human. It was like a butcher's shop. After that . . . it gets a little vague."

His wife looked at him in surprise.

"That's never happened before. You always like to tell me what you've been doing. I hope it's not the start of something."

"It's not," said Alfie. "Wait a minute. I'll tell you what I did."

He pulled his jacket from where he had left it, over the back of a chair.

He would examine his wallet and see how much money he had spent, whether he had any cocaine left, or if he had collected phone numbers, business cards or taxi receipts that might jog his memory.

He was fumbling in his inside pocket when he found something strange.

He pulled it out.

"What's that?" his wife said. She came closer. "It's a penis," she said. "You've come home with a man's penis— complete with balls and pubic hair—in your pocket. Where did you get it?"

"I don't know," he said.

"You better tell me," she said.

He put it down on the table.

"I don't make a habit of picking up stray penises." He added, "It's not erect."

"Suppose it does start to get hard? It's big enough as it is." She looked more closely. "Bigger than yours. Bigger than most I've seen."

"That's enough," he said hurriedly. "I don't think we

should keep looking at it. Let's wrap it in something. Get some kitchen roll and a plastic bag."

When it wriggled they were both staring at it.

"Get that thing off my kitchen table!" she said. She was about to become hysterical. "My mother's coming for lunch! Get it out of here!"

"I think I will do that," he said.

A few minutes later, to his surprise, he was walking down the street with a penis in his pocket.

His instinct was to drop it in a dustbin and go straight to work, but after a few minutes' consideration he thought he would take it to an artist whose hair he cut, a sculptor who usually worked in faeces and blood. The sculptor used to work in body parts, but had got into trouble with the authorities. Nevertheless, he might find the opportunity to work with a penis irresistible. The art dealers, who yearned for more and more horrible effects, would be fascinated. Alfie would get paid. His wife had told him that he should become more "business minded." More than anything she wanted him to appear on television.

Alfie was heading in the direction of his friend's house when he saw a policeman walking towards him. Quickly, he pulled the wrapped penis out of his pocket and let it fall to the ground. People threw litter down all the time. It wasn't a serious crime.

He had scarcely gone a few more yards when a schoolgirl ran up behind him, waving the bag and telling him he had dropped his breakfast. Thanking her, he stuffed it back in his pocket.

His teeth were chattering. He didn't want the "thing" in his pocket one more second.

He turned a corner and found himself crossing the river. Making sure no one was watching, he tossed the penis over the side of the bridge and watched it fall.

Then he noticed that under the bridge a passing cruiser was taking tourists down the river. A voice was commenting through a megaphone: "On the left we can see . . . and on your right there is a particularly interesting historic monument."

Meanwhile, the penis, coming loose from its covering, was hurtling towards the upper deck.

Alfie fled.

Less than a mile away, Doug, an actor, got out of bed and strolled into his new bathroom. He was in his early forties, but looked superb.

The next day he was about to start work on the biggest film of his life. It was a costume drama, a classy production, which meant he didn't have to take his prick out of his breeches until the tenth minute. The director was excellent and Doug had chosen his female co-stars himself, for their talent as well as their size. Doug had intended to spend the day in the gym. After he would get his hair and nails done, before retiring early to bed with the script.

It wasn't until he passed the mirror on the way to the shower, and looked at himself for the first time that day, that he realised his penis was missing. The whole thing had gone, penis, scrotum, even his pubic hair.

Doug thought he might faint. He sat on the edge of the bath with his head between his legs, but the position only reminded him of his loss.

He had been "in" pornography since he was a teenager, but recently the market had started to boom. Pornography had penetrated the middlebrow market and he, coupled with Long Dong—the professional moniker he had given his penis—was becoming a recognisable star.

Doug had appeared on TV chat shows and in mainstream magazines and newspapers. He believed he was entitled to the gratitude and respect that comedians, singers and political impersonators received. After all, distracting the fickle public was arduous and required talent and charm. Uniquely, Doug offered that which most people never saw: the opportunity to witness others copulating; fascination and intoxication through the eyes.

Many men envied Doug his work and some had even attempted it. How many of them could keep it up, under hot lights and with a film crew around them, for hours on end, year after year? Doug could sustain an erection all day and sing something from *Don Giovanni* while checking his shares in the *Financial Times*. Hadn't hundreds of thousands of people witnessed his stick of rock and the jets of gushing, blossoming jissom that flew across his co-stars' faces?

If he lost his manhood, his livelihood would go with it.

Thinking fast now, Doug conjectured whether, late at night, he had taken Long Dong out somewhere and slapped it down on a table. In bars and at parties, all over the world, the public loved asking questions about his work. Like most stars, he adored answering them. At some point someone, usually a woman, asked to see Long Dong. If the time and place was right—Doug had learned to be wary of making the men envious and causing friction between couples—he would let them peek. The "eighth wonder of the world," he called it.

However, he had never mislaid his greatest asset before— his only asset, some people said.

Doug went to the bars and clubs he had visited the previous night. They were being cleaned; the chairs were upended on the tables and the light was bright. Someone had left behind a shoe, a shotgun, a pair of false eyelashes and a map of China. No penis had been handed in.

Bewildered, he was standing outside on the street when, across the road, he saw his penis coming out of a coffee shop accompanied by a couple of young women. The penis, tall, erect and wearing dark glasses and a fine black jacket, was smiling.

"Hey!" called Doug as his penis stepped into a cab, politely letting the women go first.

Doug hailed another taxi and told the driver to follow the first one. In front he could see the top of his penis. The girls were kissing him and he was laughing and talking excitedly.

The traffic was bad and they lost sight of the cab ahead.

After driving around, Doug decided to go into a bar and consider what to do. He was furious with his penis for flaunting itself round town like this.

He had ordered a drink when the barman said, "If it's quiet in here it's because that penis from all the films has gone into a bar along the road."

"Is that right?" said Doug, jumping up. "Where?"

The barman gave him directions.

A few minutes later he was there. By now it was lunch time and the place was so crowded Doug could hardly get through the door.

"What's going on here?" he asked.

"Long Dong's arrived," said a man from a TV crew. "I've seen all his films—at a friend's house, of course. *Dickhead* is my favourite. The big guy's a star."

"Is that right?" said Doug.

"Are you a fan?"

"Not at the moment."

Doug tried to push through the crowd but the women wouldn't let him through. At last he scrambled onto a chair and spotted his penis standing at the bar, accepting drinks, signing autographs and answering questions like a true professional.

"You people have put me where I am today," he was saying, grandly. "I feel I should repay you all. What are you drinking?"

Everyone cheered and called out their orders.

"What about me!" shouted Doug. "Who made you?"

At this Long Dong looked up and caught the eye of his owner. Quickly he made his apologies—and bolted. By the time Doug had shoved his way through the crowd, the penis had disappeared. Doug ran out into the street, but there was no sign of it.

All day, everywhere he went, he heard stories of the remarkable penis, not only of its size and strength, but of its warm way with strangers.

The one person Doug did run into was Alfie, drinking alone in the dark corner of an unpopular bar. Alfie was distraught, convinced the police were pursuing him not only for stealing a penis and trying to sell it, but for dropping it on the head of a Japanese tourist passing beneath Tower Bridge on a pleasure cruiser.

"I recognise you from somewhere," said Doug.

"Yes, yes," said Alfie. "Maybe. I have the feeling we were together last night."

"What were we doing?"

"Who knows? Listen—"

Alfie explained that he felt terrible about the whole business. If Doug ever wanted a free haircut, he'd be very welcome. He even offered to give him one immediately.

"Another time," said Doug.

He didn't have time now to consider such things. He had embarked on the search of his life.

"Just let me know when you want a trim," said Alfie. "The offer will always be open."

It wasn't until the evening, wandering about the city at random, that Doug caught sight of his penis again, this time sitting in a workman's caff. It was in disguise by now, with a hat pulled down over its head and its collar up. Doug could see it was suffering from celebrity fatigue and wanted to be alone.

Doug slid into the seat beside it. "Got you," he said.

"Took you long enough," said the penis. "What do you want?"

Doug said, "What do you think you're playing at—making an exhibition of yourself in this way?"

"Why shouldn't I?"

"We've got to take it slowly. If there's one thing that makes everyone nervous, it's a big fat happy thing like you."

"I've had enough of your nonsense," said the penis.

"Without me, you're nothing," said Doug.

"Ha! It's the other way round! I've realised the truth."

"What truth?"

"You are a penis with a man attached. I want out."

"Out where?"

"I'm going solo. I've been exploited for years. I want my own career. I'm going to make more serious films."

Doug said, "Serious films! We're starting the follow-up to *Little Women* tomorrow—*Huge Big Women*, it's called."

"I want to play Hamlet," said the penis. "No one has quite understood the relationship with Ophelia. You could be my assistant. You could carry my script and keep the fans away."

Doug said, "You mean, we won't be physically attached ever again?"

The penis said, "I would be prepared to come back under your management, as I quite like you. But if I do, the arrangement would have to be different. I would have to be attached to your face."

Doug said, "Where on my face exactly would you like to be attached? Behind my ear?"

"Where your nose is now. I want to be recognised, like other stars."

"You'll get sick of it," warned Doug. "They all do, and go crazy."

"That's up to me," said Long Dong. "There will be cures I can take."

The penis took a sausage from the plate in front of him and held it in the middle of Doug's face.

"It would be like that, only bigger. Cosmetic surgery is developing. In the future there'll be all kinds of novel arrangements. What do you say to being a trendsetter?"

"What of my scrotum? It would . . . ahem . . . hang over my mouth."

"I'd do the talking. I'll give you an hour to decide," said the penis, haughtily. "I'm expecting other offers from agents and producers."

Doug could see that Long Dong was beginning to shrink back into himself. It had been a fatiguing day. When at last his eyes closed, Doug picked the penis up, popped it into his pocket and buttoned it down.

Doug rushed across town to see a cosmetic surgeon he knew, a greedy man with a face as smooth as a plastic ball. He had remade many of Doug's colleagues, inserting extensions into the men's penises, and enlarging the breasts, lips and buttocks of his female colleagues. Few of these actors would even be recognised by their parents.

The surgeon was at dinner with several former clients. Doug interrupted him and they walked in the surgeon's beautiful garden. Doug laid the sleeping penis in the surgeon's hand.

He explained what had happened and said, "It's got to be sewn on tonight."

The surgeon passed it back.

He said, "I've extended dicks and clits. I've implanted diamonds in guys' balls and put lights in people's heads. I've never sewn a penis back on. You could die on the table. You might sue me. I'd have to be recompensed."

As the objections continued, Doug begged the man to restore him. At last, the surgeon named a sum. That was almost the worst blow of the day. Doug had been well paid over the years, but sex money, like drug money, tended to melt like snow.

"Bring me the money tonight," ordered the surgeon, "otherwise it will be too late—your penis will become used to its freedom and will never serve you again."

The only person Doug knew with such a large sum of cash was the producer of *Huge Big Women* who was, that night, entertaining a few hookers in his suite. The women knew Doug and soon made him aware that news of his misfortune had got round. He blushed and smarted now when the women called him "big boy."

To Doug's relief, the producer agreed to give him the cash. Handing it over, he mentioned the interest. It was a massive sum, which would rise daily, as Doug's penis would have to. The man made Doug sign a contract, pledging to make films for what seemed like the rest of his life.

Travelling back to the surgeon, Doug considered what life might be like without his penis. Perhaps he had been mercifully untied from an idiot and they could go their separate ways. But without his penis how could he earn his living? He was too old to start a new career.

The surgeon worked all night.

Next morning, when Doug woke up, the first thing he did was look down. Like a nervous snake charmer, he whistled an aria from *Don Giovanni*. At last, his penis started to stir, enlarge and grow. Soon it was pointing towards the sun. It was up, but not running. He and his love were rejoined.

A few hours later Doug was on the set. His penis swung between his legs, slapping against each thigh with a satisfying smack.

Doug was glad to be reunited with the most important part of himself; but, when he thought of the numerous exertions ahead, he felt weary.